Lethal Authority

A Novel

By

Joseph D'Antoni

Book 2 of the Wade Hanna Series

This book is a work of fiction. Names, characters, places and incidents are products of the author's imagination or are used fictitiously. Any resemblance to actual events, locales or persons, living or dead, is entirely coincidental. However, the backdrop and historical context of this novel is based in fact.

All Rights Reserved, including the right to reproduce this book or portions thereof in any form whatsoever.

ISBN-13: 978-0-9830816-4-7

Library of Congress Control Number: 2015942008
ROYAL OAK PRESS*, PASADENA, CA

Chapter 1
New Orleans, Louisiana, 1974

A year had passed since Wade Hanna returned from his perilous submarine deployment. Early school problems had already kept him back a year in grade school. The unexpected recent call to active submarine duty caused yet another three-month delay from reaching his goal of a high school diploma. School delays seemed behind him now as Wade relished the thought of finally graduating from high school and moving on with his life.

But Wade had more to worry about than final exams. His last year was spent working undercover as an inscribed agent for the New Orleans Police Department which put him squarely on the wrong side of now imprisoned New Orleans mob boss T.J. Coletta. He was on Coletta's hit list and whoever remained of Coletta's splintered gang had orders to shoot Hanna on sight. A handsome payout was waiting for anyone who brought him down. Wade went about his school classes and a few social activities in a quiet manner always looking over his shoulder for the unwelcomed intervention from the mob.

This was no way for anyone to live especially someone in their late teens. Wade knew his life had to change and one of those changes had to include less exposure to organized crime figures from his former undercover work. He realized he could no longer depend on luck and divine intervention to keep him alive. Whatever fate had kept him breathing to this point wouldn't always be there to pull his butt out of the fire.

He had kept in touch with his now-friend and former handler Jake Pisano who headed up the Organized Crime Division of the NOPD. In his last conversation with Jake, he learned that mob boss T.J. Coletta was seriously ill in prison.

1

Since Coletta was the reason why Wade's name was on the mob's hit list, perhaps his illness – or death – would soon remove this uncomfortable threat. All Wade had to do was wait for his problem to go away.

As Wade waited, Jake Pisano was busy on the other side of town investigating a new crime wave. A phone call from an old classmate suddenly brought Pisano back to an earlier time when he and Wade had worked on the same case

Pisano was deep in thought when his phone buzzed, breaking his concentration. It was his secretary on the intercom line.

"Assistant Prison Director Mark Elbray from Angola is holding on line two."

"Hi, Mark, it's good to hear from you. How are things at Angola?"

"I'm good, thanks. All the usual disgruntled inmates. The reason for my call is that one of our guests has requested to see you."

"Who might that be?"

"Your old friend, T.J. Coletta."

"He's not my friend, but how's he doing?"

"Not well. He has stage four stomach cancer. It doesn't look like he's going to last much longer. They operated last week and just sewed him back up. The cancer was too advanced to do anything."

"How long does he have?"

"They're talking a matter of a few days. He's already been given last rites. Twice he's asked to see you. Says it's important."

"What does he want with me?"

"I don't know. Maybe he wants to confess, or maybe he has something useful for your old case. If you decide to come, let me know. I'll have a pass ready for you at the hospital gate."

"Okay. Let me give it some thought."

From that moment on Jake's curiosity stuck to him like molasses on cornbread regarding what Coletta had to say. There were lots of unanswered questions about where Coletta's money had gone. The investigation and prosecution team had been able to trace the money up to a point, but were never able to discover the location of his stash. They'd never found any evidence of Coletta's local political connections or been able to track the payoffs.

Unanswered questions had bothered Jake since the trial. He'd gotten his man, but was never satisfied because they hadn't found the money or the larger supporting cast that had allowed Coletta's operation to prosper.

Jake couldn't let go of the thought that Coletta might now be willing to give up the last piece of that puzzle. When he called his friend Mark back at Angola, Jake had already rearranged his schedule so he could spend the day after tomorrow at Angola.

Coletta was a tough, hardened criminal, who had murdered dozens of people. He deserved harsher treatment than the easy life sentence he'd gotten by slick lawyering. The few years behind bars before becoming ill didn't begin to pay for the crimes he'd committed. Pisano felt no sympathy for Coletta – only frustration that he hadn't spent more of his life's sentence in prison before his illness.

Jake reviewed the case file and made a list of all his unanswered questions, which kept rolling around in his mind the entire 136-mile drive to "The Farm." The trip gave Pisano a rare opportunity to think in silence. He made good use of his privacy, reviewing the trial and the troubling unanswered questions that lingered. Where had the money gone? He wondered which politicians Coletta had in his pocket, and drooled over what evidence he might uncover to prosecute them. Who else of the out-of-state organized crime kingpins worked with Coletta, and what evidence did he have on them?

In addition to the questions and evidence, Pisano wanted several of his men removed from Coletta's hit list, including his friend and former undercover operative, Wade Hanna.

Perhaps this trip would involve little more than listening to a long confession of Coletta's sins, but he had doubts. He couldn't see Coletta getting religious even in his hour of death. Coletta probably wanted something from him, but Pisano couldn't imagine what that might be. Whatever game Coletta intended to play, though, Pisano wasn't going to be a player.

The two hadn't seen each other since the trial, and there was no love lost between them. It was Pisano who had stung his operation and brought the mobster and his organization down. It was Pisano and his cohort Hanna who had used Coletta's wife to buttonhole other members and put them in prison for life.

Jake kept wondering what, if anything, Coletta might want in return for his cooperation. Coletta didn't have any leverage and nothing to bargain with, or did he?

This visit would not be the first time Jake had seen criminals on their death beds. They often told the strangest of tales, including bizarre confessions, hoping to avoid eternal damnation. He was anxious to see what Coletta had planned.

The Farm hadn't changed much since Pisano's last trip three months earlier on another matter. Tall stalks of corn had been cut clear to the river. Jake gazed out at the landscape, realizing how beautiful this property must have been as a former cotton plantation at the turn of the century. Reflections flashed off the Mississippi River as it meandered like a silver ribbon down and across three sides of the property.

The river framed an almost perfect setting, except for the high barbed-wire electrified fences surrounding the prison buildings. Even if you ignored the fences, you'd still get a bad taste in your mouth from its notorious residents – the murderers, rapists, and thieves – who occupied those buildings.

As he approached the East Gate of the prison, Pisano's mind was somewhere around the turn of the century. He enjoyed the afternoon sunset as he passed through the barbed-wire enclosure into what locals called the "Alcatraz of the South."

As he headed toward the hospital building, though, Pisano's mood changed. He thought about all the criminals he'd had a hand in putting in this institution. None deserved it more than T.J. Coletta.

Recalling Coletta's vicious killings of nineteen innocent people, and the ordered hits of several dozen more, including some of his own men, caused Jake's blood to boil. He wasn't interested in seeing Coletta for any other reason than to get information on unsolved crimes, dirty politicians, and the money they never found before his trial. And, of course, getting the contract hits removed on his men.

If Coletta wasn't going to cooperate, Jake wasn't going to waste time playing priest, listening to some self-serving confession. Perhaps Jake's message would drive home the point - that there was no salvation, and that only damnation awaited him. If he delivered that message right, it might even hasten his demise and save the state some carrying costs.

5

Pisano passed the elevators and took the stairs to the fourth floor. He took every third step in rapid succession to burn off the built-up tension.

Coletta had been moved to a private intensive-care hospital room for the meeting with Pisano. Two armed prison guards stood in the hallway outside the room. Acknowledging the guards, Pisano nodded before entering the room, and was immediately taken aback by what he saw. If death hadn't already knocked on Coletta's door, it was certainly hovering in the doorway waiting to come in. Pisano's face tensed; he barely recognized the fragile body.

Gone was his hair and most of his eyebrows from chemo. Tubes and wires ran from every part of his body, beginning or ending in fluid bottles or a wide array of colorful monitors. Coletta's eyes were closed, set in deep sockets surrounded by dark rings. His pale, white face was tinged with yellow, and his chapped blue lips appeared to have been kissed by death itself some weeks ago.

The hulk of the former six-foot, six-inch, 300-pound killer now looked like a pile of skinny corpses stacked on top of one another. Protrusions of flesh and bone stuck out in all directions from under the sheet.

A nurse stood on the other side of the bed, injecting medication into Coletta's IV tube. She glanced across the bed at Pisano and turned back to check the monitors as the new medication entered his veins. Some number on the screen seemed to strike her as important, and she wrote it down on the chart before turning to Jake.

"He goes in and out of consciousness."

"That's fine, I'll wait."

In a few moments, Coletta's right eye partially opened but didn't seem to comprehend the blurry image it saw. His one eye closed again; the other never moved. Moments later, both eyes opened in a blank stare that still showed no sign of registering Jake's presence.

Coletta was doubtless trying to overcome the effects of pain and the drugs that interrupted links between his brain and eyes. His eyes drifted shut again for a few seconds before opening again.

In a barely audible, raspy tone, Coletta struggled to get out a word. "Hello."

"How are you, T.J.?"

"Dead."

"I heard you wanted to speak to me."

"Yeah."

Coletta tried in vain to coordinate his eyes, tongue, and brain but nothing was working very well. He blinked several times to clear the cobwebs in his head. He tried clearing his throat, which triggered a painful cough, and he grimaced, causing his facial muscles to flex, and folds of skin to move along his jawline down his neck as he tried to speak.

"Thanks for coming."

"Not a problem."

His eyes closed for a short moment then opened again. "They cut me open for nothing."

"I heard."

"My little sister…" Only disjointed pieces of the sentence came out. He uttered a few more incomplete thoughts before his eyes closed. Jake responded, hoping Coletta's hearing was working better than his speech.

"I remember your little sister. She was never arrested."

Coletta opened his eyes again and from somewhere found the strength to respond.

"She moved to South Carolina. The Feds are still harassing her."

"Does that have to do with the missing money?"

Coletta had to think about the question before he answered. "I guess. She don't know nothing. She only worked for me for six months before you shut us down."

"She was your bookkeeper, right?"

"She don't know nothing. I kept her out of everything to protect her. Can you get the Feds off her back?" His eyes closed, and his face involuntarily contorted into a grotesque expression.

"I have some people at the Feds I can talk to, but I can't promise you anything."

Coletta shut his eyes and drifted off into another morphine dream for the next thirty seconds. Then his eyes fluttered open again. This time he looked intently at Jake as though he had never seen him before.

Before Coletta could put a thought together, Jake asked a key question. "Where's the money, T.J.?"

Coletta paused, closing his eyes, his face grimaced. "I can help."

"You're going to have to do better than that, T.J."

A raspy sentence sputtered out beneath the oxygen tube running from his nose. "I made a deal with Lugassi."

Frank Lugassi was the mob boss in New Orleans, and at the top of Pisano's personal most-wanted list.

"What kind of deal?"

Trying to be coherent, Coletta explained his deal with Lugassi. "When you started marking my money with that invisible blue dye crap, I couldn't use the cash without it being traced. You know, the blue stuff is what brought us down. So I went to Lugassi."

"What was your deal with him?"

"He said he could use the marked cash in European and South American operations. So I gave him $12 million in cash. He was going to launder it through his operations and give me back $8 million in clean bills. We transferred the cash at the docks, mixed in with some auto parts going to Panama, but the rat stiffed me. I never got my $8 million back. Then you guys shut us down. My little sister, she didn't know anything about the deal."

Coletta had no sooner finished his last sentence then he started to cough. He couldn't clear his throat, and his coughing became uncontrollable. He grimaced as pain shot through his body with every agonizing breath.

Pisano patiently watched until Coletta finally got himself under control. "I'm surprised you made that deal with Lugassi. You know what a rat he is."

"I got some information on Lugassi's operations before we made the deal. It was my insurance policy. If I hadn't gotten sick, believe me, he wouldn't have pulled this on me even in prison."

"What kind of information do you have on Lugassi?"

Random syllables tumbled out of Coletta's mouth before he finally spoke coherent words. "I have information on all his drug operations in Central and South America – including companies he owns, attorneys, bank accounts, everything on his operations. I got it from his accountant before we wasted him. We did his accountant clean. Lugassi still doesn't know it was us. I have all the information."

"Where is all that information now?"

"It's in a bank vault box. My attorney has the key and password, but he doesn't know anything about what's in the package."

"Are you willing to turn over that information to me?"

"Yeah. I can't use the money where I'm going. I just don't want my little sister brought into this. Let her live her life. That's the only thing that means anything to me right now."

"Like I said, I'll talk to some people at the Feds. If your sister isn't involved in any of this, maybe they'll leave her alone."

"Thank you. That's all I want."

"I have a few other things I need from you. I know you had state and local politicians on your payroll. I want those names, and evidence of what you paid them."

"Yeah. I can get you that. I don't need them or their influence anymore. I'll need to make some phone calls to get you that information."

"I'll make sure you have access to a phone."

Coletta just nodded. Jake saw his opportunity with Coletta beginning to dwindle. He jumped in with his next request.

"Another thing – you have hit contracts out on a couple of my men. I want those contracts canceled."

"My men won't follow up on those contracts – they're all in prison now just like me. But there is one problem."

For the first time Jake sensed Coletta was trying to smile.

"What's the problem?"

"Lugassi took over my contracts. I made that part of my deal with him, thinking it would protect me in prison."

Coletta started to laugh at his own revelation but went into another coughing spell, unable to catch his breath. One of the monitor alarms sounded loudly, accompanied by a flashing light. The nurse quickly opened the door as Coletta began to contain his cough. The monitor alarm stopped, and Pisano waved the nurse away just before she reached the bed. Pisano wanted an answer to his question.

"Why is that a problem?"

"You know I can't take back my contracts with Lugassi."

He made the statement like a proclamation Pisano should know - that the order was irreversible and unbreakable under syndicate rules.

"Isn't your boy Hanna out at sea with the Navy?"

Pisano was surprised that Coletta knew or remembered anything about Wade, and he was quick to respond with ambiguity. "I'm not sure. I haven't spoken to him in a while."

"That was a smart move on your guy's part. They can't touch him out at sea. But he'll have to watch himself when he comes back."

Coletta seemed to manage another small smile followed by a grimace of pain, or perhaps it was a smirk. Jake couldn't tell what control Coletta had over his facial muscles or what expression he was trying to make. Coletta was now in a semi-conscious state. His eyes focused in a blank stare on the walls around the bed like he was seeing his room for the first time.

Jake felt his time with Coletta ending as the mobster drifted off to sleep again. He lightly nudged Coletta to ask another question.

"How do I get the key to the bank box?"

"I'll call my attorney and you can pick it up."

The nurse anxiously stared through the window of the door. She came in without invitation and checked Coletta's monitors.

Already knowing the answer to his question, Jake asked anyway. "Is he asleep again?"

"He's worn out. I'm afraid that's all he can provide you with today."

"If he wakes up, please remind him to call his attorney. It's very important. I'll make certain you have the authority to get a phone to him. Hopefully, he'll remember the number to dial."

The nurse looked down at Coletta and then waved Pisano over to the other side of the room out of ear shot. She whispered, "I don't think he's got much longer."

"I can see that, but I have to get access to some vital documents in a bank vault. I can have a court order issued, but I don't trust his attorney, and there may not be enough time for that. Knowing Coletta, he's probably got a fail-safe mechanism to have them destroyed when he dies unless I get to them first. I need you to make sure he calls his attorney."

"I'll work on that as soon as he wakes up."

Pisano left the prison hospital uncertain about what he'd accomplished.

Chapter 2

Naval Submarine Reserve Facility
New Orleans, Louisiana

It was his weekend for reserve duty. Wade squirmed uncomfortably in the oak student desk as the instructor droned on about Southeast Asia's geography and the waters surrounding Vietnam. Shiny new maps of Southeast Asia hung from the classroom walls, telling their own story about what the Navy was thinking.

The instructor rapidly ran through a list of nautical distances between the coastal cities of Qui Nhon, Hai Phong, and Cam Ranh. The glassed-over eyes of the students were steadfastly ignored by the instructor. He must have expected the class to either be familiar with the Asian coast line, or have photographic memories.

Bored beyond understanding, Wade drifted off into another world as the instructor went on lecturing about ocean depths and key navigational land reference points in the South China Sea.

During the break, members gathered around benches under a tree not far from the classroom. Wade went over to sit with his friend and classmate, Chief Shaun Ellsworth and asked him, "Where are they going with all this Southeast Asia stuff? Who the hell cares?"

"We're being set up. Can't you see that?"

"For what, exactly?"

"Unit activation. I've been there before. The Navy likes to sneak up on us. They never tell us what's really happening."

"Do you think our unit will be activated?"

"Yep. You can bet on it. I don't know when, but they wouldn't be doing all this because of some sudden interest in

Southeast Asian geography."

"You've been around for over 16 years. It's not a sea battle over there. Why the hell are U.S. submarines needed off the coast of Vietnam?"

"China. And perhaps Russia. That's where North Vietnam is getting all their weapons."

"Do you see us getting into undersea battles with the Chinese or the Russians?"

"Only if they themselves become active in the war. I think subs will mainly be used for surveillance and reconnaissance missions, perhaps Special Forces deployment."

"What's your best guess on timing?"

"If I were to guess, I'd probably say in three to six months."

"I just can't believe it. I'm trying to finish school, and barely survived the *Prowfish* deployment interruption, and now this?"

"All this has messed up my life too. I'm supposed to retire in two years. It's the Navy, man. You'd better believe they'll be in the thick of things if the Vietnam War moves forward."

Class resumed with more nautical distances and reference points to land sites. Next they went over sea depths from positions in the Gulf of Tonkin and Gulf of Thailand. After the class, Wade stayed behind to ask the instructor a question.

"Lieutenant, why is Southeast Asia so much a part of our lectures now?"

"No particular reason. Locations around the world are randomly chosen to use as examples. Next month we may be talking about the waters around Denmark."

"Not likely, Sir. We've been talking about Southeast

Asia for three months now."

"It's a big continent, surrounded by large bodies of water."

Wade left, shaking his head in disbelief at the ludicrous answer.

The following week, Wade received a call from his former XO on the *USS Prowfish,* Lieutenant Commander Charles Benson.

"Wade Hanna speaking."

"This is Commander Benson. I'm calling on behalf of Captain Hodges. We're trying to locate prior shipmates for our upcoming deployment, and were interested in knowing if you might like to serve with Captain Hodges again, along with some of your old *Prowfish* crew."

The direct question caught Wade off guard. He had to think quickly before he stuttered, "I-I really enjoyed serving with you and Captain Hodges."

"We have a great new nuclear ship under our command. The Captain thinks he can get your extra nuclear shore training waived. You can pick up the training while onboard with us. For your rating, there are only a few new navigation equipment changes you'll need to learn. That should be a snap for you."

"Sounds interesting. Do you know where you'll be deployed?"

"We don't have orders yet, but rumor has it we'll probably be off the South China Sea, just off Vietnam."

Wade's mind was racing. He wanted to be diplomatic, but he wasn't about to commit to a three-year deployment in the South China Sea. He knew his longer-than-normal silence was conveying uncertainty. He tiptoed over eggshells, choosing his next words carefully. "I would consider it an honor to serve with you and Captain Hodges again." Then he quickly thought, *I can't end on that note.*

"It's good to hear that. I'll be sure to convey your sentiments to the Captain."

"I just want to let you know, though, that I'm still dealing with some personal issues right now. My mother died recently, and I'm trying to hold things together at school for the next few months until I graduate."

"I'm sorry to hear about your mother. But it sounds like your school issues might be under control soon. I'll explain that to the Captain. Call me when everything gets sorted out, but don't wait too much longer. Some final decisions will have to be made soon. You wouldn't want to miss out on a great opportunity like this one."

"I'll do that. Thank you for thinking of me."

The call ended with some relief, along with overarching worry. The muscles in Wade's jaw tightened, thinking about how the conversation had gone. He knew whatever time he had left before his status would change had just gotten shorter. His brow line contracted as he hung up the receiver and thought nervously about the call. *Hodges snatched me right out of my reserve unit in the blink of any eye when he needed men for the Prowfish. He could do it again.* His stomach tightened with a new sense of urgency.

Two weeks after the Coletta meeting, Jake called Wade to meet at the Old Grill. The two men arrived at the same time and walked over to Jake's favorite table. Wade saw the strained expression on Jake's face. He'd seen it before; this meeting wasn't going to include a lot of idle chit chat.

"Good to see you again. Your message sounded urgent."

Jake began without preamble, "I met with Coletta before he died last week in prison. He transferred $12 million of our marked blue-dye currency to Lugassi just weeks before we made our arrests. The deal was that Lugassi was supposed to give Coletta $8 million back in clean currency. But Lugassi never paid Coletta the $8 million. That's why we never found the missing funds."

Wade shook his head in disbelief. "Those two guys hated each other. Why would Coletta just give Lugassi the money?"

"Coletta had an insurance policy. He has records on Lugassi's drug operations in Central and South America. They were also going into the auto parts business together in Central America."

Wade sighed aloud. "So the marked money has already been disbursed through multiple offshore banks and is now probably all over the world."

Jake nodded in acknowledgement before Wade spoke what was uppermost in his mind. "Well, at least Coletta is out of the picture now. Things should calm down for me."

"That's partially true, but it's not all that simple. That's the reason I called you."

"What else?"

"The other thing Coletta said was that he transferred all his 'hit contracts' to Lugassi - and that you're on that list. If it's any consolation, I'm also on the list, but then I'm on every criminal's hit list."

Wade frowned. "What? That's all I need to hear right now. Lugassi's mob is fifty times larger than Coletta's gang. I thought with the Coletta guys in prison, things would cool down for me. Damn it! I just got off submarine deployment and missed a lot of school. And now the Navy is getting ready to activate our unit for Vietnam. I'm totally screwed."

"Did anything ever come of that meeting with the intelligence group?"

Wade's voice sounded morose when he answered. "Yeah. I met with Jenkins a couple of times. I put together the proposal they wanted, but I don't have any commitment from them yet. I'm still waiting for a response. They've told me they're interested, but the thing is taking forever to finalize."

"According to Coletta, Lugassi thinks you're still out at sea. That's a good thing for a while."

"Yeah, good until someone sees me."

"Then you have to make yourself less visible. Stay away from public places, the Quarter, any mob restaurants or hangouts. If you want to carry a weapon again, I can make a permit happen."

"I don't go out as it is. I have no social life - no life at all. I haven't been to the race track for ages. In fact, I don't even go to the damn movies anymore."

"Have you ever considered going to the police academy?"

"No. I promised myself and my parents I was going to finish college before I do anything else with my life – assuming I survive that long."

Seeing Wade's discomfort, Jake tried to mollify him.

"One good thing about Lugassi is that he's so busy, it'll take him a long time to get to you. You aren't a threat to any of his businesses, which means you probably won't get his immediate attention. His operations are all over the state. In fact, they're so big their size works against them. With Coletta gone, you probably fall under "old business." He's got much bigger fish to fry."

"I need to make something work in my life. I'm graduating from high school in three months, and then I need to find a way to get out of town and start college before someone grabs me."

Wade paused with his head down. He continued to think out loud, open for any suggestions Jake might be able to provide. Jake was silent, also thinking about what he could do to help.

Wade spoke next. "I'll go back and contact the Agency to see if I can arrange another meeting. I also have my summer reserve sea duty coming up, and that'll take me out of town for a few weeks. I guess I'll have to just spend more time in the swamp."

Jake offered what little advice he could. "I think the Agency is a good option for you, at least in terms of the mob. You'll be out of town for training and assignments, and you'll have the Agency behind you. The mob thinks twice before they target someone in the Agency. Hitting an Agency guy will bring down a whole lot of hurt on them."

Wade squirmed in his chair. He had the sudden urge to change the subject. "Have you tried Dean's Seafood lately? I heard they changed management."

Jake looked into Wade's eyes, ignoring the question. But before he could conjure up some response to the last question, Wade changed the subject again.

"I'm going to need that permit to carry a concealed weapon."

"Just fill out the application and drop it off at my office. I'll take care of it."

Wade took the time to fill out the permit paperwork never believing he would need it, since most of his previous work had been on behalf of the NOPD. The hope of a calmer existence with Coletta out of the picture was gone with the wind.

Wade oiled the hinges to the hidden trap door under the dash. He put in his old Colt .45 ACP where he always kept it. It wouldn't be a long wait for the permit to come back, and Wade knew that Jake would cover him if he had to use the gun before that time.

His routine fell into a normal pace. The goals were clear and simple. Finish high school as quickly as possible before the mob found him or the Navy deployed him. Sometime in the next few months, he had to find out if the Intelligence Agency wanted him. Whoever got to him first would change his future in ways he could not imagine. None of his alternatives seemed very bright right now, and a few seemed downright deadly.

Chapter 3

Wade was preparing for a final exam at his friend's house, a half block off Magazine Street near the upscale "Garden District." As the study session ended, exam questions rolled around Wade's head like they were on a loose sprocket wheel. After hanging over books most of the day and evening, a milkshake from the drive-in sounded like a good idea. The drive-in was on the way home, and Wade was long past being ready to leave.

Thoughts of milkshakes quickly faded two blocks from the Dairy Queen. The same headlights that had shown in Wade's rear view mirror for the last six blocks were still there.

He slowed down, allowing the tail to come closer. The vehicle didn't pull around him, but instead backed off when it got within a car's length of Wade's rear bumper.

It approached close enough for Wade to get four digits of the license plate number as they showed in reverse in his rear view mirror. Wade wrote the numbers down in the proper sequence on his hand with a ball point pen. By the number sequence, Wade knew his follower was not an unmarked police patrol car.

Wade pulled forward again, resuming normal speed. He made a left turn, and then followed it with a right turn at the next block. The tail was still following. Wade slowed down again. The car behind pulled closer and then fell back as it approached his vehicle.

He repeated the same pattern several more times. Wade slowed again, trying to get a better look at the passengers. The two men inside were middle-aged, wearing dark suits. They looked like mob enforcers. When the trailing car backed off this time, Wade down-shifted the four-speed floor transmission into second gear just before releasing the clutch and slamming the accelerator to the floor.

The two four-barrel carburetors sitting atop the Corvette manifold made a deep whooshing sound like air sucking through an industrial vacuum. The high-performance 283-cubic-inch Corvette engine screamed like a wild pig. Tire rubber squealed, and white smoke enveloped the rear fenders of Wade's `55 Chevy. The acceleration pushed him back against the bench seat as he grabbed a tighter hold on the steering wheel, trying to control the beast.

Residents of the serene Garden District had either gone to bed or were watching the last late-night program on TV. Restful Garden District or not, Wade had no choice but to lose his followers before they got to him.

A click of the under-seat button with his left hand brought the bottom of his hidden dash compartment down. The handle of his old 1911 semi-automatic Colt .45 ACP popped out like a welcome friend who had come to join the party. Wade put his companion on the front seat next to him to enjoy the ride.

The black sedan following picked up speed, but the sound told Wade his followers had a smaller engine and was no match for what he had under the hood. And there would be no stopping to ask, *Why are you following me?* If these men got close enough to Wade, he'd be showered with bullets. If he stopped to engage them in a gun fight, the two probably had more fire power than a small army – with more men waiting nearby to jump in for help.

He was alone in this chase, and while Wade loved his '55 Chevy, he didn't want it to become his coffin. His only option was to lose or outrun his tail. As he picked up speed, his mind raced, trying to identify both the tail and the route he'd take.

He thought of old adversaries from the race track, gang members or Coletta's old mob. These were older men, though. *Could they be Lugassi's men?* Regardless of who'd sent them, this was no time to stick around and find out.

Approaching a red light, Wade quickly checked for oncoming traffic and down-shifted into third gear. The wheels squealed again as he blew past the red light doing sixty mph. He suddenly slowed back down to forty to make a left turn.

The black sedan was still following several blocks behind. He confirmed that they'd pursued him around the last turn. They weren't particularly fast, but they were persistent, staying the course at a reasonable three-block distance. Wade's frequent turns and ability to accelerate didn't seem to bother them. They just kept coming.

Notwithstanding the docile neighborhood, Wade decided he had to go for it. He made several more left and right turns at high speeds. He thought: *If nothing else, a high-speed chase in an upscale residential neighborhood should prompt someone to call the police.*

He laughed out loud at his own thought. *Here I am, wishing someone would call the police for my own protection.* Wow, what a concept. If these were Lugassi's men, by the time the police got there, he'd be dead. He pressed the pedal to the floor again, trying to create greater distance from his adversaries before the next turn.

Wade took the sharp left on Melpomene Street. He was now headed toward the comfort of St. Charles Avenue. The avenue was a tourist attraction, with a large neutral ground where the trolleys ran. It offered a greater hope of seeing patrol cars and more public witnesses. His followers couldn't possibly want public attention, or better yet, to literally run into a police car. As they approached St. Charles Avenue his followers would soon be on public display. *Let's see if they blink.*

The wheels of his '55 squealed when Wade took the sharp right turn on the avenue headed toward Lee Circle and downtown. It was 11:30 in the evening. The avenue was quieter than Wade expected. *Where the hell are all the tourists?* Streetcars were no longer running for the evening. His hope for police protection and an avenue full of tourists quickly faded.

Wade considered driving down the neutral ground between the trolley tracks to draw more attention. He changed his mind when he suddenly saw an opening in the avenue that allowed him to make better time.

He gunned the engine, knowing the elevated statue of a stoic General Lee would soon come into view. Checking the rear view mirror, he could see that his pursuers were still there but had become inhibited by a double-parked car on the avenue. He could see men in each car honking and yelling out the window at each other. The delay allowed Wade to gain three more car lengths as he approached his next crossroads.

It afforded him a few more seconds to think about his options. Lee Circle was approaching. He didn't like the idea of going around the General's circle – too many uncertainties with approaching traffic.

He knew his best overall option was to get to Jake Pisano's police building in the Quarter, but that was still a long way away. If he could get close to the police precinct building, his followers would drop the chase. The goal still seemed out of reach, and he was out of time and options.

Approaching Robert E. Lee atop his column at this speed might even cause the General to turn his head. The General had been surrounded by enemy soldiers many times before, after all. Wade just wanted a nod from him that he was making the right decision.

He checked the rear view mirror again. He now had a five-car lead. Lee Circle approached more quickly than he expected. Considered judgment could wait for another day. There was no more time to consider options; he had to rely on instinct.

Instinct indeed took over when he pulled down hard on the steering wheel under General Lee's statue. Wheels squealed as he took a sharp right on Andrew Higgins Avenue at high speed. The old Confederate Museum on his left passed in a blurry flash.

The force of the turn made the left side of the car feel like it was coming off the ground. There was no more time to think. No sooner had he navigated the right turn then he made a hard left, in part to counterbalance the car. Dazed, the second turn put him on Camp Street facing Canal Street and his ultimate downtown destination.

Before readjusting from his turn on Camp Street, a large yellow light appeared as a square across the street. It was as though someone had painted a bright yellow direction sign for his benefit, and instinct alone told Wade to follow that light.

He pulled the wheel hard left again, not understanding where the light was coming from. Wade hit his brakes hard after making the turn to avoid the side of the building. Everything was happening so fast that his surroundings were a blur. When the car stopped, he was parked under the source of light. He had somehow landed in a commercial building that happened to have a roll-up door open at midnight while a crew unloaded a truck.

As he took in the building surrounding him, he noticed the two structural columns he'd barely missed on either side.

He hadn't even seen the concrete wall in front of him. His brakes stopped the car less than a foot before he would have plowed into a concrete loading dock.

Wade didn't know where he was or how he got there. He looked around the large building and thought, *Who could possibly be open at this late hour?*

He shut off his engine and got out of the car in one fluid movement. The car was still rocking from the sudden stop. Warehousemen in blue coveralls holding boxes stood frozen in place with their mouths open in disbelief at the sudden intrusion and near collision.

A sign across the top of the dock area read "Standard Import – Export." He grabbed the pipe railing and raced up the concrete stairs to the loading dock. Slowing to a brisk walk, Wade moved toward the center of the dock, now realizing he had his gun in his hand.

A middle-aged man stood at a warehouse podium in a short-sleeve shirt and tie, checking off items as they were unloaded. A printed form was attached to a clipboard. When the man saw Wade approaching with his gun, the pen curled over his forefinger and dropped to the clipboard. The rest of his body remained motionless.

Workers looked back and forth at each other, waiting for a sign from their foreman. Packages in their hands remained suspended in midair. The men didn't know whether to put their packages down, their hands up, or run. Wade approached the podium with a calm but urgent look on his face.

"My name is Wade Hanna. I'm undercover NOPD. I'm being followed by two mob guys, and I need to use your phone."

"Our offices are closed, sir. We're just finishing a late night shift. We'll be unloaded very soon. You got a badge?"

"I was off duty when this happened. I work for Detective Jake Pisano of the NOPD downtown division. I don't have time to stand here and discuss this. I need to get into your offices to use the phone to call for help. Just show me where the phones are."

The man paused, looking into Wade's eyes for some confirming sign of truth. He definitely saw conviction in Wade's face, but wasn't sure about truth or what this crazy man might do. He knew his job and his life might soon be on the line if he guessed wrong.

Seconds passed as the two men stared at each other in silence. Wade slowly raised his weapon, and placed his hand with the weapon on the podium. The manager briefly glanced down at the well-used weapon. It didn't look like police issue to him.

Wade could tell he had to be convincing. "We can do this the easy way or the hard way. I can arrest you if I need to."

The man looked Wade hard in the eyes. Neither man's expression changed. The barrel of Wade's gun was less than a foot away from the foreman. The foreman had to think quickly for himself as he looked into Wade's eyes. *He's definitely got conviction. Conviction isn't always 'truth,' but it will have to do for the moment.*

The foreman finally broke the silence. "I've heard the name Jake Pisano on the news before. Come with me."

They briskly walked to a door leading into the darkened office building. The foreman reached for the long chain of keys hanging from his belt and opened the door to dark offices.

"I'll turn on the lights for you."

Wade noticed a line of dim safety lights along the baseboard used for hurricane emergencies. "No, leave the lights off. Just tell me where the phones are."

"Go down that hall and make the first turn to your left where all the accounting desks are. They'll all have phones on them."

"Have your men close those outer doors until the police arrive. By the way, what's your name?"

"I'm Mike Cusso."

"Thank you, Mike."

Still fearful of what he done, Mike tentatively extended his hand.

"My pleasure."

Chapter 4

Wade quickly moved down the darkened hall to the accounting desks, picking up the first receiver he found to dial Pisano. The extension button at the bottom of the phone glowed in the darkness – not very strongly, but enough for Wade to see the surface of the desk.

While Jake's line rang, Wade slid the breach of his gun back to confirm he had a shell in the chamber, before resting his gun back on the desk. Jake was accustomed to getting late night calls from his men. He had his phone calls transferred to his home when there was an operation in progress. This evening, though, he was just working late. Finally Wade heard the familiar voice: "This is Detective Pisano."

"It's Wade. I'm being followed by two guys with bad intentions. I pulled into a warehouse on Camp Street next to the Confederate Museum. The building just happened to be open. The car following me was a late model black Ford sedan. I think they could be Lugassi's boys."

"Stay put. I'm on my way."

Wade looked around the darkened room, thinking about upcoming arrivals. There was a dim light at the other end of the large room. When he removed the telephone headset, the small extension lights came on at the base of the phone. He moved the phone around and used the light to check desk drawers. Nothing in the first desk appeared helpful.

He moved to the next desk and picked up its phone, using the light to check the drawers. Again, nothing helpful. He repeated the same procedure on the third desk. In the bottom left hand file drawer, he found what he was looking for--a small flashlight.

Using the flashlight, Wade quickly scanned the layout

of the room. There was a door to another room halfway down the line of cubicles to his left. He went to that door, opened it, and checked the wall panels. That wall didn't have what he was looking for.

He spotted another door across the room near the elevators. Flashlight in hand, he ran across the room, opened the door and found a wall with the electrical box and breaker switches. He scanned the labels next to each switch and turned off all the breakers for the first floor lighting.

Wade knew the darkness would likely slow down his tail, who wouldn't be expecting it. Darkness was his friend, and any hesitation he could create might compensate for his out-gunned position.

Now he had to find the best location from which to confront his adversaries. He ran to another door, which opened off the main hall to the employee lunch room. He beamed his light across the lunch room, over chairs and tables, to another door. That one opened into a storage room. Though he found the storage room door unlocked, it could clearly be locked from the inside, keeping out anyone in the lunch room. Wade liked what he saw.

The storage room was lined with partially-filled shelving. Another door in the storage room opened to the dock area and could also be locked from the inside. He liked the option of a second escape route to the dock. He flashed his light around one more time before deciding that was the place he would make his stand.

A position behind a shelving unit and heavy boxes offered some protection. He moved the boxes around and opened a small space between them for a shooting platform. Wade locked himself inside and took his position in the dark room. Checking his watch with one last flash from his light, he estimated another fifteen to twenty minutes before Pisano arrived.

The next few minutes in darkness seemed like hours. Tension gripped Wade every time he heard the slightest noise. He had never realized how many noises an old building made throughout the night. At one time he thought the building was breathing in a rhythm not dissimilar to his own, creaking as it stretched tired old bones.

The next sound Wade heard wasn't from inside the building; it was someone pounding on the outside of the metal roll-up door. Wade listened carefully. A loud voice penetrated the outer steel roll-up door.

"This is the police. Open up."

The same voice repeated itself. "This is Jake Pisano of the New Orleans Police Department. Open up."

Wade breathed a sigh of relief when he heard Mike open the outer door.

Pisano and two detectives with guns drawn greeted Mike, showing him their badges. The three detectives fanned out in the warehouse, and another two began searching the street and sidewalk outside the building.

Mike showed Pisano where he'd let Wade into the offices and opened the door for him. Jake called out loudly into the darkened room, hoping his voice wouldn't be met with gunfire.

Immediately recognizing Jake's voice, Wade responded with a yell of his own as he left the storeroom to meet Jake in the hallway next to the darkened offices.

"There was no sign of your tail when we got here. Tell me what happened."

"Let me get the lights on first."

They walked across the room behind Wade's flashlight. Pisano watched as Wade switched the overhead lighting back on. Jake and Wade sat down at the first cubicle across the desk from each other.

Wade provided a detailed account from the time he'd left for school that morning. While telling his story, Wade wrote on the desk pad the four digits of the license plate number and handed it to Jake.

"They were probably waiting for you at school and followed you to your friend's house," Pisano remarked.

"Do you think they were Lugassi's men?"

"I'm not certain, but they could be. So much for your being out at sea."

"What should I do now?"

"It's time for you to get out of Dodge. We'll follow up on the license plate and pay a visit to whoever owns this vehicle. Call me in a few days. I'll make sure the Lugassi boys know we're watching them closely. That may hold them off for a while."

Wade followed Jake's advice and headed out of town. For Wade the trip meant returning to his beloved swamp and his family's camp sixty miles west of New Orleans. Before leaving town he placed several calls to Jenkins at the Intelligence Agency, finally getting through to him.

"This is Agent Jenkins. How may I help you?"

"Hello Mr. Jenkins. My name is Wade Hanna. We met two weeks ago, and I just wanted to know when I might be hearing back from you on my proposal?"

"Your proposal is in the right hands now. I'm expecting a call back any time. It shouldn't be much longer."

"I'm thinking about going out of town for a few days and didn't want to miss your call. I can cancel my trip if you think you're going to hear something soon."

"You don't need to cancel your trip. Why don't you call me at the end of next week? I should know more by then."

The Louisiana Swamp

Wade couldn't wait to get back to the swamp. He not only needed to be away from prying eyes in the city, but the swamp was the only place in this world where he could really clear his mind. The primitive surroundings were still the place he'd called home since childhood.

He called a few friends to join him, but they were too busy with other things. The more Wade thought about being alone, though, the better he liked the idea. The two-hour drive to the swamp included frequent checks of the rear view mirror for any unwelcome company. He thought to himself: *Anyone crazy enough to follow me into my darkened domain does so at his own peril.*

Every new mile away from the city further improved his outlook. His thoughts jumped from one topic to another. He kept in mind his promise to his father to keep the camp in good repair, and wondered what damage might have occurred since his last visit a couple of months ago.

He'd already agreed to take care of some minor repairs during this trip, but wasn't sure if his father was thinking about selling the camp because it was getting so little use. Wade was against the sale, wanting the camp for himself, but he understood his father's reasoning, especially in light of his own uncertain future.

If his father did sell the camp, Wade knew that one day he would have one of his own.

Since Wade couldn't control when – or if – the government would respond to his proposal, all he could do was spend time thinking about his other options. *No place better than the swamp to consider my alternatives.*

Wade motored down the long drive under the overhang

of branches and Spanish moss. He pulled up to the camp and started unpacking his provisions. The few areas that needed repair were obvious, and easily repairable if he used the ladder in the garage.

Pausing from his unloading, Wade reflected on the crossroads where he stood in his life. Melancholy washed over him as he realized he had few choices regarding his future. It hit him that the vast majority of the rest of his life would be determined by others, and that caused his stomach to tense when he saw the truth. No matter which path he chose, or had chosen for him, this was the last time he would see his beloved camp for a long time – perhaps forever.

The quiet of the swamp struck him as never before. His senses weren't coping with the absence of city noise; his ears actually rang from the silence.

He took a deep breath and inhaled familiar earthy scents from the surrounding swamp. He gazed out over the pond. The soft afternoon light reflected white cumulus clouds in front of a blue sky over the still water. The weather report had said a cool breeze was coming in from the north that evening.

His surroundings were all-consuming now. He caught himself staring into space as if taking part in some long-forgotten spiritual ritual. In the trance, he seemed like an observer too young to be allowed by the spirit to fully participate in the ceremony. Perhaps it was penance for his long absence from the swamp?

When it came to unpleasant childhood memories, Wade's mind was normally like a crawfish net trying to hold water. They passed through holes, were buried deep, or no longer existed. But something strange was going on here. Unwanted childhood visions played before him like a projector spinning a celluloid reel, and he couldn't walk out of the theater. Images were coming fast at him with no particular order or purpose. He reached out, bracing himself against the bark of a nearby oak tree, hoping to slow the memories down. Good idea, but it didn't work.

The images contained harsh childhood images of beatings and being left alone in locked rooms whose details he didn't want to recall or couldn't remember. Past and present times were all the same. Wade knew his mind wasn't playing these tricks on him. There was definitely a swamp spirit behind all this.

Perhaps it was reminding him of who was in charge and not to stray too far from the swamp again. The experience took his breath away and he abruptly gasped for air, wanting all this realism to stop. Moments passed before a light flashed in his brain.

As fast as the images had come, they slowed and disappeared. Wade took another deep breath, not knowing what he was supposed to do with the trapped memories. His mother had been dead now for several years, yet she stood out among the images next to him speaking in a loud voice about his upcoming journey; then it became a whisper and disappeared with the other images.

He acknowledged the spirit from childhood that had just paid him a visit. Though he tried to shake off his experience, he remained staggered by the spiritual power of whatever had just happened. There was no message about how his upcoming journey would end - just that he would have company along the way.

Chapter 5

A few days after returning from the swamp, Wade made a call to Jenkins. In a cordial but unrevealing response, Jenkins said he wanted to schedule their next meeting at the Wave Restaurant because of the probability of inclement weather. The bureaucrat was hurried and short with Wade, clearly unwilling to chat.

After a few more moments of contemplation Wade felt Jenkins had been dismissive, and that fact didn't sit well. Perhaps Jenkins' demeanor was a way of preparing Wade for bad news. At least he was going to tell him in person rather than over the phone. Wade wondered if there was anything he could do to prepare for the meeting.

Wade began to assume the worst and prepared himself in advance for an unwelcome response. Time in the swamp had allowed him to focus on a Plan B option, which was what kept him going. Just knowing there was a Plan B anchored him. *If I can get the Navy to do my shoulder surgery and rehab, it would give me at least another twelve months before they could deploy me for undersea service.*

He kept reciting his Plan B option to himself. It wasn't that bad. Everything was going to be just fine. The Plan B alternative wasn't ideal, but neither was deploying for sea duty in the next six months, or staying in New Orleans. Under Plan B, assuming he could avoid being seen by the mob in New Orleans, perhaps he could go to an out-of-state college and have the Navy do his surgery. This would give him another year before he could be called to sea duty.

He might even call back Commander Benson and take Captain Hodges' offer. Perhaps college was not going to happen for Wade right now. Regardless of how events turned out, though, he couldn't stay in New Orleans any longer. Wade kept his affirmations positive: *Everything is going to work out fine.*

At the last meeting, Wade had presented Jenkins with a detailed outline of what he wanted in order to work for the Intelligence Agency. He felt the outline was fair to both parties, while capturing what he needed in order to be part of the dangerous world of intelligence work.

But proposals were behind him now. He didn't know if he would even have the chance to respond to Jenkins' questions, assuming he had any. At this point everything was in the government's hands, and they controlled the rules of hire. Jenkins would unfortunately be the only "government" in front of him, and he couldn't do anything about it.

The Wave Restaurant was set back from the road, nestled in the corner of an oyster shell lot across the water inlet from the lighthouse where West End turned into the yacht club.

Jenkins and Hanna arrived at the same time and proceeded to an isolated table at the back of the largely-empty restaurant. The heavily nautical motif emphasized seafood but also life under the sea – an environment Wade was trying to forget.

Images of sharks and undersea plant life seemed real behind the polished brass portholes lining the wall. The underwater scene made you feel you were looking out from a sunken ship's hull. Several large aquariums with colorful fish complemented the wall décor, suggesting guests might be swimming with the fishes.

Thoughts of his near-death undersea experience caused Wade to wonder if Jenkins had purposely selected the restaurant for its subliminal messages. The undersea images did seem to have some effect on Wade as he fought flashbacks of his *Prowfish* experience.

Seafood gumbo was the house specialty, and both men ordered a large bowl. The waitress first brought freshly-baked French bread. Both men reached for slices before the waitress's basket rested on the table between them.

Jenkins seemed sullen and unusually quiet, giving no indication of the government's position or how this discussion would proceed. His stoic posture suggested there would be no celebration at this meal. Wade thought he would break the ice with some small talk. He knew Jenkins' travel schedule must be grueling and thought the subject might conjure easy stories to share.

"Do you travel much?"

"A bit."

"Where do you normally travel?"

"All over."

Jenkins wasn't in a sharing mood. They finished the rest of their delicious gumbo in silence before Jenkins stiffened his posture even further. Caught off guard by this new "official posture," Wade wondered what he was about to say.

The stiffened posture projected bureaucratic authority, which seemed a bit misplaced in the dark corner of an almost-empty restaurant. The only audience was Wade and perhaps a passing waitress, so it was hardly the place for a public announcement.

Jenkins cleared his throat several times, calling attention to his uncomfortably erect posture.

"I think we should get this meeting started."

With that announcement, Wade expected to hear a drum roll, but there was no drummer in sight. He couldn't figure out what the hell Jenkins had in mind and why he thought it was necessary to give a formal announcement that the meeting was starting. *What are all the theatrics about?*

Instead of speaking, Jenkins pulled some papers from

his briefcase as though he were testifying before a congressional hearing. Positioning the documents upright, Jenkins created a white paper wall between himself and Wade. For some reason he held the papers as if to discourage Wade from grabbing them. The thought of reaching for the documents hadn't even occurred to Wade.

The last expression on Jenkins' face was resolute as he disappeared behind his newly constructed paper wall. Jenkins read in silence, clearing his throat every few minutes as a reminder of his importance.

After a long silence Jenkins finally lowered the paper wall. He stared into the empty restaurant as though trying to reconcile some complex legal dilemma in the text. Wade waited patiently, focusing on the tableware.

Wade wasn't about to give Jenkins the satisfaction of showing either anticipation or fear, although both were crossing his mind at the same time. For the third time he smiled and craned his head toward the cute waitress checking silverware placement at empty tables.

Jenkins was either having fun at his expense or was enjoying the importance of his own power for some perverse reason. Perhaps the old bureaucrat was making the best of the remaining few authoritarian roles he had left in an otherwise thankless career.

For no obvious reason, and without further dramatics, Jenkins broke the silence.

"I have good news to report. The government has accepted your proposal as written."

With Jenkins' long-awaited comment Wade offered a guarded smile. He stifled a happy cry and hid the frustration Jenkins had just put him through.

Wade simply responded, "I'm pleased the government found my position acceptable. What's next?"

After reshuffling papers in his hand, Jenkins answered while handing Wade several typed pages. "I have a draft employment contract for you to consider. Your outline is attached as Exhibit A to the contract. Please take a moment to review the agreement and take whatever time you need to have your attorney review it."

The agreement had been prepared in detailed legalese. To Wade it sounded both governmental and official, and after quickly reviewing the document, he looked up at Jenkins.

"I understand most of this, but I'm going to have our family attorney check it over."

"You can have your attorney call me with any questions. If I don't have the answer, I'll have someone from our legal department get back to him."

Wade sat back in disbelief. It finally sank in that despite all his fears, his Plan A had succeeded. This meant he would soon be employed by the Agency, his college education costs covered, his complicated shoulder surgery paid for, and he would receive his intelligence training – and all of this out of town and out of reach of the New Orleans mob.

Outwardly Wade maintained his reserved demeanor with Jenkins. A few questions were asked and answered about certain paragraphs referencing training locations and dates.

"If there's anything vague in timing or schedules, it'll have to be worked out as you move forward in the program."

"I understand. What Agency group will I actually be working for if I sign this?"

Jenkins' response was evasive. "That depends on what project you're assigned to. It could be any one of several intelligence organizations."

Jenkins saw Wade recoil from his answer.

"You see, the program you're coming into is new – well, new in the sense that the government wants to consolidate intelligence training activities and control costs. The government's feeling is that there's too much empire building between different organizations and not enough sharing of resources, cooperation, or coordination in performing intelligence work."

After pausing, Jenkins continued. "This administration wants to see divisional walls broken down and organizations utilizing people across lines, all with the same core skills. It's a new concept and something internal politics hasn't fully embraced. I suspect it will take some time before it's fully implemented. Most new Agency recruits will come in under the new system with the same training you will receive."

"Under the program, you'll be accessible to any one of three or four intelligence organizations. I know that may not satisfactorily answer your question, but it's truthful, and all that I can go into for now. Perhaps we can have another chat if you decide to sign the contract."

As the two men approached the front door, the rain pounded the green metal canopy over the restaurant. Ominous gray clouds in the far southern skies showed no signs of dissipating.

"I have a lot of traffic to fight before my next meeting," said Jenkins.

"I'll be back in touch as soon as I meet with the attorney."

The two men shook hands before ducking under large black umbrellas and moving quickly across the wet parking lot in different directions, toward their cars.

It didn't take Wade long to choose a medium-sized college

located in a quiet Alabama town near three military air bases. His intelligence training schedule required him to be at one of those bases to fly out of, almost every weekend and even on holidays. The Agency came through on his transfer out of the Navy into the intelligence service. No more submarine classes or worries about being called back to sea duty. He just had to manage the next six years of his life between college and intelligence training, spending the last two years of his contract in full-time service with the Agency.

The quiet, laid-back town of Greenstone, Alabama suited Wade just fine. It wasn't long before he settled into a grueling schedule of college and intelligence training. There was little time for himself or any social activities, and whatever hopes he had of a normal college social life were soon eroded.

The next three years of Wade Hanna's life passed in a blur. Between college and intelligence training, no time remained for anything else. His feeble attempts at a traditional college social life were all unsuccessful. He was handsome and easy to talk to, but few potential dates were interested because of his long and frequent absences.

Heavy doses of core classes were the mainstay of Wade's college schedule. He was also prone to taking unconventional classes. Questionable class electives like locksmithing, gemstone appraisal, art valuation, magic, and theatrical make-up were considered supplements vital for covert assignments, but caused the agency to wonder. Wade became proficient at persuading the agency to accept his strange course curriculum, arguing that he would make good use of every single skill he acquired.

His magic class actually turned out to offer a surprising

application to undercover work. A large part of the class was spent on how human perception works and how the mind tricks itself by filling in the blanks for what the brain thinks it actually sees.

The fundamental principles behind illusion intrigued Wade. He made connections between magic tricks and what he was learning in other intelligence classes. He learned that "objects" in an illusion were not as important as the method of misdirection. The visual diversion had to be created while everyone was watching. His winning classwork brought surprise and praise from his classmates and a seasoned instructor who had performed professionally several hundred times. The class project at the end of the term had students design their own illusions and perform them in front of the class.

He convinced himself that underlying illusion principles would serve him well in real undercover assignments, but he didn't know how or when such tricks might come in handy. But at least now he was ready to use them.

Life for Wade was not all about taking fun courses. Intelligence training occupied most his weekends, holidays, and even his summers. The government expected a high commitment to the training courses that consumed every spare moment of his time. Wade was a sponge, though, and loved almost every minute of his extensive training.

Government, law enforcement, and various forms of intelligence classes drummed into him every aspect of intelligence work. Intelligence classes took him across the country to numerous alphabet soup locations with the CIA, NSA, Customs, Secret Service, DIA, DEA, and FBI.

For field training, he attended classes at base after base throughout the country, including remote specialized training facilities operated by the Navy, Army, Air Force, Marines, and Special Forces. There were even a few remote clandestine facilities that trainees were taken to blind-folded.

Under Wade's government-mandated training program, all military, intelligence agencies, and federal law enforcement courses offered, became available for his training. Scheduling and coordination of these training activities for each new recruit was complex and almost impossible to achieve for the uninitiated. They were handled by an assigned intelligence officer officially called a Training Coordinator, and informally called a *handler.*

The handler assigned to Wade was Megan Winslow, who was part wizard, part task master. Megan herself was an intelligence officer and recent graduate of the program. She was based in Washington D.C. and considered her role important, but temporary.

Megan's career goal was to be a field operative, and she hoped to get a permanent posting in the next couple of years. Until then, she took her handler role seriously. She knew every trick in the book and didn't take lip from recruits or any of the military officers she had to deal with.

Like tracking a covert target, Megan knew Wade's whereabouts every moment of the day. She made sure he was where he was supposed to be at the correct time. Whatever little spare time Wade had, Megan was busy scheduling it. She knew every school holiday, when each of his college classes began and ended, homework assignment schedules, exam dates, and when a class had been canceled, often before he did.

She was Wade's constant telephone companion and oftentimes his wake-up call. Megan saw something in Wade that she didn't see in other recruits, and she liked what she saw. A mutual feeling of trust developed and began to grow to something more than just recruit and handler. Romance was in the air, but only a possibility at the end of her tenure as Wade's handler.

Wade performed well in his intelligence classes and field work. Superior ratings were common in both classroom and field training. Performance write-ups over his three years of training suggested that his strongest skill was his ability to improvise.

Many of the courses were Special Forces training sessions for both Navy SEALs and Army Rangers. Intelligence trainees, although not expected to achieve the same level of proficiency as a Ranger or SEAL, were expected to show significant proficiency in weapons, explosive devices, navigational skills, encryption, and surveillance.

Wade wasn't the strongest or most skilled at hand-to-hand combat, but he demonstrated good techniques on certain defensive moves and poise in making directed "kills" when so ordered. More importantly, Wade exhibited an ability to find ways to achieve results when resources were limited and the odds were stacked against him.

His methods were not always pretty or conventional, nor did they necessarily follow protocol, but somehow he nearly always found a way to succeed. As one field officer and instructor wrote in Wade's course review, "He finds ways to win or neutralize his opponent in situations where the odds suggest he should not prevail."

Now only five intelligence classes were left before Wade was scheduled to graduate. Two of those classes were field classes, and the remaining three were classroom instruction. It was important to Wade to do well and graduate high in his class.

One of the more difficult field classes he faced was yet

to be scheduled: the Sniper and Navigation Special Forces class at Fort Benning, Georgia. He and Megan had discussed the class for more than two months.

The class was always full and had an incredibly long waiting list. Megan was determined to get him in before the graduation deadline, however. She wasn't going to have her record tarnished because any recruit of hers missed a class she was supposed to have scheduled. To accomplish this, Megan was not opposed to going over a base training coordinator's head. A call to the assistant base commander at Fort Benning at the suggestion of the Assistant Director of the CIA got her the audience she needed to do the convincing.

Over the last three years, Wade and Megan had become constant telephone companions but had never met in person. Long personal talks lasting into the early hours of the morning were not uncommon as their personal relationship grew. There was more than a hint of a much stronger relationship to come. Each was sensitive to their professional positions, though, and cautious about how they approached the topic.

Their next big step was meeting for dinner the next time Wade was in D.C. Megan made sure an important event in the near future would make that trip happen. Secretly, their relationship was already much closer, but always expressed in playful banter. After all, both worked for the same employer – an intelligence agency. Who knew what calls were being monitored?

"I've got a tentative commitment for you at Fort Benning. I hope you can appreciate that it took an act of Congress to get you in."

"I'm not looking forward to that class. I heard it's a bear. Can I get it waived to graduate?"

"Not a chance. Besides, after all I had to go through to get you in, you're not going to bail on that class now."

"You're so damn determined! You would make an impossible wife."

"Try me."

Chapter 6
Fort Benning, Georgia

It was 4:30 on a Friday morning when the phone rang.

"Time to rise and shine." It was Megan's mellow voice at a most unpleasant hour of the morning. "Are you awake?"

"I am now." A groggy response was all Wade could muster.

"You need to be at Fort Rucker in an hour for your flight to Fort Benning. I was able to get you in the Sniper-Navigation Course with Special Forces because of a last minute cancellation. You're supposed to be in the course with three other intelligence agency members from other groups."

Wade's sleepy mind tried to recall whether the Sniper Course was three or four days long and what problems it might create with his class schedule. Megan anticipated Wade's next questions, already knowing his school schedule better than he did.

"Before you ask, Monday is a school holiday, and you'll be returning Monday evening for your Tuesday Econ class. This training should be right up your alley - there's a swamp at the base. In fact, one session is a "No Weapons" cache exercise that will test your mettle. Good luck. I'll give you a call next week to see how it went."

Responding while still half asleep, Wade tried to ask what he thought was an important question, but it came out as a dumb observation. "Do I need to take anything other than my normal backpack?"

"Just yourself and your backpack. Anything else they'll provide – or not provide, as the case may be. I went through the course a year ago. It's a real challenge."

A military transport plane was waiting on the tarmac

when Wade arrived at Fort Rucker. Several military passengers in fatigues were already seated on board. After the short flight to Fort Benning, an Army bus delivered them to a staging area on base.

The bus unloaded next to a dock below a sign marked with the course name and number. Everyone was arriving on different buses from locations all across the country. Other individuals had already assembled under the sign.

Most participants were dressed in traditional camouflage fatigues. Intelligence training personnel were not required to wear uniforms and stood out as civilians among the sea of drab military fatigues. Wade had dressed in his usual jeans and plain t-shirt, carrying a dark green Navy sea bag.

Wade quickly spotted another individual in jeans and walked over to him. The gentleman seemed lost, mingling among the unfamiliar military crowd. Wade approached and introduced himself. They shook hands. The man said his name was Harold Yankovich, but quickly followed his name with, "Everyone just calls me Yari."

"When did you arrive?"

"About a half hour ago. I just came in from D.C."

Quickly Wade surmised that Yari might be NSA or Army computer intelligence from his dress and the studious-looking round metal-rimmed glasses he wore.

"Are you originally from D.C.?"

Yari answered, "I've been living in D.C. for two years now, but I'm originally from Indiana."

"Are you in intelligence?"

Yari responded with an affirmative nod, turning back to Wade with a question. "How about you?"

"Yep."

Both men scanned the crowd, trying to find anyone else

in civilian clothes. There was no other non-military clothing in the camouflage crowd. Yari responded to the observation.

"It looks like it's going to be all military except you and me."

"It's still early. I heard there might be other intelligence folks joining us. We'll see."

In the middle of the gathered fatigues, one Army Special Forces guy spoke up loud enough for Wade, Yari, and the assembled crowd to hear.

"Someone said we're going to have spooks in our class?"

No one replied, but smiles came over many faces that confirmed an obvious shared displeasure.

Wade turned to Yari. "Here we go again."

"What's going on?"

Wade didn't want to respond to the already fragile recruit. He had faced the same attitude in other training sessions. Some military personnel saw intelligence services people as a class below real soldiers, and many were not shy about sharing that sentiment.

Some soldiers took unkindly to sharing training facilities with "spooks." Wade had found in other instances the negative attitude abated as the group started working together, but this particular guy seemed to be starting with a head of steam.

A surprised look came on Yari's face when Wade decided to confront the soldier right away. Wade knew from past experience it was best to try to defuse the situation early. He left Yari standing with an "Oh, my God" expression on his face.

Walking directly over to the boisterous soldier, Wade politely introduced himself and extended his hand for a handshake. The soldier turned his head away, leaving

Wade's hand suspended in space.

The patch over the boisterous soldier's chest pocket read "Lockhart," and his arm patch insignia indicated Special Forces Recon. Bulging muscles stretched his fatigues, giving him the look of an NFL linebacker covered in camouflage. Lockhart's massive figure towered over Wade. He turned his head back toward Wade with an aggressive, confrontational glare. Wade casually let his hand drop to his side. It was obvious that Lockhart had something to say.

Turning to look directly into Wade's eyes a few inches from his face, he started. "Look, spook, I've had two tours in 'Nam. On my last tour my platoon got wasted on a mission that a spook determined was necessary. His so-called intelligence was crap. He didn't have a clue where the enemy was or that my guys were walking into a trap. It got them all killed because bullshit intelligence guys don't know what the hell is going on in real combat."

"I'm sorry to hear about your friends."

Lockhart continued his rant. "We're out in a real war getting our asses shot off, and you guys sit behind desks pretending you know what's happening in the field. Most of the time your so-called "intelligence" isn't worth a damn."

Wade thought better than to continue the conversation, which was becoming louder as Lockhart's elevated animosity drew the attention of a growing audience. Surrounded in a tight circle of fatigues, Wade excused himself, gently pushing his way out of the circle back to where Yari was standing.

"What was that all about? Is he blaming us for what happened in Vietnam?"

"This is going to be an interesting training session. I don't think this Lockhart guy is going away."

Two army transport trucks arrived to take everyone to the barracks area. Wade and Yari were dropped off at one of several four-man housing facilities arranged in a large quadrangle.

They were the first to arrive at LQ-8. Lying on each bed was an envelope containing instructions on where to assemble, times to meet, where to eat, and a general map of the Fort Benning facilities, along with a set of camouflage fatigues in each man's approximate size.

It was obvious to Wade that Yari was the shy, studious type, perhaps skilled in computer programming, research, or encryption, but without much combat or surveillance experience or interest. Wade had the sinking feeling he might end up on the same team with Yari, and had to find out more about his new-found friend.

The next scheduled activity was an orientation session beginning in an hour. The location was close to the barracks area. The lecture took longer than scheduled because they had to wait for another truckload of trainees to arrive from a delayed flight. After the orientation, Wade and Yari walked back to their barrack.

It was 5:30 p.m. local time, and Wade asked Yari if he wanted to go to the mess hall before it got too crowded. Yari replied, "Sure." They took their map and navigated down the path from the barracks to the mess hall. Yari kept turning the map in different directions, seemingly disoriented about the direction of the mess hall. Wade thought to himself, *This is not a good sign for a navigation-sniper class.*

The mess hall was a newer facility, well-appointed on the inside. Wade was anxious to see if there was a real difference in food between this facility and other military bases where he had trained.

The food offering was impressive by military standards.

Attractive food layouts included several appetizers, a selection of three main courses, dessert, and fruit. Both men commented that the Army might have gotten an unfairly bad rap for their food service if this was any indication of what food was like on this Army base.

Yari was not much of a conversationalist. His shyness kept him from answering questions with anything more than a minimal response. In fact, talking to Yari was like pulling teeth. Answers to Wade's questions hung in the air without the offer of new information, comment, or opinions on anything.

Wade thought about topics that might loosen him up. Perhaps he could find something out about his new roommate.

"Did you say you grew up in Indiana?"

"Yeah."

"I heard Indiana is beautiful, but it gets real cold."

"The winters can be brutal."

"Did you live in the city or the country?"

"In the country, about fifty miles outside of Indianapolis."

"Which branch of Intelligence do you work for?"

"NSA."

"What do you do there?"

After some silence: "I'm a computer programmer and analyst."

"Why did you select this particular training class?"

Yari had a puzzled look on his face. "I'm not really sure why I'm here. They assigned me this class as part of a new NSA field-training requirement."

Yari's confusion soon also reflected on Wade's face. Most intelligence analysts Wade knew didn't set foot in the field. He wasn't sure why the NSA would suddenly ask an analyst to take field training courses. The only thought Wade had was, *Perhaps the NSA is gearing up for some new type of field operations.*

The more he thought about it, the less sense it made. They were both confused about Yari's training directive, and continued speculating on why he was there. Nothing made sense. Maybe someone had checked the wrong box. Yari repeated several times that he just wanted to work behind a computer screen. He seemed inordinately tentative and uneasy about the topic throughout the dinner hour.

Wade wondered how his new friend's computer background would transfer to a military sniper exercise in the field.

"Have you had much weapons training?"

"No. I don't really like guns. My father took me out shooting with a .22 when I was about ten years old. I remember the snow in the woods behind our house in Indiana. We shot a few times. I remember it was just too cold. I shot at targets, but didn't hit a thing."

Wade shared a few stories about his childhood in the swamp. Yari was stunned that Wade had grown up in the swamps and had already served in undercover operations in addition to active duty on a submarine.

They finished the meal in relative quiet and were ready to leave when Lockhart suddenly approached their table. He had in tow several of his Special Forces buddies.

"Glad to see you guys are leaving because we like this table, and we don't eat with spooks."

His comment was followed by loud, unnatural laughter. Wade was about to suggest that Lockhart join them at the table, but saw that Yari was very uncomfortable. He decided to initiate their departure from the table. As they left, Lockhart made a parting comment.

"Can you believe these guys? I can't wait to get these guys in the field. It's easy to get hurt out there if you don't know what you're doing. You guys should really consider dropping this class."

Returning to the barracks, Wade tried to engage Yari in more conversation, but could only get a bare minimum response. Yari wasn't going to suddenly become sociable. It was clear he had been affected by the Lockhart confrontation.

Training on the first day started at the sniper firing range, which was separated into two different sections with short and long-range targets. The class instructor divided individuals into two-person teams consisting of a sniper and a spotter. When assigning teams, the instructor's finger quickly paired off Wade and Yari.

The spotter did the calculation for wind, distance, elevation, impact point, and sightings after impact. Wade was comfortable in the sniper setting. It was his third military sniper training class, and he'd also had years of experience hunting in the swamps. He understood the technical features of the M-21 sniper rifle and how its 147 grain bullet behaved during its 2,733 feet per second flight.

There was always more for Wade to learn, however, especially how ballistics changed over very long distances and varying weather conditions. Wade also knew from his swamp experience how terrain and shadows played tricks on a sniper's eye.

Shadows and diffused light in the swamp made targets appear farther or closer, depending on the sun's angle and time of day you were shooting. Swamp people had spirit names for the mystical aberrations created by light in the swamp. Wade's natural comfort with the rifle combined with excellent eyesight made the range a familiar place.

Unfortunately, the same was not true for Yari. His shyness about the weapon and target protocol were obvious to Wade from the start. Yari wasn't blessed with good eyesight and clearly didn't feel comfortable with an M-21 rifle in his hands. He also knew nothing about ballistics.

Covering the role of both shooter and spotter wasn't a problem for Wade in this exercise. He would teach Yari what he could, hoping the assigned pairing was not a preview of how things would go during the rest of the training. Wade wondered, *What score is Yari going to shoot? Will his score be combined with mine for a team score?* A combined score might ruin Wade's rating on this exercise.

They were first assigned to the short range: targets ranging between 150-250 yards down range with a 5-mph wind blowing from left to right. The short range target appeared the size of a frozen ant that could only be seen with strong binoculars or the 5x power high resolution rifle scope.

Wade started explaining the differences in ballistics between the short and long ranges, but got only a blank stare from Yari. After a brief discussion of shooting principles, it became clear Yari was in complete overload. It was so bad that Wade wasn't convinced Yari knew which end of the gun to hold.

At that moment, Wade was determined to help Yari get out of the class. He did his best to get him through the short range targets, though. Perhaps he would be paired with someone else for the long range.

"I'm going to walk you through each step of the shooting procedure. Listen to what I'm saying and watch everything I do. I'll do my own spotting and shoot first; then I'll turn the weapon over to you, and I'll do your spotting for you. Now, after you get into your shooting stance, the first thing you do is dope your scope."

As Wade explained, Yari listened, seemingly understanding general concepts and the math about ballistics from what Wade explained. He didn't seem eager to learn, but at least he was more than happy to comply by following Wade's instructions.

Handing the binoculars to Yari, Wade explained what he was supposed to be observing. Using the scope, Wade made his own calculations for target distance, windage, and drop. He then adjusted the scope, explaining as he went through each step.

Wade fired his first round. He was high and to the right by an inch of the center of the target. He took some time to explain to Yari where the round had landed and why his initial calculations were slightly off.

Yari again seemed to comprehend the math, but was clueless how to make the scope adjustments. Wade made two adjustments, and his next round hit the target dead center. He continued making his spotting calculations out loud and shooting while trying to explain to Yari what he was doing and why.

Yari continued to grasp the math and was starting to do some of the calculations in his head as Wade spoke. Wade soon learned he was doing the math without understanding how a round performed when it left the barrel. Except for the first shot, all of Wade's seven rounds were within a half inch of each other.

The instructor called out for teams to switch positions. Wade got the rifle in Yari's hands and positioned properly. Yari reluctantly followed Wade's instructions. Even with Wade's instruction, Yari's groupings weren't very good. Wade tried to coach Yari as he looked down-range through the binoculars.

"You've got a 9-inch spread, with one round missing

the target completely. You flinch anticipating the kick of the rifle, causing movement just before you fire."

"I don't like how hard this thing kicks."

"You have to ignore the kick. By the time you feel the kick, the bullet has already left the barrel. It's your flinching before you pull the trigger that's causing the problem, not the kick itself."

After several rounds Yari was still anticipating the kick. It seemed like a lost cause. Still, Wade didn't want to see Yari fail his target test, because they might record the session as a combined team score. He placed a few of his own rounds dead center on Yari's target. Wade managed to score high on his target test. And thanks to Wade's helping rounds, Yari got a minimal passing score, but Wade wasn't sure how much longer he was going to be able to help his friend.

Chapter 7

For the session at the long range, the instructor switched team members, and Yari was sent to someone outside of Wade's line of sight. He wished Yari well and reminded him of the steps to follow as he turned to leave.

Wade's new team member was an experienced spotter by the name of Max Yeoman. Max had just returned from his first tour of duty in Vietnam and had applied for Special Forces training. The two men bonded, and by the end of the long-range exercise they had scores high enough to have gone into battle as a sniper team. The tight groupings on the long range target by both men showed what a coordinated effort between experienced spotter and shooter could produce.

During the long range exercise, Wade looked around periodically for Yari, but his vision was blocked by the number of bodies and curvature of the range. After the long-range session ended, the class went over to a group of buildings for a small arms close combat exercise. Team members were switched again, and Yari was assigned to yet another team. Wade worried about Yari in unknown hands, but there was no way to protect him.

On the next team, Wade was blessed again with another good spotter and teammate by the name of Charlie Moorefield. This exercise finished with Wade scoring a tight grouping of nine shots in the rapid fire exercise. Again Wade looked for Yari, but only saw him once entering one of the simulation buildings with an automatic pistol in hand.

The sight of Yari entering the combat training building caused Wade to remember he hadn't given him much in the way of safety instruction. He hoped Yari knew to keep the pistol pointed away from himself or anyone else. Wade wondered if the instructors would pick up on Yari's inexperience. They might do him a favor and kick him out of the class, or worse, there would be a weapons accident. Wade feared for instructors and other innocent people who might be in the exercise with him.

It wasn't until late that afternoon when the men returned to the barracks that Wade had a chance to speak to Yari again. Asking Yari how things had gone didn't get much response. Yari thanked Wade for helping him, but he clearly didn't want to talk. At the mess hall that evening, Wade finally got Yari talking a little about his day. None of what he said seemed encouraging.

"My assigned team members after you just laughed at me, calling me an asshole."

That wasn't the whole story. Yari wanted to let the conversation drop, and Wade didn't push, but waited until Yari was able to continue.

"The NSA never explained to me what I was getting into here. I would never consider shooting anyone or even *at* anyone. I don't even like guns."

In Yari's world, the outer limits of aggressive combat was decoding encrypted messages or hacking into someone else's computer. Coming to terms with his predicament was good, but Wade wasn't sure what alternatives were still open to him. He was registered in the system for the class. To have a drop-out on his record now might negatively impact his career. It was time to have a serious discussion with Yari about leaving the class before they started the live exercise.

"The next several days will be spent in the woods and swamp, having to navigate unfamiliar terrain and carry out surveillance against other designated enemy teams. In the next round, we'll have to evade teams seeking us out as targets."

An expression of bewilderment, or even defeat, covered Yari's face. Trying to put on the best spin possible, Wade pointed out, "It's still very early in the training session. You might want to consider opting out of the class by calling your NSA director or explaining your situation to the training commander here."

By that time, Yari had become sullen and unresponsive.

"Sleep on it tonight. You can make your decision before going in the field tomorrow. There's no disgrace in opting out of a class you never intended to take."

He wondered if Yari would be paired with him for the next exercise. For all his weird tendencies, he had grown on Wade. He was becoming like a kid brother, and Wade didn't want to see him expelled from an exercise or physically harmed. And Wade knew some of the hostile Special Forces guys and the instructors would have little mercy on him.

The next morning the men attended a briefing about the upcoming field exercise. Yari said nothing at breakfast about dropping out of the class, but was clearly discouraged and moody.

Only a few moments remained before he could drop the class. Once the exercise started, there would be no way to quit or change teams. Unless Yari was on Wade's team, he would be in the woods on his own. Wade felt the exercise would break Yari if he became isolated or was part of a hostile group.

The cache, as it was called, was a no-weapons exercise, but still dangerous, as teams were buried in isolation throughout the 180,000 acres of Fort Benning. It was easy to get lost or injured. Wade visualized disgruntled Special Forces soldiers running Yari in circles for their own amusement. But the two had already had their discussion about Yari dropping out the previous evening, and Wade didn't feel he could push the subject further.

At the end of the briefing, pairs of four-member teams were assigned to face each other in the cache exercise. Much to Wade's surprise, his team included himself, Max, Charlie, and Yari. Upon hearing the team make-up, each glanced at the others before turning to hear the instructor recite the rules of engagement.

Yari seemed excited, and Wade felt somewhat relieved. After the briefing, the team assembled. Wade was quickly elected by the other men to lead Red Team in the exercise.

It didn't take long before Wade gave his first directive. "I want to go around and have each of us briefly describe our combat and surveillance experience. Let's start with Charlie."

"I was on several night raids and recon missions in 'Nam, where my team navigated hostile terrain and known enemy positions."

Max was quiet and reserved. He didn't like talking about Vietnam, but had a great deal of combat experience that would serve this team well. "I served as a lead in my unit and was on point for a lot of recon missions in 'Nam. I also headed several of what we called live-fire missions."

Charlie inquired for clarification, "What are 'live-fire' missions?"

"We adopted the enemy's tactic of hiding along well-traveled trails in ambush. We usually wiped out entire teams of Vietcong before they knew what hit them. I was also on several sniper kill missions."

Wade added to Max's comment. "Didn't you also get accepted for Special Forces training?"

Max was holding his head down, avoiding Wade's gaze. "Yes."

Everyone turned to look at Yari. He was pale and in awe of his team's experience. "I don't have any experience in either combat or surveillance."

The next morning each man received an envelope containing maps, training objectives, and rules of engagement. Red Team's opponent was Blue Team, who was assigned the defensive position. Wade's team was on offense, which meant they had to capture the caches without being caught by Blue Team.

Rules of engagement seemed simple, on the surface. The winner on offense was the team that obtained the most caches before getting caught by the opposing team. The defensive team's goal was to capture the offensive team before they completed their mission. The winner on defense was the team that captured the offensive team with the fewest number of caches in hand.

However, the simple instructions didn't reveal much about the complex strategy needed to successfully deploy offensive and defensive team tactics.

Pairs of opposing teams were spread over a wide area to reduce the chance of contact with other groups in the exercise. Multiple quadrants within the Fort Benning territory were laid out on the map as boundaries. Crossing a boundary meant team disqualification, which would appear on one's training record. The five caches were spread out within the assigned territory boundaries.

Defensive teams were provided with the general area of the cache, but not the cache's specific location. Offensive teams, on the other hand, knew the exact location of the hidden cache, but didn't know where the defensive team would deploy their observers. The only way to know was to conduct recon missions.

Red Team's first recon mission produced a sighting of

only one Blue Team member, which was disconcerting to Wade.

"We have to do this again and expand our search area. We know too little about where Blue Team is deployed. We can't approach the caches until we know where the other team is positioned."

With maps in hand, Wade broke their boundary down into numbered sections based on the location of the caches and the location of the single Blue Team member sighting.

The search area started with the cache located farthest away from Red Team base camp. The second mission for Red Team proved more productive, identifying all but one member of Blue Team. As the sun began to set over Red Team's base camp, the men marked the map locations of all the sightings from the second mission.

A circle of gathered rocks enclosed a small fire, offering both light and warmth against the chilly night air. Wade summarized the second recon mission findings.

"Blue Team's deployment tells us they've assumed that we'll approach the caches in a certain order. So if, we pursue the caches in a different order, some should be available for the picking. But we have to be careful Blue Team doesn't change their observation postings."

A discussion of a plan to counter Blue Team's positions continued among the group. Pointing to the newly marked map, Max summarized his observations.

"Stations 3 and 4 each have two men. They're leaving Stations 1 and 5 open, but you have to cross the exposed dirt road to get past Station 3 to reach Station 1. They're almost daring us to take that route. We have to get to Station 1 or 3 a different way."

Pointing to an open area between Station 3 and 4, Wade suggested an alternative. "If we create a diversion in this location, it might draw Blue Team off their stations." The approach needed more thought to avoid being captured. Late that afternoon, Wade's team discovered that two caches remained unmanned, and they could be easily obtained without being seen. Wade called the team together to review their next strategy.

"We have to assume Blue Team believes that all three caches are still in place. If they believe any one is missing, they'll redouble their lookouts to cover the remaining ones."

"Why do you think they still believe all caches are in play?"

"Because they have a man covering a spot where the cache has already been taken. We have to assume the worst case scenario in our planning until we get confirming recon information."

The small campfire helped take the chill out of the night air. It was after midnight on the second day of the exercise. Red Team joked and relaxed, in high spirits, recapping their day after having achieved four of their five objectives - capturing caches without getting caught by Blue Team.

Wade was concentrating hard on getting to cache 5 undetected. Everyone except Yari was sitting or lying on the ground, unwinding from the past two days' events. Wade was sitting with his back against a large tree, making small notes on their area map.

Yari was the only one still standing, leaning against the trunk of a tree and still going on about what life was like growing up in Indiana. None of the other men were interested in listening to Yari's stories or his newfound energy. They just wanted to shut the day off.

Yari's vocal recital accompanied the setting of the sun. His sullen demeanor during the day changed to non-stop talking as the sun disappeared below the horizon. However, after more than an hour of listening to Yari, everyone had simply tuned him out. Wade was the closest one to Yari, but was only listening with one ear to Yari's white background noise.

As was the case for so many computer analysts, most of Yari's work was done at night, when his brain seemed to function better than most. Storytelling compensated for the absence of computers in the field, but his only interested audience was night owls and tree branches.

The other men were half asleep, soaking up whatever warmth the dwindling fire provided. The low drone of Yari's background noise didn't keep anyone from going to sleep in his face, but neither did he seem bothered by the fact that no one was listening.

Charlie, lying with his head on his hand, glimpsed bright stars in spaces between fast-moving dark clouds. Max turned quietly to his side with his eyes closed. Wade, concentrating on the team's next move, had his eyes focused on some mysterious point in the dark forest. He knew sleep would soon overtake him as he readjusted his position, nestling a few inches lower onto his rucksack. Yari went on speaking to himself, which didn't seem to bother him.

With one eye half open Wade heard Yari mention something about the beauty of Indiana girls. He opened the other eye to catch the rest of the sentence, and that was when he heard the familiar sound of a pop followed by a sharp crack. Wade instantly realized that a high speed projectile had invaded the camp's perimeter in a no-weapons space.

Wade looked up to see a small piece of bark fly off the tree branch a few inches from Yari's head. It was like a light just went on. He put the two incongruous sights and sounds together and yelled, "Get down!"

Still oblivious to what had just happened, Yari turned to

Wade and asked, "What?"

Wade grabbed Yari's shirt and pulled him to the ground, repeating, "Down!"

Wade immediately knew that what came through their camp was a high velocity silenced round – that had just been fired at Yari's head.

Jolted by Wade's pull, Yari lay on the ground and asked, "What's going on?"

Wade responded, "You were fired on. Roll." And he pointed across the clearing to where the other men were lying.

In an instant, Max was on full alert in a prone position tucked against the thick bushes that surrounded the encampment. Charlie instinctively rolled twelve feet from Max and stayed tight to the bushes lining the camp area.

Everyone except Yari reacted with alertness and instinctively moved closer to the outer perimeter of the campsite. All eyes were on Wade.

Yari was still asking, "What happened?"

Charlie, who was next to Yari, turned and said, "We were fired on."

"What?"

Wade rolled over next to Max and spoke quietly. "We took a round about three inches from Yari's head." He pointed to the barren piece of branch next to where Yari's head had been.

By now they were all awake and attentive, their backs tightly pressed against bushes lining the edge of the clearing.

"Stay as flat to the ground as you can," Wade ordered.

Whispering and using hand signals, Wade explained what happened and indicated the direction from which he thought the shot originated. "I'm pretty sure it was a silenced M-21. I heard the round hit a branch on its way in." For

Yari's benefit, Wade once again pointed to the branch with the missing bark, so everyone was aware of the projectile's direction.

Wade turned to Max and said in a low whisper, "I think the shooter is about seventy yards out."

Wade drew a pictogram in the soft dirt: two semi circles and a straight line. Max knew exactly what Wade was thinking. Now that everyone was flush to the ground and safe for the moment, Wade explained what he wanted to do.

The campsite was higher than the ground around them and buttressed by a thick stand of large trees and bushes. Lots of dried twigs and leaves covered the ground for fifty yards around the campsite, making it difficult for anyone to approach without being heard.

Wade whispered to Max that he was going to roll to the other side of the clearing and suggested that he and Max begin a flanking movement in a semi-circle toward the shooter. He directed Max to stay low and referenced his diagram in the dirt for the pattern he wanted Max to follow. Wade's impromptu plan would have them approaching the shooter from two different angles, meeting at the apex where the two semi-circles crossed, about seventy yards out. Max immediately understood Wade's plan and signaled that he was ready.

Before giving the signal to Max, Wade wanted to think a moment more to ensure that he was making the right decision. He and Max would be approaching an armed sniper with nothing more than a field knife. If they tried to run or stay in place, the shooter could instantly pick them off one-by-one. They had the cover of a dark night with fog rolling in; maybe if they could get close to the shooter from two positions, he might get unsettled and leave the area. It wasn't a great plan, but it was all he could come up with at the moment.

There were really no other options. He wasn't going to sit still and remain a target. He had to move. After all, a trained sniper who already had them in his scope was repositioning for his next shot.

Chapter 8

Wade turned to Max looking for confirmation of his plan. "We have the cover of a very dark, overcast night on our side."

As a seasoned sniper, Max anticipated Wade's thought process. "A frontal flanking approach should give us maximum effect, assuming the shooter can't get a clear shot at us."

"That's right. We'll have to make sure he doesn't get that shot. Remember the shooter probably has PVS 2 night vision goggles or a Starlight scope. Hug the ground like a snake. Keep obstacles between you and the shooter. Don't let him get a clear shot."

Max agreed and was ready to deploy. "I'm ready when you are."

"I'm going to roll back to the other side. Move out when ready."

"Copy."

Wade rolled to the other side of the clearing to give final instructions to Charlie and Yari.

Still stunned by everything that happened, Yari asked, "This may be a dumb question, but why would you go after an armed sniper in the middle of the night with nothing more than your field knife? Am I missing something here?"

"It's our only chance. Otherwise, he'll pick us off one at a time."

Trying to make logical sense of Wade's last statement, Yari couldn't think of a decent follow-up question.

"You and Charlie stick together," Wade continued. "I'm putting Charlie in charge of your team. Stay flat on the ground for thirty minutes to give us time to draw the shooter's attention. After that, belly crawl 100 yards to the south. There's another clearing. Wait there flat on the ground, preferably with trees between you and the direction of the shooter until we return. Understand?"

Yari and Charlie nodded.

"When you make your move to the new location, stay as close to the brush line as possible. Give the shooter the smallest possible target at all times."

Yari started to ask another question when Wade cut him off. "Just listen to Charlie and follow his instructions. I've got to deploy."

"Good luck."

Inch by inch, Wade and Max pulled their bodies forward, relying only on elbows and knees for locomotion as they had been trained. Every few feet, the men stopped and listened for sounds and movement.

Keeping his head low to the ground, Wade saw the heavy fog rolling in from the south. He thought to himself, *You can't see more than a foot in front of you. Even with a night scope the conditions are not ideal for a sniper.* He hoped the sniper was dwelling on the same thought.

Twenty minutes passed, and the men advanced a few feet further. Branches and leaves were becoming wet from descending fog and mist. Their position wasn't comfortable, but the moist leaves and wet ground ensured greater protection from discovery as they moved closer to the sniper with every pull.

After fifty feet of alternating crawls and stops, Wade heard something in front of him perhaps twenty yards away. The sound appeared to come from a thorny thicket to his left. His first thoughts were of a deer or one of the many animals which roamed the woods, often feeding at night, but he couldn't be certain. He assumed Max heard the same noise.

Wade stopped his crawl and just listened. His senses,

keen from so much time in the swamp, focused on a single point of sound. The soft sound pattern he heard was movement over wet leaves – which meant it wasn't being made by an animal or something that crawled.

Wade changed the timing of his intermittent crawl-and-stop pattern to one with longer pauses in between. His mind raced, trying to identify the sound he heard for the second time. It sounded like the quiet steps of a boot exerting pressure against wet leaves. One slow step up, then a pause before the down step. After hearing the sound again, he was certain it wasn't coming from a four-footed animal.

Wade wanted his next movement to be quieter than his last. He slowly collected wet leaves under his body, and then tested the padding with a gentle roll to his right. His roll made no sound at all. There was no new sound from his shooter, but Wade was two feet closer to the source. His immediate thought was, *This shooter is well trained.*

He could no longer continue to move in a straight line. More leaves and another quiet roll put his new position behind two large tree trunks at a different angle to the shooter. His change in direction might cause the shooter some confusion about Wade's actual position. He was now comfortable with letting silence work its magic on the shooter's mind.

Snipers usually position themselves for the best possible visibility, not sound. Wade stayed behind the large tree trunks. His low profile made a clean shot extremely difficult. To lessen his infrared signature, he covered himself with cold, wet leaves, hoping they would lower his body temperature and thus the chance of visual recognition.

Wade wanted the shooter's recognition of him to be based solely on sound. He once again rolled twice to his right, stuffing more wet leaves over and under him to muffle his sound and signature. Wade crawled another two feet closer to the sound he'd last heard.

This time Wade broke his pattern by remaining still even longer. He hoped the silence would cause the shooter to think he was closer than he really was. With two people coming closer on both flanks, sooner or later the sniper would figure out his position might be compromised, and either fire or leave the area.

After two more rolls to the right and several short crawls forward, Wade heard nothing. He wondered, *Are the two of us playing the same game*? Wade could only hope Max was approaching in the same manner.

His stomach tightened as he felt the increasing stress of waiting. A flash back to the *USS Prowfish* came vividly to mind, with visions of the cramped, even claustrophobic submarine quarters. Remembering the strain of not knowing the location of the Soviet sub or who would fire first, he remembered how it felt to be so close to death, and sweat poured from his body.

Wade slowed his breathing, telling himself he had better control over his current situation. He had gotten as close as he could; the next move was in the sniper's court. Wade froze himself in time. Seconds seemed like hours before he heard the crack of a twig. Another crack soon followed. The pattern of sounds became synchronized. The target was moving *away* from his position.

He lay still to confirm the sounds were footsteps. It could still be a trap if there was another shooter involved. Wade carefully raised his head a few inches to better position his ear. He noted the direction of the sounds and counted footsteps in order to estimate the distance and how rapidly it was being covered.

Wade had to be certain there was not a second shooter.

He heard an unfamiliar sound to his left and wondered, *Could that be Max?* He didn't want to give away his position until he was sure.

Wade signaled by making a bird call with his cupped hands. It was something he'd learned in childhood from hunting in the swamp. Max heard the call and recognized it was Wade. He replied with a simple, "Yo."

Wade responded in a low quiet tone, "Forty feet to center slowly. Watch for second shooter."

"Confirmed."

The two men crouched behind two large spruce trees, just weary from their "pull." Wade turned to Max. "The shooter went off in a westerly direction from my position. He had a good stride once he cleared those thickets. He was really hauling."

"He was good. I think he sensed us but wasn't sure of our positions."

"We were lucky to have this dark overcast night."

"You'd better believe we were lucky."

"I think we should try to preserve some evidence here until we can report the incident. Let's see if we can find his shooting position. There may be a spent cartridge or footprints. Get some twigs to use as markers."

Wade began tearing his undershirt into marking strips. A few yards away, the men found the shooter's lair. The area was surrounded by bushes strategically arranged for maximum cover and a stable platform. The floor of the clearing was trampled down to ensure steady footing. There was even a cleared escape path leading off to the south for his departure.

"He was here quite a while before he shot. That tells me he was waiting for us to return from our mission," noted Max.

"I don't see any spent cartridges. He may have removed his brass. There are some footprints leading out in that direction," Wade said, pointing to several indentations. "Be careful where you walk – don't destroy any footprint impressions."

"There's a wet area over there that has some good prints on the other side of the puddle. We should mark that."

"I see it. I'll tag it."

The men followed the shooter's escape path for thirty yards until it ended at the beginning of an open field. There was a thicket on the other side of the open field, but it was too dark to see much on the other side. Wade couldn't see much past the mist that had settled over most of the field.

"We need to stop here. We don't want to be exposed in that open field. He's probably on the other side of that thicket, scoping us right now."

The men continued marking evidence in the dark and returned to camp. Red Team was once again huddled in a second bivouac but without the benefit of a fire. They set up doubled watches around the perimeter. No one got much sleep the rest of that night.

Dawn came early with a hot rising sun and little sleep. The group had assembled around two large stones in the center of the clearing to discuss their next steps.

"We have another cache to capture, but I'm more concerned about what happened last night. The incident needs to be reported. Problem is, I'm not sure at this point who we can trust. We have to cross a dirt road about two klicks west before reaching the last cache. Just to be on the safe side, let's move toward the last cache, staying out of sight until we get to the road. There might be a training monitor on the road."

"If we find a monitor, we'll report the incident, but

probably blow our chances to win the exercise. If we don't find a monitor, we'll move forward with our planned diversion for cache five, and report the incident when the exercise is over at noon."

Yari could barely contain himself. "Who gives a damn about the exercise? I almost got killed last night."

No one responded to Yari's comment. They spread out silently, moving through cover toward the road. No one said it, but Wade, Max, and Charlie were of the same opinion, that the sniper might still be on their tail. After a quarter mile of hiking, staying within the forest thicket, Wade held up his fist as a sign for everyone to stop.

Each took cover under or behind the closest bush or tree. The road was visible in the morning light. Off to the left stood a training monitor with a bright green arm band, standing in the middle of the road near his jeep.

The team members went a short way back into the thick forest to quietly converse. Unanimously the team asked Wade to approach the sergeant in the road while the others remained out of sight and under cover.

Wade went around the forest and approached the road from a different direction from where his team waited. Waving his hands and yelling as he left the protection of the forest, he called out to the monitor. He crossed the ditch and walked up the grade to road level, carefully watching the monitor's eyes and movement.

He explained to the sergeant what had happened the evening before, and the sergeant immediately went back to his jeep and called headquarters on the two-way radio. Wade gave the signal for his men to come out of the woods.

The sergeant repeated what he'd been told by headquarters. "You and your men wait here. Colonel Miller will be over shortly."

The Red team members came out from behind assorted bushes and assembled on the road around the sergeant.

It wasn't more than ten minutes before Wade saw the rooster tail of dust behind a vehicle heading quickly towards them. Like a lizard crossing a hot asphalt road, the Colonel's vehicle moved with purpose and then came to a quick stop just fifteen feet in front of the sergeant's jeep.

Colonel Miller emerged from the passenger seat, and his driver followed, leaving both vehicle doors open.

Turning to the sergeant and then to Wade, the Colonel asked, "Are you the one reporting the incident?"

"Yes, sir."

Miller wanted to isolate Wade from the rest of the group. "Step over here, son. The rest of you stay where you are. Let's start with an introduction."

"Yes sir. I'm Wade Hanna from Intelligence in Washington D.C., taking part in the Sniper Navigational Training Class. For the last two days, we've been participating in the cache exercise. I am leader of Red Team and those are my men." He pointed back to his men standing in the road.

"I'm Colonel Miller, second in command at the base. Tell me what happened, Mr. Hanna."

Wade quickly recounted their response to the sniper's action of the previous evening, careful not to leave out any important details. Miller listened intently, following every step and waiting to ask Wade for more details.

"How do you know it was a rifle shot?"

"I've heard the M-21 with a silencer and fired it myself many times, sir. I believe the crack I heard was the incoming round hitting a branch a split second before hitting the tree next to Yari. I believe that incoming branch probably diverted the round just enough to miss his head."

The Colonel commented in a doubtful tone. "Last night was a dark, overcast night. Sometimes in the field you hear strange sounds..."

"Sir, I am certain of what I heard. It was dark last night. I think a night vision scope or night goggles would be the only way that shooter could come that close with a round. I think the evidence at the location will speak for itself, sir."

Miller waved over his driver, who was standing a few feet from the car. "Get Captain Padilla on the radio."

Colonel Miller turned back to Wade. "We have a forensics team on base. I'm calling them in on this. I hope your facts are correct, or I'm going to have egg all over my face. Do you understand that, son?"

"Yes, sir."

The driver turned and said, "Captain Padilla is on the line, sir."

Handing over the phone, Miller and Padilla spoke for some time. Wade overheard the Colonel say he wanted the forensics team on the site right away as part of a crime scene investigation.

Handing the receiver back to his driver, Colonel Miller started walking toward the men of Red Team standing with the sergeant. He turned to the sergeant and said, "Let's wait until forensics arrives."

The Colonel then addressed the rest of the waiting men. "We're going to call off the cache exercise at this point. I want Sergeant Martinez to find Blue Team and have them return to the barracks and report to my office. I'm going to wait with Hanna and go over details with forensics. You men return to the barracks, get cleaned up, and grab some chow. Meet at my office for a debriefing at 1100 hours. Someone from my office will handle the debriefing."

"Yes, sir," the Red Team acknowledged in unison.

"Sergeant Martinez, I want Red and Blue teams kept separated – no discussions between them until after debriefing."

"Yes, sir."

Chapter 9

Dusty rooster tails rising from the road caused Miller and Wade to turn their heads at the same time.

Pointing to the dust trails, the Colonel said, "I suspect that's our forensics team." Miller then turned to Wade. "Show me where the incident took place."

"About a half a click south of this point." Wade pointed into the woods where there were no roads.

The Colonel turned to his driver. "You stay here, and have the forensics team follow us. Turning back to Wade he said, "Lead the way, son."

Wade proceeded into the forest with Miller following. They walked slowly but deliberately on and off small paths deeper into the forest toward the clearing Wade knew would soon appear.

Approaching the clearing, Wade pushed two branches away so the Colonel could pass. "Here's our first bivouac."

Wade showed Colonel Miller the branch in the tree where the round impacted. The Colonel came in for a closer look as Wade pointed to the source of the projectile, saying, "The round came from that direction and impacted small branches in this area."

Wade stood where Yari had been standing and used his arm to simulate a straight line into the bush. "I figure the shooter was about seventy yards away in that direction."

The Colonel went over and stood behind Wade's shoulder, sighting down his arm.

Wade explained the position of each man around the campfire, pointing so the Colonel could see their relative positions. Colonel Miller was not focused on the damaged branch. It was clear the branch had suffered a high velocity impact from the direction Wade previously indicated.

"Sir, there are probably lead fragments in that tree bark that might help identify the composition of the bullet."

"I agree. Good point. I'll have forensics take that branch back to the lab."

Wade showed Miller where he and Max had rolled and started their crawl toward the shooter. The Colonel remained silent, mentally reenacting the sequence of events as though they were all occurring at that very moment.

"Did you hear any additional shots?"

"No, sir. I felt we were dealing with a trained sniper just from the way he moved. I think he was surprised to find us coming toward him."

"Why do you feel that way?"

"I had the sense that he knew approximately where we were, but because of the bush, heavy fog, and dark night, he couldn't get a fix on our position or a clear shot."

Miller wanted to know when they first heard a change in the sniper's movement. Wade replied, "We were thirty yards from the target when we heard him change positions. He was moving to our right."

Wade walked to the spot where he'd heard the movement and pointed in the direction the shooter took. The Colonel continued walking slowly down Wade's crawl path.

"How could you tell he was on the move?"

"I could hear the leaves move under his feet. I also heard several small twigs break. If you look at this terrain, it's almost impossible to move without making some sound."

Miller was now in a crouch, rubbing handfuls of leaves in his hands to sense the moisture content and replicate the sounds the shooter may have made before commenting. "The morning sun has already dried out these leaves a little. Was he moving slow or fast at this point?"

"He was moving very slowly, and trying to make as

little sound as possible."

"At what point did you hear the sound pattern change?" The Colonel followed Wade down his crawl path to the larger stand of trees Wade used as cover.

Wade stood behind the trees and pointed to where he'd heard the steps.

"Did you ever catch sight of him?"

"No, sir. By the time I felt certain there was only one individual, he was pretty far away. Max and I followed his path to the edge of an open field and couldn't see far into the field from that point."

"Let's walk over to that field," said the Colonel.

When the dense undergrowth opened to the field, Wade pointed to the where they had been standing.

"A heavy fog had rolled in, covering the field up to about seven feet high. We didn't want to take the chance of entering that fog bank unarmed. I suspect the shooter was either in the fog or on the other side in that thicket."

"Do you have any idea who this shooter might be, or why he targeted you or your men?"

"No, sir, not for sure."

"What do you mean 'not for sure'?"

"Well, sir, our team had several run-ins with one of the other team members after we arrived for training, but I have no evidence to suggest the shooting was done by that person or anybody else."

As the Captain turned to respond to Wade, they heard voices of the approaching forensics team.

"We're over here," called Colonel Miller, and he walked twenty feet to meet a uniformed man he introduced as Captain Penata. They exchanged greetings before the Colonel pointed in an arch from the bivouac area to the trees bordering the open field.

"I want the entire area taped off as a crime scene. Have your men walk through it carefully. The shooter's position was off in that direction, about sixty yards from the bivouac. Hanna here has already marked off several sites for possible foot impressions. I want all the foot impressions taken, and I want that branch with lead fragments brought in and analyzed at the lab. Once you set up your perimeter, I want your men to fine-tooth comb the area looking for any evidence, including spent shells. This was no accident. We have a shooter in our midst in a no-weapons area, and we have to find out who's responsible for this breach. I'm taking Hanna back with me for debriefing."

The forensics team was shown the location of the footprints and Wade's markers, as they walked the path taken by the shooter. When he was satisfied that the team was equipped to handle the detail Miller motioned to his driver to pick them up.

Colonel Miller's car stopped at the barrack to drop Wade off. "Clean up and grab some chow and be at my office in an hour."

"Yes, sir." Wade turned toward the steps of his barrack still amazed at the detail with which Colonel Miller approached the incident. But for some reason he couldn't identify, he felt anxious, not knowing what would happen next, and wondering where his men were.

Wade opened the door to his barrack to find that the premises had been vacated. All the beds had been stripped, and his duffel was the only one in evidence. His backpack lay on the floor at the foot of his bed. Resting on the mattress was a neatly folded square piece of paper.

Wade looked at the folded paper but decided to leave it until after he showered. After showering, he sat on the side of his bed and unfolded a hand-written note.

Dear Wade,

I realized I might not see you before I had to leave. I just wanted to thank you again for saving my life last night. I realize that you didn't have to watch out for me like you did. I will always remember what you did for me. Please call me sometime when you're in D.C.

Thank you,
Yari

Wade folded the note and put it in his backpack. He was due in Colonel Miller's office in forty minutes, so he grabbed a burger at the base snack shack before walking to Miller's office in the main administration building.

Wade entered the building and asked where he could find Colonel Miller's office. Without looking up, the desk sergeant pointed to the right corner of the floor. Wade walked over to the desk, where a soldier in fatigues sat typing an Army form.

"My name is Wade Hanna, and I'm reporting as requested by Colonel Miller."

"Take a seat. I'll let him know you're here."

A row of chairs lined the wall outside of the Colonel's office. After a ten-minute wait, Miller's assistant said, "He will see you now."

Wade approached the door and knocked twice before hearing a voice. "Enter."

The Colonel was sitting with another gentleman in uniform. He motioned for Wade to come closer and take a chair opposite his desk.

"This is Major Jarvis. Dr. Jarvis is our base psychiatrist. I want him to assist in our debriefing."

Wade and the psychiatrist acknowledged each other, shaking hands as Miller continued the introduction from his chair.

"I have given Major Jarvis an overview of the incident. We just want to ask you a few more questions about last evening and what led up to it. Why don't you explain what happened in your own words to Major Jarvis?"

Wade felt strangely comfortable in these surroundings even though he was speaking with the second-highest-ranking officer on the base and a psychiatrist he had never met before. As Wade started summarizing the events of the previous evening, he looked directly at Major Jarvis, realizing he had never met any other psychiatrist. That thought made him a little nervous.

He repeated his story nearly word for word while the other men took notes. Dr. Jarvis had an analytical look about him, although his close-set eyes darted back and forth when he concentrated, giving Wade a creepy feeling.

Jarvis asked his first question. "Were you at all suspicious of anyone on Blue Team?"

"No. I don't really know anyone on Blue Team except in passing, and neither do any of my men."

"Isn't it true you've out-maneuvered Blue Team on caches since the exercise began? You were winning the exercise, were you not?"

Before Wade could reply, Dr. Jarvis came in with another question. "In fact, isn't it true you only had one cache left when the incident happened?"

"That's correct. We were winning and only had a single cache left to capture."

It wasn't clear where Jarvis's questioning was headed.

Wade thought but didn't say: *Jarvis sounds more like an attorney than a psychiatrist. Is he trying to establish some kind of motive for the incident?*

Wade took Jarvis' question to imply that his team might have provoked or had something to do with the shooting incident. It wasn't long before the doctor's questions began to rub Wade the wrong way. His tone seemed somehow confrontational. Perhaps he was looking for some weakness or contradiction in Wade's responses. Wade wondered if this was some kind of psychological profiling. He reacted by becoming extremely cautious in his responses.

Perhaps that was the reaction Jarvis was looking for. The whole thing bothered Wade more than he wanted to admit.

Colonel Miller caught the tension between Wade and Jarvis and jumped in to provide some balance.

"Hanna, you started to tell me about a confrontation your group had with another person or group when we were interrupted by forensics. Please tell Dr. Jarvis about that situation. It may be important."

"Sometimes I find animosity directed at me when taking training courses at military bases. There seems to be a general distrust of intelligence officers on most military bases. So I wasn't surprised when that situation came up here. Usually those feelings blow over after the people get to know each other. In fact, it's not uncommon to become quite friendly with those who initially mistrusted me before the training is over."

Wade paused to see if Jarvis' expression had changed, but his head was down and he was taking notes as fast as he could write.

Wade continued, "We had a couple of situations occur since arriving for this training session. My team member

Milton Yankovich and I are from intelligence. When we arrived, we were harassed during assembly at the loading dock by some Vietnam Special Forces vets."

"There was one person in particular that became extremely boisterous and aggressive towards us. He made his comments primarily at me, about the inadequacies of intelligence officers in the field. He was speaking loud enough so that everyone within shouting distance could hear. A group of Special Forces guys gathered around me in a tight circle, and that man was their leader. He indicated that members of his recon team were killed in Vietnam because they took orders from an inept intelligence officer."

"He was clearly blaming the entire intelligence community for the problem. The evening before we started the cache exercise, this same Special Forces guy approached Yari and me in the mess hall and asked when we were leaving the table, because they wanted to sit there, and not with us. The soldier said how pathetically we had performed in the team firing exercises, and at another meal they even accused us of cheating. He said that if we weren't careful, we might not make it out of the next exercise alive."

Jarvis paused briefly from his note-taking and looked at Wade. His eyes were darting rapidly back and forth. "What did you say or do after he said that?"

"Nothing. We ignored him like we did his other threats."

Colonel Miller jumped back into the conversation. "Who was the soldier making these comments?"

"James Lockhart."

"Was Lockhart a member of Blue Team?"

"No, sir, I believe Lockhart was on the Orange Team, far to the east of our location during the cache exercise."

"Did you have a feeling that Lockhart may have been

involved in the shooting incident?"

"I have no idea who was responsible for the shooting. I'm just recounting the only incident I can think of where there was some animosity during this whole exercise. I don't want to see Lockhart or anybody else get in trouble if they weren't involved in the shooting."

Colonel Miller pushed a button on his desk. Within seconds his assistant was standing in the open door at attention.

"Get me the personnel file on James Lockhart. He's Army, Special Forces, and part of this training exercise group."

"Yes, sir."

His assistant did a formal about-face and left the room. While Wade was debriefing with Miller and Jarvis, the cache exercise had ended, and from the window he could see men returning to the barracks. The debriefing discussion continued for another half hour as Miller and Jarvis continued asking small details about different parts of the incident.

Wade was explaining how his team had intended to approach the fifth cache when a firm knock on the door interrupted his thought. Everyone turned toward the door.

"Enter."

Miller's sergeant came in holding a manila file under his arm, which he handed to Colonel Miller.

While Miller was opening the file, the desk sergeant spoke up. "Sir, I thought you'd want to know that we just received a call from exercise command, that Orange Team reported to the finish station missing a man. They reported that Lockhart was missing. He left the prior evening on a recon mission and didn't return to camp."

The Captain took the personnel file, looked at Jarvis,

and told his aid, "Call the exercise coordinator. I want the Orange Team held for questioning and debriefing."

"Yes, sir."

The sergeant executed an about-face as before and left the room. Colonel Miller turned to Wade with an expression that said Wade's part of the meeting was over.

"Is there anything else you can add to the events of last evening?"

"No, sir."

Turning to Major Jarvis, the Colonel asked, "Do you have any more questions for Mr. Hanna?"

"Not at this time, but I may want to ask him more questions after I've done more investigation on this matter."

Colonel Miller asked, "Do we have all your contact information?"

"Yes, sir."

Miller asked Wade about his flight plans, then indicated that one of his aids would give him a lift to the airport, compliments of the base.

"Thank you, sir."

The Colonel got up from his desk and followed Wade to the door. He waved his aid over.

"See that Mr. Hanna gets a lift to the airport. You can use my staff car."

Chapter 10

Greenstone, Alabama

The uneventful return flight and drive to his apartment gave Wade time to think. Lack of sleep, combined with the stress of the last two days, made Wade realize how tired he was. He was glad to finally be back in comfortable surroundings.

Mail had piled up behind the slot in his front door. Stepping over the stack, he headed for the refrigerator. Finding only a half-filled jar of jelly and a single bottle of beer, he opened both and made a peanut butter and jelly sandwich on stale bread and headed toward the mail on the floor.

He picked up the mail before sinking deep into his favorite overstuffed armchair. His mind slowly readjusted to familiar surroundings. Flipping through the mail, he quickly discarded junk promotions and put the unpaid invoices in a stack which he tossed on the table next to him. He was annoyed to see the light on his answering machine flashing a bright red. Looking across the dining table, he saw the economics book he'd left and remembered that he had a test the next day.

His jaw muscles tightened as he tried to remember what his economics test would cover. He vaguely remembered his professor talking about "cobweb theorems." The only cobwebs he could think of were the ones in his brain right now from lack of sleep. There would be no studying this evening. He was already half asleep.

Wade walked into the bedroom to set his alarm for 4:30 the next morning to give him time to study before the test at 10:00 a.m. He then turned to the recorded messages on his answering machine and pressed the replay button.

The machine promptly replied, "You have five

unanswered messages." Wade pressed the start button and heard Megan's voice.

"My God, we just got word that there was some kind of a shooting incident during your training. Are you all right? Call me as soon as you get in, no matter what time it is."

The second and third messages were also from Megan – all similar, each showing increasing signs of worry.

"You should be back by now. I haven't heard from you. Call me at home anytime – as soon as you get this. Where are you? Don't you dare forget to call me! Call anytime. You know the number."

Wade didn't want to go through another long description of the last two days, but thought he'd better answer her call. *How did the Agency find out about the sniper incident so fast?*

He looked through the bedroom door at the bed that seemed to be calling his name. He put his hand up to hold his head and closed his eyes for just a moment's rest, to catch a mental breath. As soon as his head rested in his hand, he was asleep.

After a few minutes of sleep, Wade's body twitched like someone had applied a small electric shock. His eyes flew open, realizing he had never made the return call to Megan. For the first time in the last two days, Wade realized he was losing the battle with exhaustion. Without thinking, Wade dialed Megan's number, hoping she had calmed down and was rested. In his condition he had no use for hysterics.

"Hi, it's me."

"My God. Are you all right?"

"I'm fine."

"What the hell happened?"

"I'm really exhausted. Can I give you the short version now and the details tomorrow, after I get some rest? I just remembered I have an economics test tomorrow."

"I was going to remind you of your test. First tell me what happened."

Wade gave a brief summary of the incident, and asked her how she'd heard about it.

"It was a big deal at headquarters. The head of the Agency was on a call for over an hour with the base commander at Benning. All I heard was that you performed well in the situation. Some Special Forces guy is AWOL, and there's a big investigation going on."

Megan had a list of questions ready for Wade, but she could tell he was running on fumes. Now that she'd heard his voice and knew he was okay, additional details seemed less important than his rest. She realized he had to focus on sleep now and the exam tomorrow. She also knew that he had a paper due on Thursday. Perhaps she would wait until he got some rest before reminding him. Megan sensed that she was losing him.

"Now don't go to sleep on me quite yet."

"I'm sorry. I really need to get some rest."

"Get some sleep and call me after the test tomorrow."

"Thank you."

He hung up the phone and crawled into his bed with his clothes on. No other sound registered in Wade's brain until the alarm went off at 4:30 the next morning.

Two days later, Wade had just learned that he'd passed his economics test, and was working to finish his second paper when his phone rang.

"Hello?"

"Hi, it's Yari. I was just thinking about you. It's good to hear your voice. Did you get the note I left on your bed at Fort Benning?"

"Yes, I sure did. Thank you very much."

"Well, I wanted you to know how much I appreciate you saving my life."

"You're welcome. You were really a trooper throughout the whole miserable exercise."

"No, I wasn't – but it's kind of you to say so and to have put up with me during the exercise. I was out of my league during the whole training. I know I held the team back. You guys were good enough to keep me around. The truth is that I'm no longer involved in field work, and I don't think the NSA is keeping that program anymore."

"What happened to you and the other team members after I got stuck with Colonel Miller and the forensics team?"

"They brought us back by Army truck and debriefed us, and then told us to clean up, strip the barracks, and get on the next bus to the airport. They said there was another training group arriving right behind us. The team wanted to wait for you, but we were ordered on the bus."

"I was hoping to stay in touch, but I never got the other team members' contact information."

"I have all that information, and can give it to you anytime. What happened to you after we left?"

"I had to stay at the site and go over everything with forensics. I was then debriefed by Colonel Miller and a psychiatrist, Major Jarvis. They kept me in debriefing for quite a while. When I was finally released, they offered me a ride to the airport. At the time I left, they were getting ready to question Blue Team and start the forensics investigation. I also heard that Lockhart was AWOL from his unit."

"Are you speaking from a secure phone?"

"No, just the one from my apartment."

"I'm calling on one of the NSA's secure lines, so we

should be okay. I'm also having our conversation encrypted, so we can speak freely."

Yari paused, and then continued. "I don't know if you know this, but the day after we left, they found Lockhart's dead body in a motel about forty miles from the base. He was found with a bullet in his head – apparent suicide."

There was silence on the line as Wade tried to process that information. "You're kidding. Where did you hear that?"

"I'm not at liberty to discuss sources right now, but the information is reliable. Remember, Wade, the NSA has access to information other people don't have."

"That's unbelievable. Do they know any more about what happened?"

"Unofficially, I'm still working on that angle. As it turns out, there was a CID Army Intelligence plant in Orange Team. I don't know why, but this CID person was there the whole time we were. He was apparently keeping an eye on Lockhart."

"That's interesting in itself. Why were they watching Lockhart?"

"I think the base knew more about Lockhart than they were letting on."

"But what exactly did they suspect or know about Lockhart?"

"Perhaps Lockhart had a mental condition, or maybe he knew something about the Army they didn't want to get out. I'm just guessing, but I know they were all over, watching Lockhart while he was in training."

"If they suspected something, why wouldn't they just bring him in?"

"I don't know, but my guess is that something went wrong with Lockhart. I think he might have found out about the CID plant in his group or flipped out or just turned on everyone, including us. It makes sense that it was probably Lockhart who took the shot at me. From what I'm hearing, it sounds like he slipped out of camp the night of the incident without CID knowing where he had gone. That's all I know right now."

"That's unbelievable! We're in the middle of something serious here, and we didn't have a clue about what was going on."

"It almost got us all killed – starting with me. I'm still having nightmares. Listen, you didn't hear any of this from me. I just wanted to give you that update. If you ever want to contact me, call my secure number. If I don't answer, leave a message, and I'll get right back to you."

Yari proceeded to give Wade his secure number. "I'm in touch with all of our team members. Max especially sends his regards."

Wade was at a loss for words as he processed Yari's new information. A moment passed while Wade tried to put the pieces together in quiet thought before Yari broke the awkward silence.

"Look, I don't mean to break this off, but I'm in the middle of a hot international incident at work right now, and I really have to go."

"Not a problem. Please keep me posted."

"Will do, partner. By the way, the detective handling the murder investigation is out of Atlanta. He goes by the name of Gabriel Morrison, or 'Gabe' for short. Fort Benning and Morrison are having a dispute over who controls Lockhart's body."

"Take care. We'll talk soon, partner."

Yari hung up the phone while Wade kept the receiver to his ear, still in shock over what he'd just heard. He stared at the blank wall across his room and tried to put together pieces of the disjointed puzzle. *We're on an Army base in the middle of a so-called normal training exercise. A Special Forces sniper fires on us, trying to kill one or more intelligence officers. The sniper goes missing and is now dead. A CID covert operative is a plant in the exercise. The base may have known about this all along. Who else is involved? How and why did Lockhart really die? Why are they fighting over the body? How does my agency know so much about the damn event? Why is Megan asking all these detailed questions about me and the event?"*

His mind raced back to his debriefing at the base. The more he thought about it, the more it felt like an interrogation than a debriefing under the guise of an investigation. Wade continued to be perplexed. *They did a good job of acting surprised by everything. Did Jarvis and Miller just want to find out what I knew? Was Jarvis trying to profile me during the debriefing? If so, for what purpose?*

Wade kept the ever-growing list of questions to himself. He needed to find out if his friend, Louisiana detective Jake Pisano, knew this detective Gabe Morrison.

Chapter 11

Two days later, Wade was anxiously awaiting the return call from Pisano, so when the phone rang he rushed to grab it. But it wasn't Pisano. It was Yari calling again.

"I've just learned more about the jurisdictional issue over who controls Lockhart's body. The State contends he died on county property – outside of the base property. The base, on the other hand, contends Lockhart was on an undisclosed mission for the Army when he died, and therefore the body belongs to them."

"Why is the location of the body so important?"

"It seems Gabe Morrison suspects foul play in Lockhart's death. He wants to run further tests, including toxicology tests. If the Army gets the body, he believes evidence could disappear."

"Really? Were you able to determine what kind of mission Lockhart was supposed to be on?"

"No. The Army's position is that the mission was covert and irrelevant to his death. They're insisting his death was pure and simple suicide, and they don't want further tests run. Right now the body remains in the County's possession, and there's a scheduled court hearing in a couple of days."

"You're looking at all the communication. What do you think is going on?"

"It's all too convenient for the Army if they get control of the body. They don't want any tests run. Morrison thinks Lockhart may have been drugged before he died. If the body goes back to the Army, they control how the whole story comes out. There's also another part of this that I'm still chasing."

"What's that?"

"The CID's undercover agent involved goes by the

name of David Mashburn. Apparently he was undercover on their team the whole time we were there. The records show he was shipped out right after training ended – on assignment to an undisclosed foreign county to do top secret covert work. They're not at liberty to discuss his whereabouts because his mission is classified. How's that for coincidence?"

"Very convenient."

Both men paused to think about the new information, especially the perfect timing of David Mashburn's disappearance.

"Good work on Mashburn. See what else you can find out about him and where he is."

"I'm digging, partner. Will let you know as soon as I get something new."

Within seconds of hanging up from Yari's call, the phone rang again. This time it was Jake Pisano returning Wade's call, asking if he knew anyone by the name of Gabriel Morrison.

Pisano replied with certainty. "In your message you asked if I know Gabe Morrison. Of course I know Gabe. Everyone in southern law enforcement knows Gabe. I worked with him on the Coletta investigation. He was one of my key liaisons with the FBI for Coletta's operation in Atlanta. He's very good. He knows his stuff, but he's old school. Why do you want to know?"

"It's a long story. I'm going to be in New Orleans to see my father. Can we meet to discuss this? I may need your help."

"Sure. When would you like to meet?"

After discussing alternative dates, they settled on 2:00 p.m. on Thursday at the Old Grille. Same table, nothing changed.

Wade found out from his father that he'd loaned out the camp to their cousins for the month, so the swamp spirit would have someone else to entertain. He hoped the spirit didn't mind his absence on this trip. Wade was also off the hook for repairs; his cousins would take care of those chores.

As Wade sat waiting, he mused that The Old Grille looked the same. It wasn't long before Jake arrived, and they got right to the point, foregoing small talk.

"It's hard to believe it's been four years since you were on submarine duty."

"I really lucked out that the Agency position came in just before they were going to ship us out. My unit got activated three months after I left."

"So what brings you in contact with Gabe Morrison?"

"I don't really know Morrison, but here's how he's involved."

Wade began to tell Jake the details of the Lockhart story and what had happened at Fort Benning.

"That's serious stuff. You may not be implicated directly, but I would recommend that you certainly tell your side of the story to Gabe. If I were handling that case, I would want to know how your story fits in. Gabe's a straight shooter, so you can trust him."

"That's pretty much how I see it. I don't have anything to hide, except that I may be under some obligation not to reveal information that either the Army or my Agency considers classified."

"If you want, I can give Gabe a call and set up an introduction for you."

"That would be great. I think I'd like to meet him in person. I want to keep everything with him confidential. Right now, I don't know who to trust at Fort Benning – or in the Agency, for that matter."

"Stay alert to what your instincts are telling you. I believe Gabe will honor your confidentiality request. I'll give him a heads-up."

The New Orleans house where Wade grew up had been sold after his mother died, and his father was now getting ready to move into a condo. Wade helped his father put together a list of household items and decide what had to go before he moved.

They spoke at dinner that evening. The shrimp and crabmeat remoulade followed by stuffed flounder and a bananas Foster dessert at Monroe's capped off a wonderful visit. He drove back to Alabama the next day, carefully checking the rear view mirror out of habit.

A message from Jake was waiting on the answering machine when he arrived home. It was already pretty late in the evening, so Wade decided to return the call the next morning.

"Hi, Jake, it's Wade. I'm returning your call from last evening. I assume it's about Gabe Morrison."

"I spoke with Gabe. He would very much like to speak with you. I gave him a little background but told him it would be best coming from you. Gabe asked about you, and I told him you could be relied upon. He was fine with keeping everything confidential."

"Thanks for the referral. I'll give Gabe a call."

"Keep me posted on how things turn out."

"I sure will."

Wade couldn't get the Lockhart matter off his mind. The next day he placed a call to Yari for an update on the results of the Lockhart hearing.

"I read the pleadings and the judge's order. The Army's attorney argued that Fort Benning should have jurisdiction because they claimed Lockhart was still on a classified mission under government supervision, and therefore Lockhart's body was still under Army jurisdiction. They also argued that there was no urgency for an autopsy since suicide was the most probable cause of death. They claim Lockhart had serious psychological problems, of the sort which often resulted in suicide."

Yari stopped for a breath before he continued. "The Army's pleadings were supported by a declaration from Major Jarvis in Fort Benning. The psychiatrist claimed the type of battle fatigue Lockhart suffered from produced hallucinations, and that Lockhart likely thought he was still in combat and had to defend himself against an imaginary enemy. His declaration argued that depression and those images sometimes caused soldiers to take their own lives. He also said that Lockhart was in psychological treatment, a veteran's therapy group."

"Countering that position, the State argued that Lockhart's body was found on Georgia County property, outside of the base's jurisdiction."

"But here's an interesting point. The State's argument was supported by a declaration from detective Gabe Morrison that a preliminary toxicology report suggested drugs were present in Lockhart's system at the time of death. Morrison contended that, based on his years of investigations, there was a sufficient suspicion of foul play to warrant a full autopsy and investigation. He didn't go into detail on the evidence, but said his toxicology evidence came from a liver biopsy and blood samples taken at the scene shortly after Lockhart's death."

"The good news is that the judge ruled in favor of the State of Georgia. So now Gabe Morrison has jurisdiction over Lockhart's body. The base has gone quiet after the court's decision, and I haven't seen or heard anything more about the autopsy."

Wade responded. "I was able to make a connection with Morrison through a detective friend in New Orleans. I haven't actually spoken to Morrison yet, but I wanted to ask a favor."

"Sure. Anything I can do."

"I want to set up a secure phone patch for a call to Morrison from Alabama. Can you arrange that?"

"Not a problem. Just call my number from a pay phone. I'll set up the secure patch in such a way that you can be sure no one else is listening from anywhere."

"How can you be sure?"

"Look, buddy, you're on my turf now. I not only have access to both sides of the secure lines, but the conversation will be encrypted going both ways, using my own encryption software. The government doesn't even have the latest version of my program yet, so no one will be able to break that encryption code. I've tested it on all my smartest buddies here at the NSA. Why are you so concerned about a secure line?"

"Let's just say I'm concerned. I think this issue is much bigger than we ever thought, and somehow I feel that either Fort Benning or other intelligence agencies may be involved – including possibly my own. "

"Really? When do you want to call Morrison?"

"I'll call tomorrow at one o'clock my time."

"I'll be waiting."

The payphone a block from the college on a shaded side street seemed like a perfect place for the call.

"Hi, Yari. I'm ready for the Morrison call."

"Give me a minute to set it up. When you hear a dial tone, just dial."

"Do I just feed the payphone?"

"Nope. All taken care of. You don't need to do anything. I've already overridden your payphone line and taken it out of service for government security purposes. For the next two hours, this payphone can't be used for anything but your call."

"I didn't know you could do that."

Before Wade got Yari's answer, he heard the dial tone and dialed Morrison's number.

"Morrison here."

"Detective Morrison, my name is Wade Hanna. I'm a friend of Jake Pisano in New Orleans. I understand you're working on the James Lockhart case?"

"That's correct. I was expecting your call. I've known Jake for quite a while and worked with him on several cases. He's a top-notch detective."

"He says the same thing about you."

"What can I do for you, son?"

"I'm an intelligence officer who was involved in a training exercise at Fort Benning. Lockhart was part of those training exercises. My team was involved in a shooting incident just before Lockhart's death. I don't know if my involvement can help your investigation, but Jake suggested that I share with you some of the information I know about Lockhart. There may be some sensitive pieces of this information that could involve Fort Benning or my employer that might be important. I'm also concerned that I or my men don't get dragged into this situation."

"I see. I'd like to hear what you have to say. I can promise you now that all of our conversations will remain confidential."

"I appreciate that. I would rather have our conversation in person, if you don't mind."

"Where are you located?"

"In Greenstone, Alabama."

"There's a small town called Manchester, Georgia, just across the Alabama state line. It's where Highways 278 and 27 cross. On the main street there's a great restaurant called the Red Squirrel Café. I've known the owners for many years. It will be safe for us to talk there. I'll leave from Fayetteville, but it's a much longer drive for you."

"That's not a problem for me, sir."

"Good. Then let's meet at 11:00 in the morning on Friday."

"That works for me."

After finishing his call with Morrison, Wade called Yari back to let him know he had a meeting set up with Morrison.

Yari had been busy in the meantime with further updates on the Lockhart matter. "I'm doing more work on this CID guy David Mashburn. It appears this guy knows his way around the intelligence community. He spent most of his time in foreign posts, including Vietnam. He speaks several languages. He first served as a medic in Vietnam before going into Army intelligence. I don't really remember him in our training group."

"Interesting about Mashburn's background. Do you remember when Lockhart confronted us that evening at dinner in the mess hall?"

"Yes."

"Mashburn was the guy standing behind Lockhart, who got him calmed down before they decided to move to another table."

"So that was Mashburn. Oh, yeah, I remember him now."

That evening Wade and Megan spoke.

"How was New Orleans?"

"It was great. My father's doing well and has gotten over his apprehension about moving to a condo. He actually likes the idea now. I saw a few old friends, and that was pretty much it."

"Have you given any thought to your incompletes? You know I'm still in charge of getting you graduated."

"Yeah, I spoke to my professor about the make-up exam, and got it scheduled for next week. I'm starting on my two papers and should have them finished in a week or so."

"What else do you have planned?"

Wade was still too cautious to confide in Megan about the Lockhart matter. He wasn't going to tell her about Morrison. The first thing that popped into his mind was his meeting at the Red Squirrel Café.

"I'm going squirrel hunting this weekend with one of my friends. I'm leaving early Friday morning and will be back late Saturday."

"How do you hunt squirrels?"

"My friend Rich has a mountain cur hunting dog named Rufus."

"How does a dog hunt squirrels?"

"With one sniff, Rufus can not only tell you that a squirrel is in a particular tree – he can also tell you the time the squirrel came and left. If he barks, the squirrel is still in the tree, and if he makes a high-pitched whimper, it means he left. This louder the sound, the longer he's been out of the tree."

Megan laughed, thinking this was one of Wade's country jokes. "What do you do with the squirrels if you get any?"

"Eat them, of course. Haven't you had squirrel sauce pecan? It's a great delicacy in the South."

"It doesn't sound like something I would order at a

restaurant."

"You can't order squirrel in a restaurant. I'll fix it for you the next time we're together."

"I can't wait." She sounded upbeat when she hung up the phone.

Chapter 12
Manchester, Georgia

Wade got an early start on his three-hour drive Friday morning. The only traffic seemed to be big rigs and the few cars darting out from between large tractor-trailer bodies.

The quiet drive allowed Wade to refresh his memory. He turned down the radio, and details of the Fort Benning experience began replaying in his mind.

The sound of a silenced M-21 sniper rifle he had shot hundreds of times on the range was the first thing that ran through his mind. Next he remembered the convex lines he had drawn in the dirt before he and Max started their crawl to outflank the sniper. He remembered the silence being broken by the sound of leaves and twigs rustling as they inched closer to the shooter.

His mind bounced back to the first confrontation with Lockhart on the loading dock as everyone assembled for class. Remembering the exact words Lockhart had used in that first confrontation somehow seemed important. He practiced similar phrases, trying to recall the right words. *"Someone said we have intelligence spooks taking the class with us."* Wade thought he had closely approximated the words, but wasn't sure they were exact. In thinking about Lockhart's statement, he started wondering, *Who told Lockhart that intelligence personnel were taking the class?*

Raindrops hit the windshield, followed by a short shower typical of this time of year. *At least I'll show up in a clean car.*

After two hours of driving, Wade passed several small towns. He stopped at a Gulf station in one of those towns for gas and picked up a soda and a snack. Another hour's drive. He was enjoying the silence and the time to think.

Wade arrived early for his meeting. After finding the restaurant, he parked a block away under the shade of a large oak tree at a public park, to make some notes. Traffic on this quiet main street was so light that it didn't warrant a stoplight, and none was in evidence.

After jotting down a few thoughts, Wade noticed a dark blue car pull up in front of the café, from which a middle-aged gentleman got out with a folder under his arm. He was wearing a suit and fedora hat. Wade assumed this might be Gabe Morrison. His car seemed happy in the cool shade under the tree, so he left it there and walked the block to the café.

The man he'd seen get out of the car was speaking with a woman at the back of the restaurant. Perhaps that was the owner Morrison had referred to on the phone. Wade was looking around at the sparsely-filled restaurant when the gentleman in the hat waved him over.

When Wade approached, the man extended his hand. "Hi, I'm Gabe Morrison. This is Karen Strubs. She and her husband own this fine establishment."

"I'm Wade Hanna - nice to meet you both."

After turning to Karen, Gabe asked. "May we take up one of your fine tables?"

"Any one you'd like for as long as you'd like. The place is yours."

"That's very kind of you." Pointing to one of the tables, Gabe continued. "The one in the corner over there away from everyone will be fine."

Wade and Gabe took seats across from each other, each laying out notes on the table. The waitress came over and filled both water glasses. Turning to the waitress, Gabe spoke in a soft tone. "Please give us a little quiet time here. We may want to order a little later."

"Certainly, Mr. Morrison."

Turning to Wade, a wide grin spread across Gabe's face. "If you get hungry, their collard greens and ham hocks are absolutely the best in Georgia."

"That's one of my favorites. I'll have to try it later."

The two men chatted a little while about Wade's trip out, but soon got down to the business at hand.

"So, you're an intelligence officer with the CIA?"

"As of just recently. I've been in training for the last four years."

"Why don't you just start with your story – and if you don't mind, I'm going to take a few notes. My memory's not what it used to be."

"That's fine. I just want to make sure everything we talk about remains confidential."

"Assuming that you were not involved in Mr. Lockhart's death, everything will remain confidential."

"No, I wasn't involved in Lockhart's death."

Gabe pulled out a blank pad and pen and pushed his hat across the table before asking Wade a question. "If you don't mind my asking, why you are so concerned about confidentiality?"

"I'm an intelligence officer with the government and carry a secret clearance. I don't know what disclosures I might have to make that would fall under that secret designation and naturally don't want to have the government coming after me."

"That's a fair concern. I'm only interested in the facts as you remember them and won't need any secret information. If at any time you feel you're getting into a secrecy area, I don't want you to continue."

"That sounds fair."

"Why don't you start by telling me your story from the

beginning?"

Referring to his notes, Wade walked Gabe through the details of the Lockhart story from the time he arrived on base until he departed, including the debriefing he'd had before leaving for the airport. He left in as many details as possible.

Gabe seemed intently interested in the story, taking lots of notes but asking very few questions. When Wade concluded his story, Gabe commented, "That's a very interesting piece of this investigation. It contains important information leading up to Lockhart's disappearance. Did you at any time have any suspicions about who did the shooting that evening?"

"No."

"You don't know if it was Lockhart or somebody else?"

"No. It could have been someone from Blue Team or anyone else."

"Has the base given you any information on the results of their forensic investigation?"

"No."

Gabe looked up from his notes. "Let me tell you what we know from our investigation thus far." For a moment Gabe stared above Wade's head, putting together details before he spoke.

"The state police initially received the call from the hotel operator that a dead body had been discovered in Room 112. I was called by my department to handle the investigation and got to the scene about an hour after the state police had arrived. We estimate now that this was about three hours after Lockhart's actual time of death."

"The county sheriff had already presumed it was a suicide. The state police were good enough to leave the scene untouched until my forensic team arrived. I immediately observed several things that caused me to think it might not have been a suicide."

"I've done hundreds of murder and suicide cases over my career, and you get a feel for putting a scene back together again in your mind. This scene had several problems that I didn't like. It looked too clean, for one thing, almost staged – not like most suicide scenes. The placement of the body didn't look right to me. The position and angle of Lockhart's arm wasn't natural."

"I was suspicious within two minutes after being on the scene. I had my forensic team take precise measurements and photographs of everything from several different angles. I wanted to preserve as much evidence as we could. I knew from the beginning there would be lots of questions about this one."

Wade's interest was piqued as he visualized the scene. "Did you have an ID on the body at that time?"

"No. Nothing more than the 'Lockhart' label on his fatigues. The normal ID you typically find in a suicide case lying around wasn't there. That also made me suspicious."

"What was gone that you thought should be there?"

"He was in fatigues, but his dog tags were gone. He looked military, and his tattoos suggested military. We searched his truck, but there were no other signs of military gear."

"Did you contact Fort Benning?"

"Not until the next day when we ran fingerprints and got a positive ID."

Gabe reached for a worn manila folder with crumpled edges. He opened the folder and passed several pictures over to Wade. They were gruesome photos taken at the scene, some with Lockhart's brains spread all over his face. There was another photo taken in the morgue after he had been cleaned up.

"Is this the person whom you knew as Lockhart?"

"Yeah. That's Lockhart."

"We took our time with forensics at the site. I had the team take blood samples. We took power burn residue samples. I wanted Lockhart's exact position documented, particularly the angle of his arm. I had his clothes in the room wrapped so they could be later tested at the lab. I had detailed photos taken of the blood splatter patterns. I even had a close-up shot taken of his pupils."

After a brief pause Gabe continued his explanation. "Lockhart had a strange look on his face. I've never seen that look in a suicide case before. It may not prove to be anything important, but it was certainly noteworthy."

"What look do you mean?"

"It was an expression like he was trying to say something, or scream, but couldn't. I can't describe it any better than that."

"When we got the body back to the lab, the blood tests started showing small traces of a narcotic type substance that we couldn't identify. We're still working on that angle. The traces were so small they couldn't be used in court."

"More extensive autopsy tests might allow us to better understand the substance. We started getting push-back from Fort Benning as soon as we recommended further testing. I felt their position claiming jurisdiction of the body was weak from the beginning."

Gabe paused and took out another file with some notes that he reviewed before continuing his explanation.

"We've had our differences before with the base on other matters. Once I heard this matter was going to go to a court hearing, I knew something was amiss. I made the decision at that time to bend the rules a little and take a chance."

Wade frowned in confusion. "I don't understand."

"In the first preliminary motion, the court ruled that the body had to remain in its current condition until the matter was heard. I became suspicious of Benning's desire not to want any testing done, so I made a quick decision that I might live to regret. Fort Benning had gotten the jump on me with that restraining order on an autopsy until the hearing. Actually, it's fairly common to have a stay when a dispute like this arises. But my instincts told me I couldn't lose more time, so I ordered my coroner to take a liver biopsy."

"Wouldn't that have been a violation of the stay order?"

"Technically, it might have been. We were dancing between raindrops on that decision because a biopsy for reasonable cause does not technically constitute an autopsy."

As Wade was trying to comprehend the difference between an autopsy and biopsy, Gabe continued.

"The liver biopsy is what found the traces of the narcotic substance. In fact, the biopsy actually found traces of two different drugs. Those results gave me enough data to confirm my own suspicions and support the motion for a more extensive autopsy."

"When you refer to these traces of drugs, what do you mean?"

"These drugs were not run-of-the-mill prescription drugs or street narcotics. According to my toxicologist, they fall in the category of 'exotics.' They're made up of a weird combination of natural and man-made compounds. The other thing the toxicologist found strange about the drugs is that the concentration of the drugs in the body seemed to be naturally dissipating. He describes it as a drug that quickly breaks down so that, in time, there's no evidence it was ever present. If we'd waited another few days, there would have been nothing to find."

Wade looked straight ahead and shook his head in disbelief.

"After we won at the hearing, we ran an extensive toxicology panel at the autopsy the same day. Once my people knew some of the chemical compounds they were looking for, they searched for traces in other places in the body like fatty tissues and organs not usually covered in a normal autopsy. That's where we are now – waiting for the results of these more advanced toxicology studies."

"That's unbelievable. What do you see as the next step?"

"While we wait for the toxicology results, we're doing extensive testing of the clothing and weapon. We found small fragments of rope fibers on his sleeve. There was a small sofa pillow used between the end of the gun barrel and his jaw to muffle the sound. It's strange that someone would care about the noise their gun would make if they were committing suicide. The location of that pillow on the floor after the shot also didn't look right to me. We're doing trajectory tests to see where that pillow should have landed in the room in relation to his body and the gun discharge position in a true suicide."

"Did you determine whether or not he pulled the trigger?"

"As we'd expect, we found his fingerprints on the trigger of the gun, but not in other places you normally find them. The rest of the gun was clean – too clean, as in wiped clean."

Wade could now see the evidence mounting. More questions were coming to mind, but he didn't want to interrupt Gabe's train of thought.

"There was only one bullet in the chamber of his gun when it fired. There was no other ammo around, and the magazine was cleaned of ammo and fingerprints."

"That's strange."

"Funny thing is that we didn't find any ammunition anywhere. There was none on his person, in his belongings, in the room, or in his truck. Strange you would only bring one bullet, even if you were going to commit suicide. We also have his camouflage fatigues and boots that were behind the seat in the cab of his truck."

Gabe paused for a moment, recalling Wade's story.

"You mentioned that you found footprints in the area of the sniper position the night of your incident?"

"Yes, I marked several footprints with flags I tore from my t-shirt. Some of the prints were in soft dirt and should make good impressions. The Fort Benning forensics team was pouring impressions when I left."

"Interesting... they haven't mentioned that to me. You can bet I'm going to pursue that angle. I have his boots to compare against those impressions."

After a short restroom break and a refill of their water glasses, Wade asked the question uppermost in his mind. .

"What do you think happened, if it wasn't a suicide?"

Gabe thought for a long moment and replied, "If I were a betting man, I'd put my money on a professional hit. Lockhart was a big strong Special Forces guy the size of an NFL linebacker. No one was going to sneak up on him or attack him by surprise.

"I think he knew the person who killed him. I think this motel was probably a meeting place of some kind – perhaps to exchange something or to pay Lockhart off. My hunch is that someone got close enough to him to administer the first drug, which probably knocked him out. I think at least one other drug was used in some way to keep him alive long enough to stage his suicide.

"We found a small puncture wound the size of a hypodermic needle on the side of Lockhart's neck. The angle of penetration was three inches below his left ear, into the muscle in the back of his neck, while he was sitting in an upright position." Gabe demonstrated the angle of the wound with his finger extended over his own shoulder.

"I believe the second drug immobilized him. My hunch is he was alive and might even have been awake watching them stage his body for the kill shot. He just couldn't do anything about it. Even immobilized, Lockhart was too big to be handled by one man. I believe two or more people were involved in this execution and clean-up."

"Could this be mob guys?"

"Could be, but I don't think so."

"Why do you say that?"

"They positioned his body to look like he was sitting at the table when the shot went off. Lockhart was probably bound with a rope to keep his arm and hand upright in the chair. His finger was probably positioned on the trigger to fire the weapon. From the stronger print impression on the trigger, I think someone else pulled his finger down over the trigger.

"Mob guys typically want to send a message by their killings. They don't care about the mess they make. This hit was done by people who cared about how the scene would look afterward. They went out of their way to try to point evidence in a certain direction – to divert attention. To me this looks more like a black ops job done by a professional hit squad, perhaps foreign intelligence. I believe the men in this squad all wore gloves. We found a few flakes of latex powder on his flannel shirt, the kind of latex gloves used in hospitals and laboratories."

"Can you guess who might be behind it?"

Gabe thought about the question, but didn't answer it directly. He continued giving Wade his opinion of what had happened. Gabe demonstrated how Lockhart was tied, emphasizing the angle of his own arm and hand.

"There was no evidence of drugs or alcohol in the room, but preliminary reports of Lockhart's stomach contents show evidence of alcohol. He might have been given the first drug with some booze. We're now waiting for more detailed test results of the stomach contents. Lockhart was a known drinker; he'd been arrested several times off base for public drunkenness, fighting, and disorderly conduct. And while the first drug was probably administered with a shot of alcohol, I think the second drug was administered with a slightly-larger needle. They tried to conceal the second injection by putting it into a tattoo on the back of his neck."

"That's amazing detective work," replied Wade.

"I figured that Lockhart's contact must have met him and paid him cash. Then they had a drink to celebrate. The hotel operator on duty that night vaguely remembers a black van parked across the street from the hotel, but he didn't get any identifying information.

"After Lockhart was out from the first drug, my hunch is the hit squad was called in to do the rest of the job. This group was all pros."

"You seem to have this all worked out except for who did the murder."

"You're correct – except most of what I'm telling you is pure conjecture on my part. We're a long way from proving any of this. We'll need a lot more evidence to make it stick."

"Is there anything I can do at this point?"

"I'm very interested in this CID guy, Mashburn, who is now conveniently out of the country on a special classified covert assignment. It would be helpful if you could provide any information about who he reports to and where he's located."

"I'll get right on that."

"I would appreciate that."

His mind still was trying to grasp the facts when Wade posed another question. "Will you be able to obtain the foot impressions taken by the forensics team at Fort Benning? I'd still like to know if Lockhart was our shooter."

"That's a good question. If I've led you to believe this will be a fight to the death over jurisdiction regarding Lockhart's body, I misspoke. Aside from this squabble, I happen to have an excellent relationship with Fort Benning. Most of the forensics people at the base trained with or know my forensics people. In fact, I can pursue some of this off-line, just between my forensics folks and theirs."

"Secondly, the base and I usually end up cooperating on almost all investigations. In the long run, negative publicity doesn't work well for the base, and ongoing disputes with local police don't buy them good press. From your story and what I know of the Fort Benning staff, I don't believe they were part of the actual Lockhart murder. I think they may have gotten caught up in the cover-up story somehow. That usually comes from orders coming from higher up, outside the base. Your question about your Agency's involvement may not be unfounded."

Before he replied, Wade reflected back on his interrogation after the incident, which they'd called a "debriefing."

"Your explanation makes perfect sense to me. During my debriefing, I didn't get the sense that Colonel Miller had a clue about Lockhart's true identity. At least that was my take on it at the time. Of course they may be really good actors who fooled me, but I doubt it."

Gabe swallowed a sip of water. "We know from his prior arrests that Lockhart was mentally unstable and carried a grudge about a lot of things. It's also possible that he might have had some information that certain parties didn't want revealed. Perhaps it was something he knew about Army operations in Vietnam, and he demanded to be paid to keep his mouth shut. It's also possible that he discovered Mashburn was a CID plant in his group and felt threatened. He might have thought you guys were somehow involved in that CID operation – and that could have pushed him into taking the sniper action."

Wade was in deep thought, absently tapping his fingers on the table. "That may be true, but why would the Army allow someone who was already disturbed to take a course in preparation for another Vietnam tour? I don't understand that kind of thinking. He was a loose cannon."

Gabe nodded. "You're absolutely right, but your story just gave me another angle to pursue. What if back in Vietnam, Lockhart discovered something that had gone wrong – with bad intelligence or a senior ranking Army officer – that got his men killed? He might have thought the intelligence community was going to take him out because of what he knew. For example, what if he discovered a cover-up over a botched job by an intelligence officer in 'Nam? Lockhart was supposed to be in the group the day that his platoon was killed. Why wasn't he in that group?"

Wade shrugged. "That's a very good question. I'm speculating here, and I may be way off base, but Lockhart survived three tours of recon missions in Vietnam. If Lockhart had proof that someone on our side was a bad guy, he could have tried blackmailing the government or someone in the government to get a big payoff. He might have assumed he would be safe in the U.S. Then when Lockhart

119

felt threatened, something snapped, and he went on his own misguided black ops mission. He obviously didn't realize or believe the U.S. would turn their own black ops team on him."

"That's an interesting angle. Let me do some digging around, and see if I can find out who the CIA intelligence officer in Vietnam was and learn some more about his platoon."

"That might not solve our local murder case, but it could help explain a lot about why Lockhart was taken out."

After a pause, Gabe continued. "Another thing still bothering me here is that we've found no money trail—at least not that we've discovered so far. In most murder cases of this type, you follow the money. You know, I have a hunch the Vietnam connection might have a money component to it, but that's just a hunch on my part."

Wade jotted a note and set down his pen. "I'll look into that angle as well."

"Can you get me the names and contact information of the others in your Red Team training group? I may want to have some private discussions with them to confirm some of the facts we've been discussing here."

"I happen to have their contact information right here." Wade pulled out a folded document from his pocket and handed it to Gabe.

"Thank you. I'll keep their names confidential and keep them out of any formal investigation."

"They would appreciate that, I'm sure."

"Now, are you ready for some collard greens and ham hocks? They also have homemade root beer and apple pie."

"I sure am."

Chapter 13
Greenstone, Alabama

During his drive back from Georgia, Wade's mind raced with killing scenarios, evidence, and possible Vietnam connections. The more Wade thought about what had happened, the more moving parts he saw in motion. He and his team had been caught up in a nefarious murder plot being played out at Lockhart's expense. His suspicions kept coming back to his own Agency, and he kept asking himself why that was so. The evidence didn't point to a direct Agency involvement, but his instincts told him differently.

There was some link between a CIA Vietnam intelligence officer and Lockhart that involved people higher up in the Agency. The mysterious death of that intelligence officer occurred by a strange hit and run car accident just after he returned from Vietnam. The hit and run driver was never found.

Lockhart had a connection to the CIA operative in Vietnam. It was Lockhart's platoon that was wiped out from bad intelligence from the CIA officer. Lockhart wasn't on the mission that evening but never forgot it was the CIA intel that got his men killed.

Mashburn and the CIA agent had also been in Vietnam at the same time. Wade had to find out more about them. Perhaps there was a person at the Agency who could quietly access that information. He knew one person there who excelled at getting that kind of information, but could he trust Megan with that task? Would she even be willing to take the risk? Wade decided to wait. He wanted to mull over and sort out these connections further.

A few days later, Wade returned home to find the red light blinking on his answering machine. It was a call from

Yari. *When does this guy ever sleep?*

"Hi, how did your meeting go with Detective Morrison?"

"Good. Things are more convoluted than you might imagine. Were you able to get any more information on Mashburn or the intelligence agent in Vietnam?"

"Yeah, it turns out that Mashburn attended security training at CID. He also took special classes at the Army's biological weapons facility over the past three years. I'm still digging out what those courses covered." Wade could hear Yari shuffling papers before he went on.

"I also found out CID has been doing joint assignments with the CIA and foreign intelligence agencies. One internal memo shows the two agencies were also dealing with organized crime figures involved with Castro during the Cuban conflict. It seems Army Intel played a part in some joint covert activities with mob characters who were trying to do away with Castro. Mashburn's record looks like it includes some of those covert activities. There were sections of his file that prove he was doing intelligence work in Vietnam after he was a medic. Much of it is blacked out even for Army eyes. I'm still digging."

"Anything on Lockhart while he was in Vietnam?"

"Lockhart was in Charlie Company Recon Platoon under Major James Wister, near a town called Moc Bai along the Cambodian border. It seems much of their work included excursions into Cambodia. Their missions were geared to breaking up supply lines between Vietnam and Cambodia along that border region."

Yari paused as he read through some of his notes. "It seems those same supply routes were also used by the Vietnamese to bring weapons and ammunitions out of Cambodia. I found one briefing memo that says this particular region was also used to bring out cocaine, which was sold on the black market to raise money for the North Vietnamese. The memo suggests that some of that cocaine might have gone through U.S. hands, but gives no details."

Yari shuffled some papers as Wade listened intently, taking notes on their conversation. Continuing with his report, Yari stated, "There was one mission where one of the platoons was wiped out because the informant they used was a double agent who double-crossed us. The platoon walked right into a Viet Cong ambush. The memo is classified top secret. That may have been Lockhart's platoon. I can't tell because the name of the platoon is redacted. I'm still trying to find out why Lockhart wasn't on that death mission."

"That's good intelligence work. Keep digging in that area."

"Sure thing, boss."

"Were you able to find out where Mashburn is now?"

"I've got a trace on an unverified phone call that he was in Spain. It's been interesting."

"What do you mean?"

"A week ago he was using a CID secure line and passwords. His CID line uses an older form of encryption, but I was able to break most of the codes and heard parts of several conversations. Those conversations kept using the code word 'Macho.' I had to do some real digging into CID records to find Macho. The code refers to the President of Spain, Francisco Franco. Mashburn seems to be on a CID assignment for Franco in Spain. I wanted to get more confirmation before I gave you that information, though."

"That's weird. I didn't think the U.S. was supporting that character."

"I was also interested to learn that Mashburn is no longer using that CID line."

"Then how are they communicating?"

"I'm still going through old messages to see what happened."

"Let me know as soon as you find anything."

"Will do, partner."

After finishing his Sniper Navigation Class at Fort Benning, Wade only had one surveillance field class and two minor classroom training classes left before graduating from the Intelligence Agency. He often compared notes on the countdown of classes when he spoke with Megan in the evenings. This evening's call was no different; Megan got right to the point.

"You still have to take your final Surveillance-Counter-Surveillance (SCS-7) Class here in D.C. But the class is given all the time, so there should be no scheduling problems. Just let me know when you want to take it."

"Is that graduation reception still taking place in two months?"

"Yes, that date won't change."

"It might be good to take SCS-7 around that time."

"We can make that work. I hope you're still planning on getting together when you're here."

"I sure am. D.C. would be very a lonely place without you."

"Okay. I'll plan on it."

"What else have you been doing?"

"Nothing. I have no time. They gave me three more recruits, since you're getting near graduation."

"That's unfair. I didn't take up the equivalent of two recruits, did I?"

"Close to it. By the way, did you ever hear any more about that shooting incident at Fort Benning?"

"No. Have you heard anything?"

"There was some discussion around here, but nothing specific. Something about an ongoing investigation."

"Well, somebody should certainly be investigating it. Did they ever find the guy who shot at us?"

"I think they found the guy dead, but apparently there's some question regarding whether or not he's the one who fired on you."

"You're kidding."

"Beats me. I'm just glad you got through it okay."

"I guess my group was lucky."

"That's not what I heard."

"What did you hear?"

"I heard you and another team member went after the shooter bare-handed in the middle of the night. That's what made the shooter leave the area. At least that's the story circulating in our office."

"I lucked out, it was a very dark and foggy, overcast night."

"Hmmm, one day you'll have to tell me the real story."

After a pause, Wade abruptly changed the subject. "Do we have anything scheduled for this week?"

"No. You've got the week to yourself. Just make sure you get those incompletes removed. I don't want any black marks on my record."

"I can't imagine you with black marks."

"I wish you were here right now."

"Me too."

A tiny part of Wade remained suspicious about Megan and the agency. He wasn't sure if the agency was directing her to pump him for information or if she just asked too many questions out of curiosity. Either way, he couldn't take a chance. His gut told him she was as honest about her feelings toward him as he was with her. The last thing he could afford now was to send a suspicious message that something might be wrong in their relationship.

Wade was working intently on his final class paper when the phone rang.

"Hi, it's Yari. I think I have the name of the CIA guy in Vietnam: Daniel Spencer. He left the agency after his Vietnam tour and went back to being an insurance agent in his hometown in Raleigh, North Carolina. He died shortly after he returned home."

"Really? How did he die?"

"According to the local newspaper article, he was killed by a hit-and-run driver. They never found the driver."

"Do we know why he left the Agency?"

"I wasn't able to find out specifically why he left, but there were a few notes about a drug investigation that might have involved him. Most of his file is buried under lock and key at the Pentagon, so I've hit a dead end on Spencer. I think there could be something in his file the Agency doesn't want discovered."

"His death seems like another strange coincidence."

"I'm also monitoring Morrison's communications. He received a toxicology report on Lockhart's death. The drugs involved go by some obscure names, which nobody seems to know anything about. One of the drugs seems to come out of India and the other out of Malaysia. There are some other high-end binding chemicals involved. These are not street drugs. From monitoring Morrison's calls, it's clear that he's spending a lot of time trying to track down the source of these drugs."

"Is there anything else going on at Fort Benning on this issue?"

"Apparently Morrison is working with someone at Fort

Benning regarding what was found at our shooting site. Benning has agreed to release their forensics findings to him."

"Anything else?"

"Yeah, actually. Remember the CID communication link I had on Mashburn?"

"Yeah."

"It's dead now. For whatever reason, Mashburn and CID aren't communicating."

"I wonder if CID cut him off, or if they're using another communication device. Maybe Morrison was getting too close with his investigation."

"I've got a tap on the phone Mashburn uses for most of his calls. But all of a sudden, CID has stopped calls in both directions. I do have Mashburn making two calls to a new number in Brussels. I'm now tracking that number."

Wade shook his head. "What the hell is that all about?"

"I don't know, but they're easy to monitor. The two calls still referenced Macho, but I'm not sure if that refers to a person or an operation. The person on the receiving end of Mashburn's calls is referred to as 'Condor.' I'm in the process of tracing that code name to the Brussels location."

"It sounds like command authority may be shifting its focus to this Condor person."

After a long pause Yari broke the silence. "There's something else going on in the conversation that you might find interesting."

"What's that?"

"They're talking about extraction routes and options out of Spain."

"That's interesting. Sounds like something has or is about to go down. Where are Mashburn's calls originating from?"

"Mostly from a town in Spain called Zaragoza, which is about midway between Madrid and Barcelona."

Wade nodded without realizing it. "It's normal operating procedure to be close to two extraction points. My instincts are telling me we have to double our efforts on Mashburn right now. I'm going to do some research on President Franco and Condor. Keep me posted on any discussions Mashburn has."

"Will do, partner."

The university library was far from Wade's apartment, and he used it often. There were a couple of things he wanted to look up at the library for his class paper, but mainly he wanted to research President Franco of Spain.

He was amazed at how much public information was available on Spain and the Franco regime. It didn't take a genius to see the U.S. was clearly shuffling its feet between blasting the guy for his brutal, tyrannical methods and maintaining some semblance of diplomatic protocol.

The contradictory political positions of the U.S. didn't explain why the U.S. would covertly support a dictator by sending in a covert assassin like Mashburn. Something was amiss. Wade's instinct had him thinking: *Could Mashburn be there as a double agent?*

The code name Condor in Brussels was next on Wade's agenda, but he wasn't going to find anything at the library except references to the near-extinct bird of the same name. Wade racked his brain, for anyone he knew in the Agency old enough to know operatives in Brussels.

In one of his international legal classes, Wade met Bob Hollings, an older European CIA operative taking the refresher course. They had exchanged contact information during the class. It was a long shot, but why not give old Bob a call? Perhaps Bob recalled something about the name

Condor that didn't refer to a bird. Wade checked the time differences in Europe and called when he thought Bob might just be home relaxing.

"Hi, Bob, it's Wade Hanna. We took the international legal class together a few months back."

"Yes, I remember. How are you doing?"

"Doing great. Almost done with my coursework and ready to graduate. I'll be glad when it's all over."

"I bet you will. What can I do for you?"

"I came across a name in Brussels I'm trying to research, and just thought you might know an operative who goes by the code name Condor."

"Yes, I know that name, but I haven't heard it in many years. I think he might be an old timer like me. There was an operative by that name who decided to leave the company about eight years ago to retire and go independent."

He paused while trying to summon up old memories.

"Last I remember was a few years ago, when the company would give him a little low-level contract work now and then. He used to operate out of Brussels, I believe. But I haven't heard of him doing any contract work in the last three or four years. I assume he's long retired by now."

"Did you know anything about him? Like what kind of operations he ran or what his real name was?"

"Let me think. He did some black ops stuff in the old days, but his real forte was making good connections with higher-ranking foreign offices in the European intelligence community right after the war. I can't remember which countries. We used him to broker information when things were politically sensitive, as I recall."

"Do you remember if one of those countries was Spain?"

"Come to think of it, Spain was one of the main

countries he focused on."

"Do you remember what his real name was?"

"I can't think of his last name, but I think his first name was Myles. I can probably get that last name for you by making a few calls."

Wade realized he had a connection to Condor and didn't want further links getting back to the man. He thought it best to cut this part of the conversation off immediately. He would explore other sources on his own if he needed more information.

"No. That's okay for now. You've been very helpful."

"Sounds like you're working on an interesting project."

"You know how research goes. A lot of twists and turns, with a few crumbs along the way. I've just been asked to pin down some of these old records."

"Let me know if you need anything else."

"Thanks for your help. I sure will."

Chapter 14

When Wade picked up the phone, he could hear excitement in Yari's voice.

"Hey, I think I have something."

"I can't wait."

"Our boy Mashburn is extracting from Spain. Condor seems to be calling all the shots. There's been no communication with CID. In fact, I think Army Intelligence is out of the picture."

"Did they say where Mashburn is extracting to? They can't be bringing him back to the U.S., because Morrison has a warrant out for his arrest in the Lockhart matter."

"He's on his way to British Honduras. I mean Belize. I keep forgetting they just changed their name."

"Interesting. Why Belize?"

"It seems Condor is setting up a meeting there. He's made calls to Guatemala, Nicaragua, and Cuban operatives. There's talk about a U.K. war game exercise off the coast of Belize."

"What's the date of the meeting?"

"They haven't said. No travel dates yet. Condor has Mashburn going from Spain to Panama, then on to Belize. He's supposed to call Condor for his next instructions when he arrives in Panama."

Wade thought about the set-up before responding. "He's on a 'need-to-know' basis. They may be concerned he could be picked up between Spain and Panama. Any information on the operatives involved?"

"No. Condor isn't giving Mashburn any details, except where to go on the next leg."

"Are you able to monitor other calls Condor is making?"

"I'm recording all his calls from the one landline in Brussels."

"If it's any help, Condor's first name is Myles. He's a former CIA operative who became an independent contractor about seven years ago. He ran black ops for U.S. and U.K. Intelligence for about three years after he left the agency. They also used him to broker sensitive information between difficult European countries. For the last few years I hear he's been retired from intelligence work."

"That will give me something to go on."

"If we need to, I can probably get a last name for Condor. I just don't want to raise any suspicions with my contact source."

Yari's voice sounded more than a little eager when he responded. "Let me work on what you've given me so far from my end."

Wade, on the other hand, saw his target coming closer to his neck of the woods. "I think I want to pay a visit to Mr. Mashburn when he arrives in Central America. Keep me posted."

"You got it."

Wade relished the thought of Mashburn coming closer. His mind started whirling, devising ways to get to Central America. His suspicions grew more each day about the Agency's involvement in the Lockhart killing and the drug activities of Spencer in Vietnam. He couldn't put his finger on exactly how his Agency was involved, but it was clear that Army Intelligence, Mashburn, and Spencer were all acting under orders. He just didn't know yet who was pulling the strings - or why.

His mind raced, thinking about how much the Agency already knew about the Lockhart murder. He thought it unlikely that Megan's penetrating questions were mere curiosity. As much as Wade wanted Megan's help to glean more details about the Agency, he couldn't put her or himself at more risk. Feeling he had no other options, Wade resolved to live with Megan's uncertain role in the Agency's involvement in the Lockhart matter. That was just the way things had to be for now.

Morrison had been on Wade's mind; it was time he got up to speed on the Lockhart investigation. But he would only make that call after taking precautions to be sure he was on a secure line.

"Morrison here."

"Mr. Morrison, this is Wade Hanna. We haven't spoken in a while, and I thought I might call to get you up to speed on the Lockhart case."

"Good idea. I just received the toxicology report. As suspected, one of the drugs in Lockhart's body was similar to a rare substance derived from the skin of an Amazonian frog that paralyzes the muscles."

"Sounds pretty exotic."

"It's a synthesized version of what jungle Indians use on their arrows and darts to paralyze prey. The substance comes from a mixture of several skin secretions of certain poisonous frogs, which you only find in remote locations of the Amazon, Malaysia, and India. The drugs were mixed with modern binding agents. After a few days, these drugs dissipate in the body, making them almost undetectable."

"That's why the Army wanted to prevent a full autopsy as long as possible."

"That certainly sounds like the motive. I still don't think the base knew much until the jurisdictional issue was brought up. They may have been instructed to fight for jurisdiction without knowing the reason why."

Wade snapped his fingers, suddenly remembering to

ask a very important question. "Did you ever get the base's forensic footprint results?"

"Yes, and those were Lockhart's footprint impressions you found in the soil. There was a slight defect in the sole of his left boot, which showed up perfectly in the impressions. He was your man, all right." Morrison paused. "Have you found out anything on your end?"

Wade thought for a moment before he replied. "Yes, from what I've been able to learn, the killer, or at least a major participant in the death squad, was David Mashburn. I don't think he'll be coming back to this country anytime soon. He's on some clandestine covert mission for the U.S. Military."

Morrison replied, "That's a convenient assignment. What about the people who gave him the orders?"

"I don't have any names yet - still working on that angle. What I found out is that Mashburn is no longer reporting to Army Intelligence in the U.S. on the new assignment. He's being handled by an offshore operative out of Brussels."

Morrison was eager to pursue that lead. "That's another convenient twist. I'd like to find out who Mashburn reported to here, the one who was giving him orders in the U.S. That's who I want to go after."

"I'm still working on that angle. I did find out something on your money theory."

"What's that?" Morrison asked.

"There was a military investigation on drug deals that went on in Vietnam involving Army Intelligence and CIA operatives. Mashburn was initially part of that group, although I think he was primarily a delivery boy. The CIA operative involved was a guy by the name of Daniel Spencer, who was the subject of a secret government drug investigation."

"After the investigation, Spencer left the agency and the military. He was killed by a hit-and-run driver in South Carolina shortly after returning to the States. They never found the driver or solved that case. Other than a few memos referencing the investigation, Spencer's records have also gone cold or disappeared. There's a Spencer file at the Pentagon which is sealed, classified as Top Secret."

Morrison's instincts told him not to buy the coincidence. "Spencer's death sounds like it may have been a hit. I've worked with some detectives in North Carolina, so I can follow that thread with them. Do you have the names of any of the military offices involved in the drug deal?"

"Haven't gotten any yet. I'll keep you posted on what I find. What are the next steps on your end?"

"I've turned up the heat on Fort Benning. I've asked the court to force the Army to produce the psychological records on Lockhart. I want to ask Dr. Jarvis some questions when I finally have those records in my hands."

Morrison had a call coming in on another line. "If anything turns up on my end, I'll let you know."

"Sounds like a plan. Thanks."

Wade hung up, thinking about Mashburn's Spain connection. Was it a legitimate assignment, or did they just want to get him out of the U.S. when the Lockhart matter heated up? A trip to Belize was certain to be in Wade's future. He couldn't wait to come face-to-face with Mashburn and interrogate him on his black ops history. Wade knew his mission would have to go unsanctioned, under the radar. He had to slip in and out of the country without the Agency, the government, or law enforcement knowing he was there. He tried putting a positive spin on the idea. *Belize is supposed to be a beautiful place with great fishing – I've always wanted to go fishing down there.*

Even though he considered his mission "company business," Wade felt the Agency wouldn't see his involvement that way. The next problem Wade faced was expenses for the Belize trip. He needed a plan that would let him use military and intelligence transportation assets to get him to the tropics without attracting unwanted attention.

Wade couldn't get Megan's help on transportation because of his continuing Agency suspicions. He had to find another way to get to Belize on the government's nickel. The military contacts he'd made during training sessions should be useful in some way.

Wade made a list of his transportation contacts. Surely one of those contacts could help him slip in and out of Belize without notice. He decided to call the people he knew best at military bases near him, hoping to find an unofficial ride to the tropics.

"Fort Rucker Army base, may I help you?"

"This is Wade Hanna. I'd like to speak with Master Sergeant Chris Cassel, please."

"Cassel here."

"Hi, Chris, Wade Hanna. I'd like to pick your brain, if I could."

"Sure."

"I'm trying to hitch a ride to Belize and back. You got anything going that way?"

"Let me check our upcoming flight schedules."

After a few moments Chris was back on the line. "Sorry, nothing headed in that direction. However, I think there are some war games being planned between the U.K. and Belize. You might try Ellington in Texas. I think that base has lots of flights going to Central America."

"I don't know anyone at that base. Can you help me

out?"

The sergeant replied quickly. "You do too know someone at Ellington. Don't you remember Ramon? He used to work with me here at Rucker. He now lives in Texas and works as an independent contractor for Ellington."

"I do remember Ramon. Do you have a number for him?"

Chris was silent as he looked up the number and gave it to Wade. As he thanked him, Chris replied with a question. "How are you getting to Texas?"

"I guess I'm driving."

"You don't have to do that. I can get you to Ellington."

"Great. What are the flight options to Ellington over the next week?"

"There are lots of options. We have almost daily flights from Rucker to Houston."

Wade's next call was to Ramon, with whom he quickly renewed his relationship. The Ellington Air Transport Wing supported regular flights to Belize and other Central American countries. The regular flights to Belize usually ran twice a month but would soon increase due to the upcoming war games. With Ramon's help and a few more calls, Wade nailed down flight details and a primary contact to schedule his trip.

His next call was to his cousin Frank, who lived in Houston. During the longer-than- necessary call Frank offered to set up dinner invitations, parties, a fishing trip, a barbecue or visits with friends, all of which Wade politely declined.

He explained to Frank that he was on official business. The term "official business" meant little to Frank. He just wanted to celebrate. It took some time, but Wade finally convinced him that "official business" meant government undercover work. In the end, Frank reluctantly acknowledged the connection and backed off the robust party agenda.

"I keep forgetting you're with the government, where you do clandestine missions and all."

Wade responded, trying to curb more unwanted attention to his mission. "Yeah, this trip is official business. I'll just be in Houston for one night. We can go to dinner that night, but I can't plan anything else. Don't worry, cuz. I'll be making other trips in the future that aren't so tightly scheduled."

"Okay, I'll make the reservations at Ciprio's for dinner. You can stay at the house and use the spare car."

"I appreciate that. We'll party next time I visit, I promise."

"Don't make promises you can't keep – spy man."

Weapons and tactics were on Wade's mind as he planned his trip. He assembled maps of Belize and in-country transportation systems, weapons, and disguises. Wade thought it best to keep his schedule flexible until he discovered Mashburn's location. There were lots of moving parts and unknowns about Mashburn and his reasons for being in Belize. Yari's monitored calls were Wade's only source for more information about Mashburn.

The payphone near Wade's apartment was convenient and more secure than the phone in his apartment. He dialed Yari's secure number.

Without preamble Wade asked, "Any new developments?"

"Condor has Mashburn taking trains and public buses to the airport in Spain for his extraction. They talked about changing passports. Apparently Mashburn is using the name Ramos on his current passport, and for some reason I don't get, there seems to be some concern about getting out of Spain."

"What kind of concern?"

"Condor told Mashburn that once they got the passport issue straightened out, he wanted to break off all communication with him until he arrived in Panama. Condor suspects their communications are being monitored."

"Well, aren't you monitoring them?"

"Yes, I am, but he's not referring to my monitoring– there's someone else. He seems to be worried about the Spanish government."

"Could he be worried about CIA monitoring?"

"No, I don't think so. I have a handle on that situation."

Wade wondered if Mashburn was in Spain hiding from U.S. investigators or if he was on another mission. What plans did CID or the CIA have for him in Belize? Wade wondered if he had any intention of slipping back into the U.S., because of its relative proximity to Belize.

"Does Mashburn have any family in the U.S.?"

"I'll have to check records, but he's not trying to make any calls to the U.S."

There was a pause before Yari continued. "I've been thinking. Are you going on this mission alone?"

Wade had the thought that Yari might want to join him. "That's what I'm thinking about. Why do you ask?"

"Well, it turns out that our old friend Max from Fort Benning might be available. He was wounded in the leg in Vietnam and is finishing a couple of months of rehab before he ships back."

Wade briefly thought about Yari's suggestion, but he wasn't keen on the idea, because he didn't know what he would find in Belize. "Let me think about it. Where's Max living these days?"

"He's living in Texas."

"Interesting."

"He says he'd really like to finish the job you guys started at Fort Benning."

Wade thought more about the idea before responding. "First I'll have to see how everything works out in Belize."

"I understand, but you might have more to contend with in Belize than just Mashburn. The calls keep referring to other guys that are part of this group."

"I know. Get busy and try to find out more about those other guys."

"I'm working on it."

Chapter 15

The evening call was strained between Megan and Wade. Megan was tired from a long day at work, and Wade seemed unusually distant. With only two courses remaining before graduation, Wade had no need to talk about schedules as they had in the past.

Humor usually prevailed during their chats about their feelings for each other, but there was nothing lighthearted in this conversation. Both understood that nothing was going to happen in their personal life until their official reporting relationship changed in the next few months.

Megan was perceptive when Wade distanced himself from her. She had become skilled at reading his moods over the phone. But the strain of the conversation got to the point where Megan had to know what Wade was really thinking, and she wasn't shy about asking.

"You sound like you're a million miles away in some distant land."

Megan's comment caught Wade day-dreaming about the mission. He quickly responded with a cover story. "I was thinking how long it's been since I've been on a fishing trip."

Megan's didn't know much about fishing but thought his response was a little strange. She responded, trying to discover what was behind his words.

"I think a fishing trip would be a great idea. Where would you go?"

"I could go somewhere nearby, but that's not real exciting. I really miss going out in the Gulf of Mexico for a few days. I'd have to pull together some friends to share the cost of a charter. I used to do that all the time when I was growing up."

Megan knew Wade's training schedule had been brutal. "You've got some time on your hands now. That is, before you come see me for the D.C. class. Listen, I know how important fishing and hunting are to you, so why don't you go ahead and take that trip now?"

Wade was eager to respond. "You're right, they are important. When I haven't been fishing or hunting for a long time, I get moody."

"I can't handle moody."

"Let me think about it. I'd probably leave from Louisiana or Texas, and go see my Dad before I leave."

Still concerned about possible Agency involvement, Wade couldn't share more details or the truth about his mission. He also didn't want her to worry about his safety.

Megan anticipated his next thought. "You really should plan that trip while you can."

"Perhaps I'll be less preoccupied once I get it out of my system."

"I think you're right. I bet you'll feel much better when you get back."

Wade's best instincts told him something was going to break with Mashburn soon. He didn't know when, but wanted to be prepared when it happened. He stepped up his workout regimen. Vigorous twice-a-day workouts followed by three hours on the shooting range increased both his target-shooting accuracy and his physical stamina.

Wade liked to alternate firing ranges between Fort Rucker and the local police range to ensure he got practice on several different target profiles. His short-range rapid fire and long-range rifle scores ranked among the highest posted at each range.

When performing his rapid-fire sequence that morning, Wade's jaw clenched when he imagined Mashburn's face on the target. Solving Lockhart's murder had by now become an obsession.

He went over and over the questions he would ask Mashburn and thought about what he would do to ensure he got the right answers. If Mashburn's lips were truly sealed, Wade was prepared to terminate him. In addition to the details of Lockhart's murder, Wade had to find out who was involved from his Agency and what they were trying to cover up. His future and well-being with the Agency depended on Mashburn's answers.

After five more days of the same routine, Wade became bored with shooting targets,, lifting weights, and three-mile runs. The same two questions kept rolling through his mind in a continuous loop: *Where the hell is Mashburn, and what is he planning in Belize?* He was ready to take action, but felt frustrated that Yari had no further news on Mashburn's whereabouts.

The small Alabama town of Greenstone was especially peaceful that afternoon. After returning from three hours on the firing range, Wade had begun to doze off in his favorite arm chair when the phone rang. He jumped awkwardly, knocking over the receiver.

"Hi, it's Yari."

"Do you have anything?"

"Yep, Mashburn made his first call to Condor from a payphone at the airport in Panama. I now have a new ID on another Condor line. From their conversation, the extraction from Spain went as planned, without any problems. Condor wants Mashburn in Belize in three days, and he gave him a laundry list of things he wants done when he gets there. Condor is treating Mashburn like an errand boy."

"Is Condor coming to Belize?"

"He hasn't said, but my hunch is no. I also get the

distinct impression that Mashburn is not running the assignment in Belize. Condor talks to him like he'll be a waiter serving cocktails on the mission."

"Do you have any more information on timing, dates, location, or the names of other operatives?"

"Hold on, partner. I'm tracking as fast as they give me information. Condor's made only those two short calls."

"Yeah, but Condor has to be talking to the other people. I thought you had a trace on all of Condor's lines."

"I don't think I have all his outgoing lines. He's probably not using the same lines for all his calls."

"Can't you monitor all of his lines?"

"I'm working on that angle, but my line tie-back comes from the original CID line he was using, and I'm pretty sure CID and Condor are no longer communicating on that line. Condor just uses that old line to speak with Mashburn."

"You've got to find out how he's communicating with the other operatives."

"I'm on it. Oh, by the way, I found out more about the war games off the coast of Belize. It's a big deal politically, for the purpose of showing off for the Russians and Chinese more than for other Central American countries. According to my internal military communications, we're demonstrating to the big boys that we control the Gulf of Mexico region. Canada and Australia have now joined in the exercise along with the U.S. and U.K."

"That seems like overkill and a bit ridiculous."

"True, but remember Cuba is still a wild card in the Gulf of Mexico, and don't forget Belize is asking for total independence from the U.K. in a few years."

"Belize couldn't survive a week without U.K. military protection. Their old adversary Guatemala or any one of the other bordering countries would crush them like a bug if they didn't have the protection of the U.K."

"I'm just sharing internal intelligence information that I read. What do I know?"

"Thanks for the information. As soon as you get anything on the operatives, location, or timing, let me know."

"Did you ever decide whether or not to use Max?"

"No, not yet, but give me his number. I'll probably want to talk to him. With Mashburn's timetable being moved up, I'll have to get down there right away."

Two days passed without any news from Yari. After a morning workout and range practice, Wade made a sandwich and was just about to take the first bite when the phone rang. It was Yari, and his excitement level had nearly reached hysteria.

"I've got new intel on Mashburn!"

"Let's hear it."

"He's rented a house in Belize for the meeting. Condor just wired him funds through a Panamanian bank. I was able to track another funds transfer to Mashburn that originated from a Brussels bank. I found out that Mashburn has a Swiss bank account as well. Condor wired Mashburn $28,000 after he left Spain."

"That may be his contract payment for the Spain job."

"I also know the general location of the house he's renting in Belize, although I don't have an actual address yet."

"Where is it?"

"It's an area called Belama, in Belize City not far from the highway to the airport."

"Good job. Anything more on when the other operatives arrive?"

"Apparently they're not arriving for another two weeks – just before the war games start. But I can't figure out why Mashburn would stay in a house instead of a hotel."

"A house would be more isolated and attract less attention than a busy hotel."

Wade's mind was racing, interpreting Yari's new information. He could see timing was getting tight. Yari continued speculating about war game events when Wade cut him off.

"I only have a narrow window of opportunity, so I have to leave now."

"What do you mean?"

"I need time to interrogate Mashburn before the other operatives arrive."

"Is there any chance that there's another operation tied to the war games? Isn't that why they're meeting?"

"Probably, but I can't deal with both issues right now. Once the other operatives arrive, they'll have resources in place that I don't have."

"What about using Max?"

"It doesn't make sense right now. I'll deal with whatever comes up after that, once I'm down there. Just tell Max to stand by. I'll call if I need him."

"What do you want me to do?"

"Keep monitoring. I want to know everything I can find out about their operation and when the other operatives will arrive. Try to get the names of dignitaries who will be in Belize during the games. Belize has payphones. I'll keep in touch. But there's no time to lose. I've got to hit the road ASAP."

"I've got your back, partner."

In fifteen minutes, Wade was packed and ready to go. He called his friend Chris at Fort Rucker and confirmed passage on the 2:00 p.m. flight to Ellington in Houston.

He made two more calls in rapid succession: the first was to his cousin Frank in Texas to let him know he was coming, and the second to Megan.

"Megan Winslow."

"Hi, it's me."

"It's not like you to call in the middle of the day like this. What's up?"

"You're not going to believe this, but that fishing trip I mentioned just came together for me. I've been invited down to the Texas coast, and I'll leave as soon as I can get out of here. The guys wouldn't tell me in advance, but it looks like it's a surprise graduation gift. I just wanted to let you know, because they don't have phones on fishing boats, so I'll be out of touch for a while."

"That's great. How long will you be gone?"

"About a week."

"I'll miss hearing your voice, so call when you can, okay?"

"I will. I'm just not sure what day I'll be back on solid ground."

"I understand. Just let me know you're safe when you get a chance."

"I'll be safe. Remember, it's only a fishing trip."

Wade couldn't shake deep feelings of regret that he couldn't be up front with Megan about the trip. But he couldn't risk revealing things that could put her in danger, especially if she was merely a pawn in a dangerous political chess game.

The air transport flight from Fort Rucker rolled to a stop on the tarmac at Ellington. Wade checked in with the flight sergeant on duty and confirmed the next day's flight to Belize. Passing through the hanger on his way to the exit door, Wade saw the smiling face of his cousin, Frank, who grinned and waved, clearly overjoyed to be reunited.

On the way to the car, they joked about childhood escapades and parties on the bayou, rodeo rides, and country music. Frank reminded Wade of a relative who was still trying to make it big on the country music charts. Frank's enthusiasm eased Wade's tension about his upcoming mission.

"I'm taking you to Ciprio's Steak House tonight. The food there is fantastic."

Wade's smile mirrored his cousin's.

"I can't wait."

"Are you going to need the car to go see your father?"

"I'll see him on my way back. I leave for the tropics tomorrow morning."

"I know you can't say much about your destination, but…" By the look on Wade's face, he knew better than to ask for details.

After a long pause, Wade changed the subject, "So what dish do you recommend that I try?"

"Have the steak with lump crab meat. It's awesome."

"I'm looking forward to it."

Chapter 16
Belize City, Belize

The flight to Belize was delayed an hour on the Ellington tarmac while they repaired a cargo door malfunction. Wade waited in the pilot's lounge, chatting with the copilot. He'd already learned that the soft-spoken man was a Belize native and had recently inherited the house he grew up in, after his parents passed. Wade turned the discussion to the upcoming war games off the coast of Belize.

"How long have you been flying to Belize?"

"Ever since I started flying, in my late teens."

"I understand the war games are a big deal down there."

"You could say that. Our command supports both land and sea operations. We'll be sending fixed wing and chopper flights down with supplies and equipment throughout the exercise."

"Is everything being staged out of the airport in Belize?"

"Yeah, the commercial airport is shared with the U.K. fighter squadron. We train with their guys on a regular basis."

"Will you be transporting any big wigs down to Belize?"

"I haven't heard. Most of the U.S. top dogs are Navy brass who'll be at sea on flag ships. I heard from the U.K. pilots that British dignitaries are coming in for press conferences and ceremonies."

Pleased to have the additional information, Wade kept asking questions because the man was so congenial.

"I guess even though Belize wants their independence, they still need the British Air Force to protect them."

"Yeah. Every so often Guatemala or one of the other

countries starts marshaling forces along the jungle border and gets everyone worked up. The U.K. boys have a number of those Hawker Harrier aircraft in their squadron that require hidden landing cutouts in the jungle. When the unfriendlies start making noise, the U.K. pilots pop up out of those jungle cutouts and run tree-top passes with full afterburners. It breaks up ground maneuvers pretty fast. After a few sonic booms, everyone goes back to playing nice again."

"Do you spend much time in Belize other than your regular flights?"

"I go back down three or four times each year to spend time with relatives. I haven't spent much time there in the last six months though. I'm too busy up here. How long will you be there?"

Wade wanted to dismiss any importance to his mission, so he quickly responded, "Oh, I'm on a fast turnaround. Just down to interview some people for the Agency."

The sergeant finally alerted everyone in the lounge that the aircraft was ready to board. Sitting in the rear compartment of a C-130 was loud even with ear protectors on. It was impossible to have a conversation with any one of the other twelve men on the flight so passengers had to be content to look around the open expanse of the immense cargo bay. The only communication came when someone had to yell instructions to be heard over the cacophony of engine noise.

The flight was bumpy due to a tropical depression off the coast of Mexico. As they touched down at Belize International Airport, the British military presence was visible on both sides of the runway. After disembarking, a flight sergeant pointed Wade to the car rental agency where the rental agent gave him a map of the city and keys to a mid-size car.

Driving out of the airport, Wade proceeded towards Belize City, taking in the white cap waves of the Gulf. He saw why Belize was referred to as a yet-to be-discovered tropical gem. The Belama area of Belize City wasn't hard to find. It stood out as a group of high-end tropical homes all with lush plantings. He couldn't wait to see where Mashburn had rented the safe house. The only problem was that he didn't have an address.

Wade passed a grocery store parking lot with a payphone attached to its outside wall. Standing in the parking lot exposed to noise and anyone with eyes, Wade dialed the international code Yari had provided. He would've preferred to call from a more secluded place, but he didn't want to spend time driving around an unfamiliar city searching for a better call spot.

As soon as Yari picked up, Wade spoke up. "Hi, it's Wade."

Yari seemed frustrated. "I've been trying to call you in Houston. Where are you?"

"I'm in Belize, near the area you told me Mashburn would be staying."

"You're kidding. You're already in Belize?"

"Yes, and I'm standing at a payphone in the middle of a grocery store parking lot. It's not exactly private."

Crackling on the line contributed to the poor connection. Yari spoke louder to overcome the static. Wade was nearly shouting when he said, "I can barely hear you."

"I was able to get the street name for the house he rented, but I still don't know the address."

"Great, that probably narrows it down to about 300 houses."

"The street is called Adam Roy Avenue. I think it's

named after some pirate who used to visit there."

"I guess I can drive up and down that street hoping I'll run into Mashburn."

"I'm still working on an address. I won't have more precise coordinates until he makes a call from that location or refers to the address."

"Okay, I'm going to check out the neighborhood. I'll call you when I get settled. Listen, cars are filling the lot so I need to boogy. Later."

Wade checked his street map. Adam Roy Avenue was just a few blocks from where he made his call. He drove down Adam Roy looking for signs advertising houses for sale or for rent, hoping to get lucky. There were no signs, and the upscale neighborhood didn't look like a rental area to him. Mashburn could be in any one of these houses. Since Mashburn had already rented the house, though, how likely would he find a rental sign still up, advertising its availability?

Wade concluded that there had to be a better way to spend his time. It hadn't been a complete loss, however, because he now had a sense of the neighborhood and how the cross streets intersected Adam Roy. Someone was laying out serious cash for a safe house in this neighborhood – if in fact he was in the right neighborhood.

After driving the area, Wade refocused his attention on finding a hotel. Two hotels recommended by the copilot made sense to Wade. They were in the right area, but he wanted something he could get in and out of quickly. He came across a small motel a few streets off one of the main streets in the area. It was a little run down, but he liked that it was single story and had two street entrances off quiet side streets.

He parked and approached the receptionist for a room

and took the weekly reduced-rate special. After checking in, he hauled his backpack and sea bag to his room. His luggage contained his disassembled SIG Sauer P-220 with an extended threaded barrel for the silencer. He assembled his gun and checked to see if the first round had ejected into the chamber.

After laying out his clothes, weapons, and disguises, he left the motel grounds for a brisk walk to stretch his legs and get a bite to eat. He walked toward the water and passed a newspaper stand on the way. He strode the three remaining blocks to the beach and stopped to cross a busy street, savoring the beautiful white sand, colorful umbrellas, and bronze bodies dotting the landscape. With no dining recommendations, Wade followed his nose for a few blocks to a restaurant with a delectable fragrance of cooking food that he just couldn't pass up. It was now approaching 4:00 pm, and he hadn't eaten since breakfast.

He randomly chose dishes with unfamiliar local names. The delicious meal of conch ceviche, local broiled lobster tails, black beans, rice, and plantains was fit for a tropical king. Once he'd finished his meal he sat back and turned his attention to the newspaper.

Two articles on the front page described the upcoming war games. Details regarding the upcoming ceremonies to be held in the new capital of Belmopan and on Ambergris Caye were listed along with the names of dignitaries speaking at those venues. One of the scheduled speakers was the Prime Minister of Belize. Other senior diplomats from the U.S., U.K., Canada, and Australia were also mentioned along with admirals, vice-admirals, and embassy officials from participating countries.

Wade turned to the classified section and drew the paper closer to read the fine print. Two of the house rental listings indicated they were in the Belama area. The same real estate company and agent kept appearing among the rental listings for the area.

Two of the rental listings indicated an address with the warning "Do Not Disturb Occupants - Drive by Only." He tore out that section of the paper, folded it, and tucked it in his pocket. Despite the waitress's wonderful description of dessert, Wade couldn't bear the thought of more food.

Once he left the restaurant Wade turned away from the beautiful ocean view and took up a brisk pace back to the motel. He was anxious to check out the two rental listings he found. The drive to the first house was short. It had open, airy windows that went right up to the sidewalk facing the street. Wade quickly eliminated that house as a prospect because of the exposure to the street.

He drove to the second house and liked what he saw. This house had all the right features that the first house lacked. Momentarily he saw an open parking spot, where he watched the house for an hour, making notes on its potential use as a safe house. The rental sign was still out front, but there were no signs of people or activities. He considered breaking in for a closer look but decided against it. Instead, he returned to his motel and called the listing agent, who happened to be the same person mentioned in other listings. Her name was Elizabeth Barr, and he hoped she might provide some useful information.

"This is Elizabeth."

"Ms. Barr, this is Marvin Baylif. I was down here a month ago with my wife, and we looked at a house for rent in the Belama area that we really liked, and hoped to rent again. but I seem to have lost my notes and can't find the address. I need to know if it's still available for rent."

There was silence on the phone while Ms. Barr racked

her brain, trying to remember the listings she had a month ago.

"I had a four-bedroom house available around that time, but that one has already been rented."

"Do you recall the address of that house, just so I don't keep chasing my notes?"

"Yes, the address was 501 Adam Roy Avenue."

"I think that might be the one my wife liked. Do you know how long it will be, before it becomes available?"

"It's rented for three months, but the gentleman who rented it is from Panama, and hasn't been by to pick up the keys yet."

"Ms. Barr, I'm just down here for a few days before I have to return to the States. If the house is still vacant, would you be willing to give me a quick tour of that house? That way I'll be able to tell my wife I found the house she likes. If that's the one, perhaps you could jot down my name and give me a call when it's available. I promise I won't take up much of your time. I just need a quick look inside to refresh my memory."

"I can set it up right now. How about three o'clock tomorrow afternoon?"

"That would be perfect."

The agent was standing in the doorway when Wade arrived. He approached looking like an ugly American tourist with money. His disguise included a wig, dark sunglasses, straw hat, bright patterned Hawaiian shirt, and Bermuda shorts. He enhanced his disguise with a distinct Texas accent—sounding much like a used-car salesman.

Wade walked under the walled arch past the heavily-timbered yard gate to greet Ms. Barr with a smile. He was keenly aware of every detail of his surroundings, reinforcing his belief this would make an ideal safe house for covert operations. The seven-foot-high stucco wall protected a thirty-foot perimeter of interior courtyard before reaching the house itself, offering an excellent kill zone.

The entrance gave Wade the feeling of walking through the walls of an old Spanish fort. The house itself was modern--a combination of contemporary Spanish and mid-century design. Narrow vertical glass windows that opened at the top would allow air to circulate without inviting outside interest. In Wade's mind, the place was a virtual fortress, and would've been his first choice for a safe house. In fact, by then he was convinced that it was exactly where Mashburn would've set up housekeeping.

Ms. Barr waited at the front door and greeted Wade like they were old friends. He returned her smile then followed her into the well-appointed kitchen. As she passed the center island, she set her red purse on the counter. A ring of four sets of keys fell with a metallic clank, to the side of her purse, catching Wade's attention. Small tags confirmed his suspicion that every key fit the lock of this house, and the number of keys probably indicated the number of people who would be staying there.

Wade moved slowly around the kitchen, checking in drawers and turning knobs on appliances. He took out a few utensils like a seasoned cook might inspect in a kitchen. His comments showed interest and attention to detail. "The kitchen seems well equipped."

Ms. Barr quickly responded. "It comes fully furnished by the landlord who had a professional chef furnish it."

"Does the place come with bed linens, bath towels, and tableware?"

"Yes, it comes fully furnished. It also includes maid and garden service. It also has central air conditioning, which you'll come to appreciate. It can get pretty hot down here during the day. In the evening we get the cooler ocean breezes that bring the temperatures down."

Wade wanted the agent to be relaxed with his questions, hoping to get more information about his true objective.

"I've noticed the nice evening breezes here. They're very pleasant. How often does the maid come?"

"She's scheduled to come twice a week. There's an extra charge if she comes more often than that."

Wade hoped to find out more about the occupants as he finished his tour of the kitchen.

"I think twice a week would be fine for just my wife and me. We may have a relative come down while we're here, though. Is the twice-a-week service the norm?"

"Yes, but I think the gentleman from Panama wanted three days a week because he's hosting three other guests while he's here."

Wade was thinking about Yari's phone tap when he asked the next question. "What about telephone service? Does the house have its own phone number?"

"Yes, it's less expensive for the owners to keep the same number. The phone company bills us separately for phone usage during the rental period. We take that expense out of the renter's deposit."

"That would be fine with us."

Wade left the kitchen area and turned down a hallway to the bedrooms. He passed a table with a telephone on it and glanced down, memorizing the number printed on the phone. Ms. Barr left the kitchen and headed for the living in the opposite direction from Wade.

As he continued his investigation, Wade kept asking questions in a louder tone so Barr could hear him. "Has the current renter told you when he's coming down?"

"He said at the end of last week, but he hasn't shown up

yet. I've tried calling him, but his phone just keeps ringing. I assume he's traveling. He's already wired us the entire rent and deposits for the full three months, so they can arrive anytime they'd like."

"That seems strange. I hope nothing's happened to him."

"I don't think so. It happens with renters down here more often than you'd think. I've had situations where they pay us and never show up."

"How often does the gardener come?"

"Once a week, usually on Saturdays. He handles several of our properties in this area."

Wade moved down the hall, checking each room and recording a mental layout of the house including distances between rooms. Three bathrooms were shared by four bedrooms. He checked the locking mechanism on the door at the end of the hallway and confirmed that it opened to the driveway and covered carport.

Another side door off one of the bedrooms opened to a lush tropical interior courtyard. Like quickly putting together a jigsaw puzzle, Wade saw ingress and egress scenarios. He noted the locking mechanisms on each bedroom door and the exterior doors.

In one of the bedrooms, Wade noticed a light that didn't work. He walked over to the jalousie glass windows in the same bedroom and noticed the glass slat was not properly aligned. A turn of the knob told him the lower louver was loose. A light push of that louver sent it to the ground outside the window a foot below the sill. It landed softly without breaking.

Ms. Barr was keeping busy in the living room checking the wall thermostat when she heard Wade call out.

"Ms. Barr, are you aware that one of the lights in this

bedroom is out, and the window seems to be broken?"

That was all she needed to hear before she responded, "Where are you?"

They crossed paths just outside the living room. Wade explained, "There's a louver missing in the back bedroom window, and the light doesn't work. The light probably just needs a new bulb. It doesn't look like the missing window pane is broken, just missing, but you might want to check the bedrooms, so you don't get any nasty surprises later."

As Ms. Barr headed down the hall toward the first bedroom, Wade strode toward the kitchen.

"Which bedroom did you say it was?"

"The last one on the right. Listen, I'm going to check out the living room while you do that."

Wade wasn't interested in the living room. He wanted to get at the key rings hanging on Ms. Barr's purse. He slipped one of the sets in his pocket and replaced the others and quickly moved to the living room. Having done her research, she soon reappeared in the hallway near where Wade was standing.

"Thank you for pointing out those issues. Those louvers are always coming loose. I'll have my repair guy come by and fix it in the morning."

"This is a very nice property, and I'm sure it's the one we saw when my wife was down here. It was on a caravan tour, and we saw so many houses that we couldn't keep them straight."

Wade was satisfied that he'd seen everything and was ready to leave. They met again in the kitchen. More questions from Wade kept Ms. Barr distracted as she picked up her purse. When the agent looked up, Wade had already prepared a piece a paper and handed it to the agent.

"Here's my contact information. I really thank you for

the quick tour. I hope it wasn't an inconvenience."

"I'll mark my calendar to contact you when this property is available again."

She smiled and handed him a business card.

He nodded. "It's been a pleasure meeting you, Ms. Barr. I can't wait to tell my wife about the property. Good luck with your rentals. I'll be in touch."

Chapter 17

After asking around, Wade found a nice quiet payphone in the lobby of the local library. It had a comfortable seat facing out into the large lobby area away from passing ears going in and out of the main library room. He took a seat and dropped a coin into the slot, hoping to reach Yari without a sea of static. But Yari had little to report. Wade proceeded to fill him in on the rental.

"I may have found the house Mashburn rented. After a check of rental ads I contacted the listing agent and arranged to tour the place. Here's the name and number of the real estate agent and the number and address of the house. I'd like you to monitor phones for both the house and the agent, if you would."

"Consider it done. I did pick up a call from Panama yesterday between Mashburn and Condor."

"So what did they say?"

"Mashburn is on his way to Belize. I listened to the call several times and think it's odd that they don't once refer to the other operatives by name. It sounds like Mashburn has no idea what's going on."

"What makes you think that?"

"Mashburn keeps reminding Condor he doesn't know anything about the assignment or have a description of the people he's supposed to pick up at the airport."

"Did you get anything more on timing?"

"Mashburn is supposed to get flight information on the arrival of other members from Condor tomorrow or the next day."

"That makes my window of opportunity even tighter."

"It appears they don't want the other guys around until the war game exercises have already started. That's still another ten days away."

Wade paused, before he responded. "I know. We have to check on the schedule of those onshore ceremonies. That is, unless they're planning some kind of attack at sea."

Yari shared his concern about their missing information. "They must have this all planned. But I still don't have a tap on that other line Condor is using."

"Keep trying. I'm going to check the local newspapers and make a list of times and dates of all the ceremonies. Once these operatives get down here, we'll have a whole different level of threat. I'm just here to get at Mashburn and get out. "

"That's a good idea. I'll continue to look at government transmissions."

"If you monitor both the numbers I just gave you, we might get lucky. Otherwise, you're telling me you won't know Mashburn's whereabouts until he makes a call from the new location."

"That's the way it looks right now."

"I don't believe in coincidence. The house I looked at was rented for three months in advance by a guy from Panama."

"Why do they need it for three months? That's expensive."

"Not if it's government money. We're still just guessing." Wade didn't want Yari straying from the task at hand. "Look, just keep monitoring both the numbers I gave you. My guess is this crew isn't staying around for any three months."

"I'm on it. Give me a call tomorrow afternoon. I may have something by then."

"I'm at the library. I'll do some research on the upcoming war game festivities while I'm here."

"Later, big guy."

Wade felt his stomach clench as often happened when he sensed that something would happen soon. He spent time doing research in the library, then took the rest of the afternoon off to exercise and burn off nervous energy. A three-mile run along the beautiful waterfront gave him the relief he needed. During the run, he spotted several new restaurants he wanted to try.

He couldn't help wondering whether he guessed right about the safe house rental. Instincts told him he was right, but there was no way to confirm those feelings. If it wasn't the right house, he was back to square one, and with the other operatives arriving soon the pressure was building. Mashburn was due in tomorrow. Wade's only hope was that Mashburn would make a call to Condor for instructions as soon as he arrived in Belize.

After an early dinner of local fish stew, Wade searched the streets around the Adam Roy house looking for observation points. He parked at one he liked and noticed a few cars were different from the ones he'd observed early in the day and yesterday. His stakeout of the Adam Roy house that evening told him who all the neighboring property owners were. Everything seemed normal.

Library research yielded press articles about the war game ceremonies in the capital city of Belmopan, just over an hour's drive from Belize City. The Belmopan capital had recently been constructed out of the dense jungle near the remains of Aztec and Mayan ruins. Both ancient and current cultures were built to avoid the devastation of hurricanes that came in from the coast.

The next day, Wade drove the eighty kilometers to Belmopan. Local maps identified the key buildings and streets surrounding the capital. The capital was well laid-out and easy to navigate. Belmopan was a shining new city that peacefully emerged from dense jungle. It was not well guarded, however, suggesting easy targets for terrorists.

How Belmopan fit into Mashburn's assignment in Belize was still a big mystery to Wade. Attacking a city wasn't in Mashburn's skill set or part of his prior assignments. Nothing felt right to Wade about the Belize assignment or where Mashburn fit in.

He sat in his car looking at a glistening high-rise building in Belmopan that yielded no answers. He needed to get back to Yari, who was his only source of information regarding Mashburn's current activities.

As Wade drove back to Belize City, he wondered what Belmopan would be like once it was filled with international dignitaries and news media broadcasting worldwide. Frequently checking his rearview mirror for tails and finding none, Wade drove directly to the library to call Yari.

Yari had difficulty controlling his excitement. "It's about time you called."

"Just checking in for any new developments."

"I just monitored a call from Mashburn to Condor at the airport in Belize. You'll soon have Mashburn."

"Did he give an address?"

"No. He just let Condor know he was at the airport."

"Anything about the other guests?"

"No. They weren't mentioned."

Wade figured that Mashburn would be on edge and suspicious right after his arrival. "I want Mashburn to relax and settle into a routine."

Yari anticipated Wade's anxiety about Mashburn's whereabouts. "I should know his location as soon as he makes his first call from the house."

"I don't want to wait that long, and I'm not sure I can make it to the airport before he leaves. He has to get a rental car and go by the real estate office to pick up the keys. I'll be in disguise at one of those positions when he arrives."

Yari sensed Wade's frustration and somehow felt responsible. He was dealing with some very smart covert operatives and was also frustrated that they didn't leave him a better trail. He couldn't help stating the obvious.

"You realize you may find him before I can get the coordinates."

"That's a good possibility. If my hunch is correct, we'll both know within a couple of hours. Either way, I'll call back this evening to confirm."

Parked across the street from the real estate office, Wade noticed the familiar features of Mashburn's face getting out of a green sedan, someone he recognized from the brief time they spent together at Fort Benning. Ms. Barr came out the front door to greet Mashburn with keys waving in her hand. After handing him the keys, she pointed in the general direction of the house on Adam Roy, giving him directions. Mashburn motored past Wade's parked car, looking up and down the streets to get his bearings and make sure he wasn't being followed. Wade knew from the direction Barr pointed where Mashburn was headed. He followed using a different route. When he saw the green sedan in the driveway, he knew his hunch about the Adam Roy safe house had been right all along.

Wade backed into one of his observation spots down the street and turned off the engine. In no rush, he wanted Mashburn to get comfortable in his new place without suspecting a tail. Now that he'd found his target and his man had gone to ground, it was time to patiently wait for him to develop a routine. Course after course on surveillance had drummed principals of good stakeouts into Wade's psyche. He had to understand his target's behavior pattern before anything else. Mashburn needed to get comfortable in his new space before revealing his routine. Only then would Wade make his move.

His surveillance position allowed a good view of the driveway and the side entrance, which he assumed Mashburn would use to unload his car. At first Wade caught no sight of Mashburn through the binoculars, just several minutes of repeatedly flickering lights. Apparently Mashburn was fastidious about turning off lights after inspecting each room. The pattern of light switching revealed the man's exact position in the house.

Once the lights were on in just two rooms, Mashburn came out the side door to unload his luggage. A full trunk and back seat revealed that he had more luggage than any one person could possibly need for lounging on the beach. Wade counted as eight pieces of luggage were extracted from the trunk and backseat and assumed by the effort it took to move them that they were inordinately heavy.

Whatever was in this luggage was not bathing suits and sandals. *Weapons, explosives, and detonation devices* were all on Wade's mind as he observed the action. This luggage clearly had to do with the mission Mashburn was on, and at least in this instance, that mission had nothing to do with death by poison via syringe.

The driveway light reflecting off Mashburn's face only enhanced the coldness in his eyes. His expression was not menacing or brutal but a blank pale stare, like that of a scientist who enjoyed injecting rats with diseases and drugs to see their effects. The body struggling with the luggage was not toned or remotely fit for combat; he was clearly built to wear a lab coat rather than body armor.

Wade saw in him the lowest form of life - a human being who no longer cared whom he caused to suffer before they left this earth. Terminating this less-than-human could only benefit society. Wade kept telling himself he was not a judge or jury. This was a target who had information he was determined to extract. *Patience, patience*; now was not the time to rush to judgment or act prematurely.

The light switching sequence told Wade that heavy luggage had gone into the living room. The light pattern also told Wade that Mashburn had chosen the bedroom nearest the back door for himself.

After several hours of stakeout, Wade squirmed in his seat, restless from observing the same two lighted rooms with no activity. He wanted to check in with Yari for an update. His biggest concern was ignorance regarding the arrival times of Mashburn's housemates. If he didn't finish with Mashburn before their arrival, the stakes would get a lot higher. Only Yari had the answer to that question.

Wade had to be at his surveillance post early the next morning to confirm the maid and gardeners' schedules. The time to grab Mashburn would be soon, before the other operatives arrived. He evaluated his options: he could either remain in position or chance missing Mashburn if he left his post to call Yari. After evaluating the risks of each alternative, he chose to leave, because he needed the intel.

When he left for the library payphone, the only light on in the house was in Mashburn's bedroom. The rest of the house had been dark for the last three hours.

Sitting at the payphone booth in the hallway, Wade was anxious to hear Yari's voice. "It's me. Listen, our man is at the house and I need to know if he's made any calls."

"Yes. He tried to make one to a no-answer number in New York. I'm tracking the owner of that number now."

167

Wade considered his next comment. "Good. The thought crossed my mind... what if Mashburn doesn't know any of the other operatives, and he's not in charge of this mission. Where does that leave us?"

"That one's got me stumped as well."

"What about going back and listening to more of the Condor's calls?"

"I've done that. Nothing there. Did you ever think that Condor may not be running the operation either?"

"Yeah, but that doesn't leave us anywhere either. The problem I have is that if I take Mashburn out now, we'll be left clueless as to the details about this op."

"It will get really complicated if they're operating independently."

"I have to make sure Mashburn gives me the information I need on the Lockhart matter first."

"How can you be sure he's telling you the truth?"

"I have my ways."

"I wouldn't want to be Mashburn right now."

"He's fine right now, but you won't want to be him in a few days."

"I'll stay on the calls. I think you should check in every day, since I don't have a way of reaching you."

"I'll do that."

Wade returned to the stakeout. For the first time since arriving at 5:30 that evening, Mashburn left the house. Keeping a safe distance between them, Wade tailed him to a food stand near the beach. Much to Wade's surprise, Mashburn found a walk-up pizza stand. He thought to himself, *With all the wonderful seafood and local cooking in the area, why would he eat a pizza? Old habits die hard, I guess. In a beautiful tropical paradise filled with fine local cuisine, and he stands at an outdoor counter eating pizza.*

How boring and unappealing.

With nothing better to do on the stakeout, Wade nicknamed Mashburn "Possum." He'd been taught to always nickname his targets as an easy way to remember them by their habits. *Perhaps Mashburn is some form of nocturnal creature who only ventures out when the sun goes down.* Wade's sense was that Mashburn might be a good assassin, but he was also weird to the core.

Wade was on stakeout from early evening until Mashburn shut off his bedroom light at 2:00 a.m. Wade wondered if this detailed stakeout of Mashburn was necessary. He wondered if he was overthinking his target. As a creature of habit, Mashburn would be an easy target to hit even if he was constantly on the move. His sloth-like movements didn't exhibit any of the evasive tendencies a well-trained undercover field operative would use.

Unless Mashburn had been spending time booby-trapping the house with explosives, he had to be bored or an extreme loner. He had enough equipment in his luggage to make whatever explosives devices he wanted. When he made his move, Wade would have to keep a sharp eye out for trip wires, fragmentation grenades, and C-4 shape charges around door sills.

By 5:00 a.m. Wade was already situated in a new surveillance position. This second position was more obscure and better for daylight observation. Wade watched through binoculars when the maid appeared to clean and noted the time. Using a master key, she let herself in. Wade was glad to see that no explosives went off. While she cleaned, Mashburn broke his usual routine, and drove off in his car, with Wade following at a safe distance.

Immediate questions came to Wade about the location of the suitcases in the living room. They must be closed and locked or covered, away from the prying eyes of the maid. Wade followed Mashburn to the grocery store. The maid was still cleaning when Mashburn returned with enough grocery bags to fill the cupboards of two houses.

It was clear Mashburn was furnishing the bunker for multiple operatives. When the maid finished, Wade followed her to her next cleaning stop three blocks away. For that job, she pulled a commercial cleaning cart from the garage, which sported a clipboard hanging from the side. Wade wanted to get a closer look at that board.

In disguise, Wade walked up to the maid's cleaning cart, clumsily brushing against it and startling the maid.

"Oh, I'm terribly sorry, ma'am, excuse me. I'm new in this area and seem to be lost. Can you tell me where I might find Adam Roy Street?"

Approaching the clumsy tourist, the maid repositioned the cart and moved to the other side so she could give better directions. A quick glance down and Wade saw the cleaning schedule on the front page of the clipboard. A few more questions showing continued confusion gave Wade a chance to see and memorize her weekly schedule for the safe house. It confirmed what the real estate agent had said. The form read "501 Adam Roy: 3-days, M, W, F, 9:00 a.m."

"Thank you so much. I think I have my bearings now."

"You have a nice day, sir."

Chapter 18
Belmopan City, Belize

Wade's stakeout notes were copious, giving details of Mashburn's routine. It included times and places he'd visited over the prior two days. His pattern was that he left the house twice each day. One outing included an afternoon walk around 3:00 p.m., always along the same path near the beach. The second occurred precisely at 7:30 p.m. and included dinner at one of three places, two of which were fast food.

Mashburn's routine suggested an obsessive pattern of revisiting designated points precisely on schedule. His bedroom light remained on well into the early morning hours, indicating he might have problems sleeping. Wade told himself that this should not be a surprise, given his profession. Wade would have to keep in mind the man's compulsive behaviors when he finally made his move.

The morning of the fourth day, the maid arrived right on schedule at 9:00 a.m. She took forty-five minutes to clean and then left for her next scheduled stop three blocks away.

Once the maid left, Mashburn pulled out, turned the car around, and backed into the driveway, then looked in all directions before opening the trunk. Moments later he reappeared with one large suitcase and two smaller ones. He placed all the suitcases in the trunk and slowly drove off. For the first time in five days, the man had broken his routine.

Mashburn craned his neck, looking side to side while driving for three blocks before he made a sharp left turn. Wade followed at a three-car distance. Mashburn doubled back on his previous route, making a standard figure-eight pattern of turns, checking for tails. At one point he stopped following his predictable patterns and took another route to a spot Wade had predicted. He let Mashburn pass before resuming his tail.

Apparently confident he was not being followed, Mashburn headed to the on-ramp of Western Highway and his intended route east to Belmopan. It was the same trip Wade had made just a few days earlier. As he followed, he wondered what Mashburn had in mind for the large suitcases in his trunk.

The jungle scenery on both sides of the highway reminded Wade of his Louisiana swamp and how much he admired the Mayan civilization for having cleared enough of this thick jungle to house a civilization using only crude tools and their bare hands.

As they approached Belmopan, he slowed enough to read the exit signs. Mashburn took the Hummingbird Highway South exit and soon left the off-ramp on Forest Drive. He turned left to Ring Road and made another right onto Cemetery Road. Mashburn slowly drove past the two columns marking the cemetery's entrance. Wade came to a stop several blocks behind him. A tree kept his car well out of sight. With binoculars Wade tracked Mashburn's route through the cemetery plots on each side.

Mashburn held up a paper from the front passenger's seat. He drove slowly past two crossing cemetery streets. At the third intersection, Mashburn turned right. He was straining, trying to read headstones and comparing it to his notes. Apparently Mashburn located the name he sought on a mausoleum three burial plots away.

Wade drove to the other side of the cemetery and parked behind the shady leaves of a large elephant-ear tree. He trained his binoculars on Mashburn as he crossed over a green patch of grass and entered the service road, which put him behind the selected mausoleum. Mashburn looked in both directions before he opened his car trunk.

The side of the mausoleum was overgrown with thick shrubs extending all the way to the road. His cautious handling of the shrubs suggested they were thorny. Mashburn pulled back the shrubbery enough to make a path. He returned to the service road and looked up and down both sides again to make sure he wasn't being observed.

Mashburn walked back to the trunk and opened the large suitcases inside. He pulled out two smaller cases made of hard black plastic that fit snugly inside the larger case. Wade sat with binoculars, well out of sight. The smaller cases he saw looked similar to heavy duty cases used to carry heavy camera or laboratory equipment.

Holding one case in each hand, Mashburn walked around the car and through the path in the shrubs he had just made. He moved the two cases into the shrubbery, handling them gently like fragile items he didn't want broken.

After the drop Mashburn returned to the back of the car and slammed the trunk, looking up and down both sides of the service road again. He backed up and took the same route in reverse. Wade waited forty-five minutes after Mashburn left, scanning the horizon to ensure that no one was watching the drop site.

At this point, Wade wasn't concerned about tailing Mashburn. He knew his prey would return to his hole by the seashore. Wade's mind was cautious but curious. *What's in those cases, and why did he make the drop?*

Comfortable that the site was clear, Wade drove over the same path Mashburn had used. He approached the shrubs and removed the two cases, carefully examining their exteriors. They were heavy for their size. Their locking mechanisms were an unusual design: a barrel lock incorporated into the strong metal handle. Rivets going from the handle permanently secured it to the case. There were four spools of alternating numbers and letters that made up the lock mechanism. Wade concluded the lock could easily be part of a detonation-trip device that might be triggered if the locking mechanism was breached.

Explosive classes had taught Wade that it was best not to fool around with locking mechanisms even if you thought you understood how they worked. He squelched a burning desire to spin the spools to see if he could hear the movement inside. Wade kept hearing his explosive instructor's voice yelling warnings as he handled the cases. Instead of maneuvering the lock mechanism, he made extensive notes and photographed the cases.

After placing the cases back in the shrubbery, he made his way back to the highway and Belize City. He had a strong feeling that Mashburn would be headed back to the safe house. In Belize City, Wade passed by the house to confirm that Mashburn's green sedan was parked in the driveway before heading to the library to check in with Yari.

"It's me – Wade. Anything new on your end?"

Yari responded with some hesitation. "Yes, lots. But it's somewhat confusing."

"Let's have it."

"I have two calls to Condor from your location. The one last evening talked about going to a cemetery drop. The one today talked about an operative by the name of 'Stephan' arriving in three days. I didn't discover much about the cemetery, but it seems he and Condor had discussed the location previously. Each seemed to know what the other was talking about."

Wade smiled at Yari's confusion. "I've already covered the cemetery drop. Two suspicious cases were placed in the shrubbery alongside a mausoleum. The cases were locked with a very strange mechanism. Did Condor ever mention what was in the cases or the combination?"

"No. They just referred to them as the 'drop'."

Wade wanted to know more about the new arrival. "Who is Stephan?"

"First time I've heard his name, but he's arriving in Belize from Panama by way of Germany. He must be part of the operations team."

"Did Condor mention anyone else?"

"No, but I got the sense that Mashburn didn't know this Stephan guy. He asked Condor to spell his name and give him a description. They had a bad connection. The way they talked, I think Stephan could be the guy in charge of the Belize operation. I think there's something else going on between Stephan and Condor, too."

"What do you mean?"

"I monitored another call between Stephan and Condor. They talked about Phase 2 and disposal of a body near the creek at a rest area off Hummingbird. It seemed like Hummingbird was a code name for something. I didn't understand it."

"No, Hummingbird is a highway that runs north and south from Belmopan. I wonder if they could have been talking about what will become of Mashburn's body."

"I'm not following you, boss."

"Look, Mashburn is a liability to Condor. Stephan may be here to disrupt the war games and then take out Mashburn. That location is where a body would be easily found. Perhaps they plan to give authorities a lead following whatever destruction they're planning. After all, he is, or was, CID – Army intelligence. If he's found dead with some incriminating evidence on him, it solves Condor's problem about what to do with Mashburn. He knows too much.

That's why Mashburn is out of the loop on everything. He may be part of this set up - only he doesn't know he's the one taking the fall."

"Wow. That's heavy stuff."

"It's still speculative on my part. I just know I've got to make my move on Mashburn before Stephan arrives. My guess is the other operatives will be working under Stephan. Timing is everything right now."

"What about the other operation? Won't your moving in on Mashburn alert them?"

"Maybe not. It depends on how I handle Mashburn. I'm still thinking that through. Pretty soon things are going to get a lot hotter down here."

"I know you can handle it, partner. I'll keep monitoring, and we'll talk soon."

The next day Mashburn went out for his usual late afternoon walk and dinner outing. Wade didn't want to take the chance that Mashburn might remember his face even though their only encounter at Benning had been brief. Just in case Mashburn got a glimpse of him, Wade wanted the added protection of a disguise. Wade gained access to the house with his key and had thoroughly searched it long before Mashburn returned from his evening dinner.

He found among other things a Walther 9mm semi-automatic pistol in a holster taped to the back of the bedside table, easily reachable from Mashburn's bed. The contents of several large suitcases were spread across the living room floor, revealing several weapons broken down into component parts. The stash included a silenced sniper's rifle with a high-powered scope and lots of ammunition. There were also night goggles, fake IDs, passports, and maps of Belmopan, Belize City, and Ambergris Caye, which Wade quickly reviewed.

A search of Mashburn's bedroom revealed more papers taped under one of the dresser drawers. Written in Spanish, they looked like details of the Spain assignment. Removing the tape, Wade folded and pocketed the documents for later translation and review.

The biggest surprise came when Wade found three interesting medicine vials cooling in the refrigerator. An assortment of needles and syringes were lying among utensils in a kitchen drawer not far away. He examined the vials; each contained a solution of a different color. These didn't look like street drugs or prescription medicine. The silver metal ring clamp holding the soft gray rubber top for needle access had clearly been professionally manufactured. He hid the vials, syringes, and needles close to where he was going to interrogate Mashburn.

Wade thought, *Perhaps these are the same or similar drugs used on Lockhart or ones left over from the Spain assignment. What are they? And how are they used?*

Wade removed a pillowcase from one of the bedroom pillows. He found more papers under the mattress, which he also folded and pocketed. There were no weapons in the other bedrooms.

A notepad, pen, and small tape recorder were placed on the seat of a chair next to where Wade would interrogate Mashburn. Based upon his previous pattern, Mashburn was expected to arrive at any time. Wade checked his disguise one last time in Mashburn's bathroom mirror.

Slightly pulling back on the side of the curtain Wade checked both windows out to the driveway. He double checked the molding around the side door for wires and looked for camera and listening devices.

It wasn't long before Wade heard Mashburn's car come

to a stop in the driveway. The engine shut off and there was dark silence in the house. Wade could hear his heart beating faster. He felt the tension as the key slipped into the door lock and turned.

As Mashburn's hand reached in for the light switch on the wall he felt a cold, round cylinder pressed firmly against the back of his skull.

The voice from behind him said, "Don't turn on that light if you want to live."

Mashburn quietly raised both hands over his head without being asked. Pushing Mashburn from behind, Wade walked slowly to a chair already pulled out from the dining room table. Wade firmly shoved Mashburn into the seat.

Believing he was being robbed, Mashburn spoke in a quivering voice. "I don't have much money here, but you can have everything I have."

There was no reply to Mashburn's plea. Wade gave a strong command in a voice deeper than his natural tone. "Sit still in the chair without turning your head."

Wade kept the gun pressed into Mashburn's back. Strips of silver duct tape were already hanging from the table's edge.

"Wrap the tape tightly around your right hand and the arm of the chair and don't speak."

When Mashburn finished strapping his right arm to the chair, Wade slipped the dark pillowcase over his head before turning on the overhead light. The pillowcase had already been checked to make sure the weave was open enough to breathe, but wouldn't allow facial recognition of an image on the other side of the fabric.

Wade tightly wrapped Mashburn's left wrist to the chair arm. Then he also wrapped both of Mashburn's arms to the chair just below the elbows.

The strapping was done in silence as he secured Mashburn's legs to the chair, wrapping them just above the ankles and again just below the knees. The heavy, carved Spanish chair with Mashburn taped to it became a single solid structure that wasn't going anywhere.

After Mashburn settled for a few minutes, he mustered enough courage to ask a few questions in Spanish, trying to determine if the intruder naturally spoke Spanish. Obviously Mashburn still thought it was a robbery. Wade understood Mashburn's questions but didn't reply.

Wade imagined the man's mind running through a progression of questions, trying to assess his position and options: Did the intruder already search the house for money? Did he see the weapons still on the living room floor? Could he buy off the intruder? The fact that he had not already been shot suggested there might be hope for negotiation.

Chapter 19

Wade's next words caused Mashburn to rethink his robbery theory. His captive's voice was strong, speaking American English with only a slight hint of a southern accent.

"Listen, Mr. Mashburn or Ramos, or whatever your name really is, we have to talk."

Mashburn was clearly confused and unsettled. His work on the dark side had never before included capture.

"If you want money, I can...."

Wade interrupted. "Quiet. I will tell you exactly what I want from you, and you will listen very carefully without speaking, or your life will end here and now. Do you understand me?"

"Yes."

Mashburn was already trying to rethink his previous assumptions. His mind jumped to "intelligence personnel." He knew there might be no negotiation under an intelligence scenario. Compared to robbery, the thought of surviving an intelligence capture made him sick to his stomach. He asked himself why he wasn't already dead, and whom he might have infuriated. The list was too lengthy to comprehend, but he kept coming back to his recent assignment in Spain.

Wade allowed the silence to continue. He knew exactly what Mashburn was thinking. The list of intelligence sources that might capture him was growing. Wade could tell that the silence was getting to Mashburn, but he let him stew before he finally spoke.

"The reason you're not already dead is because I want information. My assignment is to get truthful information from you – or eliminate you as I see fit, so you're no longer a problem to my current employer. Do you understand that?"

The pillowcase bobbed up and down acknowledging his

agreement.

"I want you to understand that I may still eliminate you after you give me the information I need. You'll just have to take that risk. If you choose not to provide me with truthful information, I can assure you that your death will be drawn out and very painful. You will never leave this room alive. Do you understand me?"

Mashburn's head once again bobbed vigorously up and down. To emphasize the point Mashburn also muttered a squeaky, "Yes."

Robbers could often be paid off, but covert intelligence operatives have different agendas, including torture. Mashburn had concluded he was at the mercy of a covert hit man, which actually made him quiver in his chair. The thought sent cold chills down his warm body. He gritted his teeth, shivering as though a sudden blast of arctic air had blown over him. Wade's message was clear enough.

The irony of his life ending at the hands of a covert black ops agent using torture techniques raced through his mind. Mashburn saw the faces of people he'd terminated pass before him. His mind kept coming back to the simple option before him. *If I don't cooperate, I'm dead the hard way. I may be dead anyway, but at least I have a chance of living longer if I keep talking.*

With a shaking voice, Mashburn mustered enough courage to ask, "Are you an American?"

"My nationality is not important. Let's just say we work for similar employers. No more questions on your part. I want you only to listen and answer the questions I'm going to ask. If I find you've lied to me about anything, you'll make my job of eliminating you quick and easy. As long as you give me truthful and complete information, you'll live. Do you understand?"

"Yes."

"In my hand I'm holding the 9mm Walther P-38 that was taped behind your nightstand."

The next noise Mashburn heard was the unmistakable sound of the breach of his pistol sliding a round into the chamber. The cold, hard barrel of his own gun pressed against his head.

"Your gun has a round in the chamber, and the safety is off. It also has a silencer. In case you're wondering about noise, I also have a pillow from the living room in my other hand, and I'll place it between the barrel and your skull to muffle the sound even further."

Wade slapped Mashburn in the head with the pillow. Mashburn recoiled from the blow like it had been an anvil. He nervously racked his brain, trying to determine which agency sent this man and what his fate would be, no matter how he answered. He was even more convinced than ever that the longer the questions kept coming, the longer he'd stay alive.

"We're going to start our discussion with a little history. You were in Vietnam between 1971 and 1973 for two tours of duty as a medic. Is that correct?"

"Yes."

"I want you to tell me how you went from being a medic to a spy."

"I was serving under Colonel Mark Baker in a forward Medivac command unit on the border of Cambodia and Vietnam. It was bad. We couldn't keep up with the wounded. We didn't have enough medical staff or supplies on hand to help everyone. It got to the point where I couldn't take the stress anymore.

"One of my wounded men told me about a supply of morphine derivative drugs that was available out of

Cambodia. He put me in touch with an intelligence officer by the name of Daniel Spencer. At least, I think he was CIA, not Army intelligence."

Mashburn paused, hoping Wade was listening to the details.

"Continue."

"I connected with Spencer, and he put me in touch with a local Vietnamese source that had access to those drugs. Spencer took care of the payments to the supplier. We started giving the drugs to the patients with the worst wounds, to ease their pain."

Reliving the experience, Mashburn had to take a breath. His anxiety was affecting his speech. Vietnam had been a long time ago. During the pause, Mashburn wondered if his captor had something to do with Vietnam. He regained enough composure to tell himself, *Just keep talking.*

"After a while, Spencer had me distribute drugs to some infantrymen who weren't wounded. These guys were paying me the money, and I was delivering it to Spencer. The next thing I know, my commander and Spencer got me transferred out of my medic unit to an Army intelligence unit, where I reported directly to Spencer. I soon got to the point where I was delivering drugs and picking up money full time for Spencer and my commander.

"I believe Army command knew all about it. No one seemed to be asking me any questions or bothering me. One day, Spencer came to me and said that Command was doing an illegal drug trafficking investigation. They were looking for scapegoats in a military drug scandal, and I was one of the targets."

"Spencer told me I could no longer stay in my current unit. He got me transferred to another Army intelligence special ops unit that reported to someone in the States. The next thing I knew I was transferred out of Vietnam and doing intelligence work in different countries. At that time it was mainly document drops for CID command."

"What happened next?"

"When my Vietnam tour ended, I was sent to CID training school and then back into the field in different countries. With my background as a medic, they trained me on the use of a new line of 'wonder drugs' Army intelligence was using."

"Was Spencer the same guy who sent the Army recon mission out on patrol that got them all killed?"

"Yeah, he's the one."

"Is that where you met Lockhart?"

Mashburn hesitated. Lockhart's name hadn't been mentioned before, but he assumed his interrogator already knew about Lockhart and Spencer by the way he asked the questions.

"Yeah. He never really recovered from Vietnam. He blamed Spencer and my commander for the deaths of his platoon. He claimed he knew everything about the drugs coming in from Cambodia and how Spencer was obtaining them and making a fortune."

Wade thought Mashburn's story was too rehearsed and defensive about his own role. He changed the subject to throw him off guard.

"What was your assignment in Spain?"

"I was assigned to covertly assist the Franco government."

"You're lying to me."

"No, I'm not."

Wade put the 9mm against Mashburn's temple. "Let's go over that last question again, unless you want to die now. Franco has already killed 300,000 of his own countrymen.

He's perfectly capable of killing anyone he wants to in his country. Why would he need you or the U.S. to do his killing for him?"

"These were special assignments when he didn't want his men involved in the terminations."

"That doesn't sound right. You'd better come up with a good example."

"There was a former general in his army by the name of Salino, who changed political affiliation and then left the country just before Franco took over. Salino was a popular political figure in Spain and was coming back into the country to oppose Franco. That was a threat to Franco and my most recent target. He didn't want his regular men to handle it."

"Who did you work for in Spain?"

"I worked for President Franco's security officer General Juan Carlos."

"I still think you're lying about Spain, but we'll come back to that topic in a moment."

While Mashburn was speaking, Wade had checked his notes and the recorder. Wade continued to break up the sequence of his questions.

"Who do you work for in the U.S.?"

"That's a good question. I'm not trying to be evasive. I'm officially undercover operations for CID, but I've been farmed out. I'm now reporting to a handler in Brussels. I just know him through his code name, Condor. I no longer have any direct contact with CID in the U.S."

Wade felt Mashburn's last answers were mostly truthful, or he at least was sticking to a well-rehearsed cover story. Wade changed the direction of his questions again to ones he already knew the answers for, to see if Mashburn was lying.

"Have you ever been to Fort Benning?"

"No, I don't think so. Is that in Alabama or Georgia?"

"You're lying to me again."

"No, I just can't remember."

"Well, we're going to have to improve your memory. I have something here on the table that might help. I've got three strange-looking unmarked medicine vials that I found in your refrigerator, along with some syringes from the kitchen drawer. One vial has a clear liquid in it. The second has a cloudy gray solution, and the third has a milky white solution in it.

"Since you claim you're not lying, and I don't trust what you've already said, I can't trust you to tell me what's in these vials. I think the only way to find out what they contain is to do some experimentation. I'm loading a syringe with the cloudy gray solution now and will soon be injecting it into you."

"If that injection doesn't do anything to help your memory, we'll try the next one. I think by the time we get to the third one, perhaps your memory will improve – or you won't be around to worry about it."

"You can't do that. The solution will kill me."

"That sounds like a truthful answer." Wade pressed the end of the needle against Mashburn's arm, slightly penetrating his skin. "Let me repeat my question about Fort Benning."

"Wait. Please, don't inject me. My memory's coming back."

Wade removed the prick of the needle from Mashburn's arm. "I'm listening. You were saying you remember being at Fort Benning?"

"Yes, I was on assignment for CID doing surveillance on Lockhart while he was in training there."

"What did your assignment entail?"

"At first I was just there to keep an eye on him."

"You're lying to me again, Mashburn. I'm loading the second syringe, this time with the clear solution. Perhaps it's only penicillin and will cure any bacterial infection you have."

"No, it's not penicillin. Don't do that. It will kill me!"

Wade saw Mashburn tighten his grip on the chair, waiting to feel the fluid enter his body. Mashburn's fear caused him to soak his pants, confirming the solutions were definitely not penicillin.

"If you continue to play these games with me, you'll soon die a horrible death by injection. I'm no medic, but it's probably a lot worse than a quick round to the head. Now tell me your entire assignment with Lockhart at Fort Benning."

"Lockhart made the overture to a CID operative that he wanted to be paid to keep quiet about the drug deals in Vietnam. I was initially sent to observe him and approach him with a deal to pay him money from the government in exchange for remaining silent."

"That wasn't the real deal, though, was it? To pay him off?"

"At first it was. But then I saw and reported how unstable Lockhart had become. I was ordered to get him alone and make the payment, and then eliminate him and make it look like a suicide."

Wade placed the needle into Mashburn's arm so that he felt the point break his skin. Mashburn tightened his grip on the armchair, shaking as he agonized over what the drug would do to his body. The details and medical effects of each drug were well known to Mashburn; he had administered them and been around to see too many people die at his hands from their use. He didn't want to die that

187

way.

Visualizing the effects of the drugs, Mashburn clenched his jaw, knowing he would soon be paralyzed. Unlike Lockhart's injection, this one would go beyond paralysis, spreading its painful venom into his organs until his heart stopped. Mashburn's stomach convulsed and he gagged, almost vomiting in his hood.

"How were you going to eliminate him?"

Mashburn coughed. "I was assigned to head the death squad. I administrated the first drug in some booze we had for a celebration drink that knocked Lockhart out. Then I injected him with the second drug, which paralyzed him without killing him. It took the other guys to set him up in the chair so it looked like he killed himself with his own gun. Those were my orders."

"I take it you're familiar with the effects of these drugs?"

"Yes."

"How many people have you killed using some form of drug?"

"I've never killed anyone unless ordered to do so. I'm not sure of the exact number... maybe thirty or more? If it makes any difference to you, I still see their faces and hear their screams at night."

"If you have such nightmares, why do you still do it?"

"I can't get out. I know too much, and there are too many people in power above me to allow me to leave. I'd be dead in a matter of hours."

"Do any of these vials contain the same substance you used on Lockhart?"

"No, not exactly. The one with the white milky substance is similar. That one paralyzes you first, but goes on to kill you. Lockhart's solution doesn't kill you. That drug paralyzes its victim for about two hours."

Mashburn took in two large gulps of air before continuing. "All the vials you have there will kill you, but in different ways, to avoid postmortem detection or tracing. After those solutions are injected and do their damage, they dissipate over time after you're dead. That's why there has to be a delay of several days before an autopsy can be done."

"So why was Lockhart targeted at Fort Benning?"

"Lockhart applied to return to active duty in Vietnam. That's why he was taking a refresher course at Benning. CID knew Lockhart was unstable and probably wouldn't survive his next tour of duty. But they had to make sure he didn't."

"So why not wait until he got to Vietnam?"

"Because of how mentally unstable he had become. They thought he was ready to go off and kill someone or tell someone about the Vietnam drug deals before he shipped out. They couldn't take that chance."

"What happened next?"

"During a night exercise, I lost control of him. He went off on his own, believing that his classmates were out to get him. He almost killed one of them. I think he was also suspicious of me. He knew me from Vietnam and thought the other guys worked for me. After the night incident, he went AWOL. CID felt they had to act. Before he broke off that night, I told him I thought I could get him the money he wanted from my commanding officer to keep things quiet. After the exercise, he contacted me by phone at the barracks. He wanted to meet at the Candlelight Motel about forty miles from the base to get his money."

"Then what happened?"

"My instructions were to give him the money, and then terminate him."

"Where did that order originate?"

"My CID unit commander - someone I inherited from Vietnam. His name is Cory Fortier. Cory told me his authority was coming from above. That's all I know, I swear."

"So you met Lockhart at the motel. What happened next?"

"Lockhart liked to drink. I told him we had to celebrate when I gave him the money. I had a fifth of his favorite single malt bourbon and drugged his drink. That knocked him out."

"Let's go back to your assignment in Spain. I don't believe you were really working for Franco. What's the real story?"

"The U.S. owed Franco some favors, but he had gone mad killing everyone. The U.S. couldn't appear to be supporting him in any way, so they sent me in to do some covert work for Juan Carlos."

"That sounds like a cover story."

Mashburn suddenly grew silent as though he had been paralyzed by the question.

Wade slapped Mashburn on the side his head with the pistol butt to jar his memory. "Well, do I need to get the syringe out again? Is this really the end of your story?"

"That was my cover story."

"Who was your real target?"

"Franco."

"So you were a double agent?"

"Yes."

"Is that when you met Condor?"

"Yes. I'd just been assigned to Condor for the Spain assignment. My orders from Condor were to carry out Franco's orders, but in reality I was to try to get to Franco himself."

"Did Condor instruct you on how to do that?"

"He pretty much left it up to me. He told me to get close to Juan Carlos first. Franco was having some medical issues at the time. I was told to find out as much as I could about his health issues, and then work that angle."

"Why is Condor involved in your current operation?"

"I don't know. I don't think he knows much about what's going on."

"What do you mean?"

"He doesn't seem to have any details or answers to my questions. I don't understand why this operation is even going on. I mean, Belize is a friendly country with strong ties to our British allies. I don't know why we're disrupting these games. I was just told to follow instructions."

"I know that. What's the real operation?"

"I swear I don't know. I just know Condor is turning me over to another operative who's running the operation. I'm now supposed to report to him and follow his instructions."

"Who's the other operative?"

"All I know is that it's a guy by the name of Stephan. I haven't met him or spoken to him yet. I can't even tell you what he looks like."

"Isn't it true Stephan is out of Germany?"

"I was never told that."

"What's in the two black cases you delivered to the cemetery yesterday?"

"I swear I don't know. They were delivered to me at my hotel in Panama before I came here. I was just told where and when to drop them off."

"You weren't curious about what was inside?"

"I took one look at the locking mechanisms and didn't even want to handle the cases. All I was told was to make the drop at the cemetery, and Stephan would take it from there."

"Aren't there other operatives who will be arriving?"

"Yes, I was to make arrangements and pick up two other operatives from the airport, though they would arrive at different times."

"When are they arriving?"

"I haven't been given flight numbers or times yet, and I don't know who they are. I just know they're supposed to arrive a few days after Stephan."

"And when does Stephan arrive?"

"In two days. I have his flight information in the bedroom."

There was a pause in the interrogation. Wade hadn't counted on getting so much information on the current operation. He considered his options with Mashburn and their consequences.

"This is the way I see your position. You've been passed from handler to handler since Fort Benning. You did the Spain assignment, which could have serious political repercussions. Your name is on lots of target boards for the work in Spain.

"You're wanted in the U.S. for the Lockhart murder, and you've always been a problem for my agency. CID has completely distanced themselves from you. You're a liability to them not only because of the Lockhart murder but because of what went on in Vietnam and Spain.

"If my agency has tracked you down, so can others. You're here in Belize as a gofer for an operation you claim to know nothing about. It's not your kind of operation. You've not been given any specifics, and you're reporting to a German-trained assassin by the name of Stephan. Is any of this smelling a little strange to you?"

"It smells like hell. I'm being set up."

"There's an old intelligence saying, 'If you ever feel you're worth more dead than alive to your agency, you'd better start looking over your shoulder.' That's because chances are you won't be around long."

"I get your meaning, and I'm not too proud to admit that I wouldn't like my position even if I wasn't sitting in this chair."

"If I were to tell you that my agency knows that your Belize operation is already designed to have a dead fall guy found at a rest stop off Hummingbird Highway, would that ring any bells for you?"

Wade let some time pass for the concept to sink in before continuing. "If my agency has the information on the dead drop, don't you think you would have been informed of that phase of the assignment?"

"I wouldn't be surprised if I'm that fall guy."

"Who can be certain of anything in our business? But you do have all the right credentials for being that fall guy, especially if they plant incriminating evidence on you. It solves the Lockhart murder, the Vietnam drug incident, and the Spain connection all at once. You're the rogue agent who couldn't be controlled."

Wade paused before going on. "Knowing what you know about the Belize assignment where do you see your skills coming into play? I don't see your skills being used here at all, and Condor has better and cheaper gofers to do the grunt work."

"If I were a betting man, I'd wager that your body will be the one found near the creek at the rest stop. Your death solves too many problems for people above who need to remain protected."

A grim silence fell between the two men. Mashburn squirmed uncomfortably in the silence before he asked,

"What happens now?"

"Quiet. I'm thinking through my options with you."

"Please don't kill me, I beg you."

"Quiet. I'm thinking."

The pillowcase over Mashburn's head was wet from the sweat pouring from his head.

Without a word, Wade got up and walked to the other room, leaving Mashburn to his own thoughts. He returned with scissors and a pair of Mashburn's socks. He placed them on the table loudly enough for Mashburn to hear the clang of the scissors. Mashburn jumped back in his chair. The silence that followed was deafening, and Mashburn couldn't wait before asking.

"What are you going to do to me?"

Chapter 20

"I'm going to take off the hood from behind you and place some of your socks I just cut over your eyes and tape them to your head."

"Then you're not going to kill me?"

"I haven't decided yet."

Mashburn heard the duct tape being torn into strips. The room was now dark as evening set in. Wade worked with just the table light on.

"Keep your eyes closed tight."

He stood behind Mashburn and placed a sock over each eye. He held the material in place with one hand as he pulled a strip across Mashburn's face to hold the socks in place. He strapped extra tape all around his head, leaving his nose uncovered so he could breathe.

"I have one more thing to convey before I decide what I'm going to do with you."

Mashburn was shaking, afraid to show his curiosity.

"The people I work for want to see you out of the assassination business – as in permanently retired. They've left it in my hands to ensure your retirement. I believe your covert skills are good enough to give you an opportunity to disappear forever from the intelligence community. If your skills are not good enough to permanently disappear, one of the agencies will find you soon enough."

Wade took a breath and then continued. "There are at least three agencies and several independent operatives chasing you in addition to Condor and his men. As I see it your only chance of survival is to hide for the rest of your life. There's no other way out. "

Wade paused to adjust the tape over Mashburn's eyes.

"I suggest you go find some small village in the

backwoods of Europe or South America. Find a village where nobody's heard of a U.S. citizen. You might even practice some real medicine, helping people in that village. But as of this moment, your days as an undercover assassin are over."

Mashburn was silent, slightly nodding his head in acknowledgment.

"My people have shown the ability to hunt you down. In fact, if they find that you're not dead or in complete hiding, they will find you and terminate you. I may be given that assignment, and I can assure you we won't have another discussion like this before it happens. Have I made myself clear?"

"Yes."

"Your cleaning lady comes tomorrow morning at 9:00 a.m. To ensure that you remain still until that time, I'm going to tip your chair backward until it rests on the edge of another chair that I've set up."

Wade checked Mashburn's chair by balancing it backward on its two rear legs. He returned it to the upright position before continuing.

"I'm going to insert a syringe of your favorite solution into your neck and leave the plunger extended, taped to the chair and your neck. You can take your chances trying to wiggle free, but I'd encourage you to remain perfectly still until the maid comes tomorrow."

Wade wiggled Mashburn's chair from side to side, showing the effects of the movement. "No matter which way the chair moves the syringe will automatically plunge the gray solution into your neck. Do you understand?"

"Yes."

"When the maid finds you, she'll initially panic. Assuming you haven't moved your chair during the night, you can show her you're still alive by making sounds. Let her calm down so she carefully removes the tape from around your mouth. She can help you remove the rest of your bindings – but not the syringe. You'll have to remove the needle yourself."

"I understand."

"After you get the maid to calm down, tell her you were robbed. You'll also have to inform the real estate agent, Ms. Barr of the robbery, and perhaps even give a report to the local police. Ms. Barr won't want the news spread that her rental property was robbed, so the report will go no further. Do you understand?"

"Yes."

"I have one more thing to do before I leave you. I'm going to put the remaining sock in your mouth and tape over it. Do you have anything to say before I do that?"

"Thank you for letting me live."

Wade put the sock in Mashburn's mouth and taped it around his head, leaving an open area below his nose to breathe.

"Remember, you're retired as of now. If I were you, I'd take the next few hours to think about how you're going to disappear so that you won't be seeing me or anyone else looking for you - ever again."

"By the time you get through with the police and the real estate agent, you'll have only one day before Stephan arrives. I left the return ticket to Panama in your bedroom. Stephan is also coming to Belize through Panama, so you'll need to be careful not to cross his path at the airport."

"Since neither of you knows each other, he probably won't be able to track you for a while. Once you leave Panama, you'll have to remove all traces of your existence. You won't have much time to disappear, but it's your only chance to survive."

Mashburn nodded his head and grunted, acknowledging Wade's advice. Wade leaned Mashburn's chair all the way back until it rested precariously against the seat of the other chair. He inserted the needle at the base of Mashburn's neck and taped the syringe to his neck and chair, leaving the plunger end extended a few inches from the supporting chair.

Wade gently rocked the chair side to side, showing Mashburn how easily the chair would trip the syringe. He collected the sniper rifle and the other weapons from the living room. After checking Mashburn's bindings one last time, Wade made sure he had all the documents and vials of solution. He gathered his tape recorder and notes before wiping down everything for fingerprints wearing surgical gloves, as an extra precaution. He quietly closed the side door behind him.

The street was quiet, with only the sound of large tropical leaves dancing to evening ocean breezes. Wade never told Mashburn that the syringe he'd left in his neck was filled with tap water.

Wade arrived at the military section of the Belize airport to catch the first morning flight to Houston. He'd accomplished one part of his mission with Mashburn, but had turned up another more serious terrorist threat that he hadn't yet addressed. Wade's stomach churned as he considered the ramifications of that threat and what could go wrong.

He needed time to think. His only hope was that Mashburn would take his offer to disappear, and that the Belize police would believe the robbery story. Stephan and Condor would have to change their plans to exclude Mashburn from the assignment, or call the whole thing off.

As Wade boarded the military flight 771-L, he looked into the faces of the other soldiers, who also seemed to have a lot on their minds. The loud flight back to Houston took place with little conversation among the passengers.

Running scenarios back and forth during the three-hour flight exhausted Wade. What troubled him most were the unknowns, especially the scenario where he would return to neutralize the terrorist threat. How was he going to take on at least three additional operatives? What if he had misread Mashburn? Instead of disappearing, what if Mashburn went directly to Condor with the whole story? Wade began questioning his decisions and repeatedly replayed the "what ifs" as the plane touched down in Houston.

Wade wondered if things would have been any different if he had terminated Mashburn, as he'd originally intended. Instead of a robbery investigation, the Belize police would have a homicide on their hands. Wade kept justifying his decision to himself. *If Mashburn's disappearance doesn't work, Stephan will terminate him in a few days anyway.*

On the other hand, if the robbery story played out and Mashburn disappeared, things would calm down and the threat would go forward with a few minor adjustments. Wade thought about his own situation. He couldn't formally explain his actions with Mashburn or the Lockhart murder without putting himself on the agency's hit list. The scenarios kept leading him back to Belize to deal with the planned threat and the other operatives. For now he just needed to distance himself and see what happened with Mashburn.

By the time Wade disembarked in Houston, nothing had been resolved. His pockets were filled with small slips of papers containing notes and lots of To Do lists that would occupy him for the next couple of days.

He called his cousin Frank to pick him up.

"How was your trip to Belize?"

"Great. That is one beautiful country. I was mesmerized by the scenery."

"I used to get down there every year to fish."

"The seafood was outstanding. I love the conch ceviche."

"How long are you going to be in town?"

"Not long. I have a lot of things to get done right away. I may be returning there shortly"

"Really? That bad?"

"Yeah, just may have to check out more of paradise."

"Well, I'm here if you need anything, including the spare car."

"That's great. I really appreciate it. Right now I have to do some copying, mailing, and phone calls."

"Why don't we just go over to my office? You can do it there."

"Works for me. Thanks."

After getting settled at the office, Wade asked for a box to pack the vials for mailing. Those he would ship to Morrison. He needed several copies of all the documents so he could have them translated.

Wade found a quiet office to place a call to Yari. "Sorry it took me so long to get back to you."

"I was worried sick not hearing from you. What's going on?"

"I'm back in Houston, at my cousin's office."

"Did you interrogate and terminate Mashburn?"

"I interrogated him and let him go."

"What?"

"It's a long story, which I don't want to get into right now. I got everything we need on the Lockhart murder, including the names above him ordering the hit. There was a recent Mashburn assignment in Spain. I recovered documents from him that are written in Spanish. They will have to be translated."

"Send them to me. I'll take care of that. Why did you let Mashburn get away?"

"I had to make a compromise decision in the field when I discovered the Belize plot. If Mashburn was terminated, Condor would just cancel the Belize mission or change tactics. I felt it was better if Mashburn just disappeared and stayed hidden. If he doesn't do a good job of disappearing, he won't survive long anyway. Keep your ears to the ground on Mashburn's whereabouts."

"What's the plan now?"

"I staged Mashburn's departure as a robbery. If all goes well, he'll be discovered alive at the house. I need you to monitor calls from the house, the real estate office, and the Belize police station. There should be a robbery report coming in on that house address. I need you to also keep monitoring Condor, especially calls between him and Stephan. We have to find out how they're going to react to Mashburn's departure and any change in plans regarding interruption of the war games."

"How much time do we have?"

"Not sure. I grabbed most of their weapons and stashed them in a safe place. That might give us some additional time while they try to replace them."

"Got it. Not a problem. What do you do next?"

"The second operation is too complex and involves too many operatives. I can't handle it alone. I'm going to have to involve some Agency resources. I just haven't determined who or how yet."

"What happened to those black cases Mashburn brought

in?"

"The black cases are still in place at the cemetery. To remove them would alert Condor and Stephan. I'm sure they're a big part of the Belize operation."

"What about Mashburn's other weapons?"

"I stashed them in an offsite storage facility. I'm hoping Stephan will conclude they were taken as part of the robbery. The police report shouldn't refer to the stolen items as weapons, just luggage and personal items."

"Did you find out how Mashburn killed Lockhart?"

"Yes. I got all those details. It involved some real exotic drugs. I have samples, which I'm sending to Morrison for analysis. We'll need to track the source of those drugs, but for right now, we need to focus on what Stephan and the other operatives are planning in Belize. From what I was able to find out, it's going to be a terrorist attack to disrupt the war games ceremonies, but I'm not sure of the motive and don't know who ordered the attack."

"I'm on it."

"We'll talk soon."

Wade's next call was to Gabe Morrison. He told Gabe about the drugs he was sending, his interrogation of Mashburn, and where and how Mashburn had received his orders to kill Lockhart.

Wade dreaded the next call – not because she might be irritated, but because of how long it had been since he had said he would call. He gritted his teeth, not sure what he was going to say.

"Megan speaking."

"I take full responsibility and am prepared for my punishment."

"Well, hello, stranger. How did your fishing trip go?"

"It got a little more involved than catching fish."

"I can't wait to hear that fish story. Where are you?"

"I'm in Houston at my cousin's office. I just got in a few minutes ago."

"Catch anything?"

"I sure did, but it goes beyond fish."

"I hope it's not a disease."

"It's not. Let's just say it's something I need to talk to you about in private."

"I take it you're not in a good place to talk?"

"That's right."

"Is the matter personal, between us?"

"No. It's really business, I guess, our business, and it needs to be handled privately."

"Why don't you call me tonight? I can have a secure patch put over my home line."

"I sure will. Is 9:00 p.m. your time good?"

"Perfect."

Wade wanted to change the subject away from his mission. He lightened the conversation when he asked, "How's everything else going?"

"Fine. Busy at work. But most of all, I miss you."

"I feel the same way."

She sighed aloud. "You know, I like having you in this awkward position where you're embarrassed to speak in front of other people. I'll have to find ways to get you in that position more often."

"That's not funny."

"I didn't say it was funny. I had other ideas. I'll wait for your call tonight."

After he hung up, Wade wasn't sure what he had accomplished with the call, although he was pleased Megan wasn't too upset. Not only did Wade have to decide what he was going to say that evening, but he wondered how secure the call would be.

Wade needed to talk with someone he trusted. The only person he could really trust with his dilemma was Jake Pisano in New Orleans, but he had to find a way to meet face-to-face. He called a short time later, and they agreed to meet the next day at the Old Grille. Wade left Houston in his cousin's car at 4:30 a.m. to make the six-hour trip.

Chapter 21
New Orleans, Louisiana

The drive from Houston to New Orleans gave Wade time to think about how much he was going to tell Jake about the Belize mission and the new threat. Wade remembered it was Pisano who had made the introduction to Gabe Morrison. Maybe that was a good way to start their conversation.

"Good to see you, Jake."

Jake was worried about Wade's call and not in the mood to dance around the issue. "Does your visit have anything to do with the shooting at Fort Benning?"

"I guess indirectly. I just got back from Belize, where I interrogated the suspect Mashburn, believed to have killed Lockhart. That's the murder Gabe Morrison is investigating."

Jake was quick to respond. "I remember. What were you able to find out?"

Wade provided Jake with details of the interrogation and the discovery of the new plot in Belize. Some of the details came fast and were overwhelming with lots of interlocking parts. Wade made it clear that he was looking for guidance. After a few pointed questions, Jake held up his hand in question.

"I'm afraid to ask, but what did you do with Mashburn?"

"I told him about the planned hit on him and let him go. I hope he takes my advice and permanently disappears and retires from the business. There's always the possibility he won't, of course. Based on what I've told you thus far, what do you think?"

"I'm still on overload, but other than breaking about sixteen federal laws, I think you did the right thing with

Mashburn."

Jake's mind was turning as fast as Wade's now. There was a pause while they both processed alternative options. Before Jake could respond again, Wade changed the subject.

"There's something else I forgot to mention."

"I can't wait."

"Before I interrogated Mashburn, I followed him to the cemetery in Belmopan, where he dropped two hard black plastic cases in the shrubbery next to a mausoleum gravesite, for future pick-up. Mashburn claimed he didn't know what was inside the cases – he was just following instructions for the drop. I examined the cases, and they had a very weird locking mechanism and a welded T-Handle that went into the case. I've never seen that before. I think they might well be explosives."

"Were the black cases still there when you left?"

"They were there the day before I interrogated Mashburn. I think they were left for Stephan and the other operatives."

Jake paused, still processing the information, before he looked up and spoke. "I'm trying to figure out a time line here. Stephan is arriving in a day or two, but doesn't know Mashburn is missing. The other operatives are supposed to arrive in a week or two. The war game ceremonies are supposed to start in three weeks."

"That's right. Oh, and there's one other thing I forgot to mention."

"Spit it out."

"Here we go again."

"Sorry, but I can't help but feel suspicious that my agency is somehow involved in the Lockhart matter. The guy heading the illegal drugs in Vietnam was CIA. After the investigation, he was released, and died shortly afterward in a mysterious hit-and-run accident that was never solved. I don't know who I can trust there about Lockhart because of his direct ties to the Vietnam drugs. I just have that nagging feeling you're always talking about."

Jake paused before summarizing Wade's options.

"Let's break all this down. For now, I would just turn over all the Lockhart evidence to Morrison and let him run with it. I wouldn't spend any more time on it if I were you. And I wouldn't worry any more about Mashburn. It seems to me you need help at several levels on the Belize threat. One is military. The others are diplomatic and probably intelligence."

Jake looked up at the ceiling, quietly running through a list of government contacts. "I know a top guy in the state department who might be able to help. I would probably go to him first. If the threat isn't foreign, it doesn't fall under him, but I think he'll know the right people to contact. I want to think on this tonight. There's a lot here to process."

Wade had some concerns about involving someone in the government. "One other thing I forgot to mention is I have pictures of the black cases. Haven't had time to get the film developed, though."

"I can have my lab do those tonight."

"Great. I'll go get the film from my car."

After the meeting ended, Wade headed for his father's condo, hoping to spend some time with him before returning to Houston. His father greeted him with a smile and a hug. His sun-tanned face and lively step showed Wade he was adjusting well to his new single life.

His father was quick to tell Wade he had taken up golf and was spending a lot of time with new friends. Wade saw a sparkle in his eyes for the first time since his mother died.

"I thought retirement would be a bore, but I'm having

more fun than I ever thought possible."

"You look great, Dad."

"I thought we could go to the driving range this afternoon. You can share my clubs, or they'll have others you can use at the range."

Wade wasn't a big fan of golf, but he wasn't about to turn down an opportunity to be with his father.

"That would be fun, Dad. Let's do it."

They talked about the condo and his father's move.

"Do you miss our old house?"

"I thought I would miss it because of all the memories there. But once I got settled and met new friends, I was able to move on with my life. I haven't given the place a second thought or even driven past it since I moved. I'm very happy here."

They studied each other for a long moment. A lot of water had passed under the bridge between them that didn't need to be discussed. An unspoken message was felt rather than spoken between them. It was clear that they were truly grateful to be able to spend time together.

His father spoke first. "Now tell me, what have you been up to?"

"Nothing very exciting. Tell me more about your golf game. What scores have you been shooting?"

As his father began describing details of the last nine holes of each of his last two games, Wade's mind wandered a bit. *What am I going to say to Megan when we speak tonight?*

"Do we still have the camp?"

"Of course we do. You may want to take a few days while you're here to go check on it."

"Unfortunately, Dad, I'm on a quick turnaround this trip. I'll spend the night, but I have to leave in the morning.

Maybe I'll have more time on my next trip."

After hitting balls at the driving range, his father went to bed early. Wade thought about what he wanted to say before making his call to Megan. He felt almost relieved when he got her answering machine and left a cordial message.

The next day the sun came over the condo balcony, lighting the dining room table as the two shared an early breakfast. Wade's father brought in the *Times Picayune* and threw it on the table in front of Wade.

"Look at those headlines. After killing all those people, that tyrant Francisco Franco of Spain finally died in a hospital from some mysterious illness. His second-in-command is now taking over running the country. I wonder if anything will really change there."

Wade was nibbling a piece of toast when he grabbed the paper with interest and starting reading the article to see if he could find a link to Mashburn.

Wade had plenty to think about during his trip back to Houston. The timing of Franco's death and Mashburn's last assignment was all too coincidental. Reading between the lines of that Franco article, Wade put the pieces together, convinced that Mashburn was responsible for Franco's death. He couldn't help wondering where Mashburn might be hiding now.

After returning to Houston, Wade made a call to Yari. "Any new developments?"

"I picked up one call between Stephan and Condor. Stephan's plane is delayed in Panama. Engine problems."

There was a pause on Wade's end. He wondered if the plane delay was real. He hoped Mashburn had somehow managed to avoid Stephan at the airport in Panama. Wade wondered if Stephan's delay was because the mission to Belize had been called off. He made some quick calculations of flight times in his head.

"Did Mashburn use his ticket back to Panama?"

"Yep."

"That means both men crossed paths at the terminal?"

"Looks like that's a possibility, although Stephan's flight from Germany was also delayed."

"I'd like you to calculate the actual arrival and departure times for both their flights, so we can see if they missed each other or were in the airport at the same time."

"Got it. I'll do the math and let you know."

"What about calls from the real estate woman in Belize?"

"There was a call from the real estate office to the Belize police to report the robbery, but I haven't seen a police report issued yet. Everything I see tells me it's been swept under the rug there."

"Any new activity from Mashburn? Phone calls, credit card transactions?"

"There was one credit card transaction in Panama, and that's it. No calls."

Wade was pleased to hear that Mashburn wasn't making calls or leaving a trail of credit card transactions.

Wade still had to make the call to Megan and wanted Yari's assistance.

"I have a strange request."

"The stranger the better."

"I have a call coming up with someone from my agency. The call is being patched through a secure Agency line to a home phone. However, I'm not sure someone from the Agency won't be eavesdropping. Can you set up a secure line that overrides an existing secure line patch?"

"That's not a strange request. We call that a 'double patch with encryption.' What it means is that whoever's listening to your call won't be able to understand either side of the conversation. My encryption will override their patch. I'll use my new encryption code. Did I tell you that no one here has been able to break it yet?"

"I think you mentioned that."

"We do double patches all the time when we think our unfriendly foreign neighbors are listening to an agent's call. Will you be calling from the number you're on right now?"

"Yes, and I don't want this number to be identified. The last thing I want is someone tracing calls from my cousin's house."

"Give me about twenty minutes to set everything up. You can make your call any time after that."

"Great. Thanks, buddy."

"What else do we need to be doing?"

"I'm waiting for a response from the State Department after my meeting yesterday. I don't have any plans until I hear back from them. I need you to keep tracking the calls to our friends in Belize, though."

"Got it. I'm all over those calls."

"Thanks. We'll talk soon."

Wade was torn about his upcoming call to Megan. Despite his suspicions, he felt he had to make the call. After setting up the double patch with Yari, he picked up the phone, still unsure of what he was going to say.

It sounded like she'd been waiting by the phone. "Hello?"

"It's me. I hope this is a convenient time to call."

"I thought it might be you calling."

He tried to make small talk. "How's everything at work?"

"The same – busy."

"I miss not talking to you every day."

She coughed as if uncomfortable. "Well, there's nothing preventing you from calling."

"I know. I get distracted with other things, but you're always on my mind. And sometimes when I call, you're out on company business."

"We're both busy. So you were going to tell me a fish story."

He cut to the chase. "Before we get into that, let me ask you something. I need a straight answer."

"Sure. Haven't I always given you straight answers?"

"Do you totally trust the Agency? I mean, are there any areas where you have suspicions?"

A long, awkward silence followed, until he thought he'd lost the connection, but he was relieved to hear her take a deep breath and let it out. It was clear that Megan was taking his question seriously – she hadn't been expecting it and was clearly cautious about how she answered.

"Well, I don't always agree with how the Agency handles things. Sometimes it does things that violate its own policies. But I can't say I have any real suspicions. What exactly are you getting at?"

"You remember the sniper incident at Fort Benning?"

"Of course."

"Well, some things have come out about that incident that may involve the Agency. Like the fact that they knew all about Lockhart. There were also some questionable drug operations going on in Vietnam that the Agency either knew about or sanctioned."

"Where are you getting your information?"

"Let's just say it came up during the Lockhart murder investigation."

"You're kidding! I didn't know anything about that investigation. Why didn't you tell me this before?"

"I was told they weren't sure who might be involved, and I was instructed to keep quiet."

"Do they think either of us is somehow involved?"

"No. They didn't say that. I'm just not sure all our communication channels with the agency are secure."

There was a pause while Megan said nothing. The silence caused Wade to wonder what she was thinking.

"Is that the 'fish' story?"

"That's part of it. I really can't go into the rest right now. I hope you understand."

"Do you feel safe?"

"I think so, but I'm not absolutely sure."

"What can I do to help?"

"Nothing right now. I can't let you get involved. You're too close to the D.C. senior people who might be implicated. I can't have you jeopardize your job – or worse, your life. I care about you."

"Let me worry about my job. I can take care of myself. You should know that by now."

"Right now, I just want you to trust me. I'm in the middle of something, and my survival instincts are dictating my every move."

"I do trust you, but I can't help if I don't know what's going on. I know my way around the Agency, and I'm good at getting information about what Agency people know or don't know. I had to learn that skill to survive here in order to do my job. If anyone should know that about me, you should."

He stood up and paced the room before finally sitting down again. "I do know that. The problem with this incident is that it goes to the top of the Agency, and heads might start to roll if it gets any closer. Other than providing the investigators what they ask for, I'm trying to stay as far away from it as possible. The investigation has now taken on a life of its own and is out of my hands. We'll just be collateral damage if we get too close."

"I understand the risk. Just let me know what I can do to help."

With Megan's last comment, Wade had to decide how much he could trust her. The thought that Megan would risk her job and maybe her life made him sick with guilt. He also needed information that he knew Megan could probably obtain.

"I need to know which Agency operatives we can trust in and around Belize. But you have to make sure your inquiries can't be traced back to you or me."

"That shouldn't be a problem. What else do you need to know?"

"That's all for right now. I'm still working on other angles."

"The obvious question is why the country of Belize?"

He sighed, feeling his frustration level rise. "That's precisely the question that will raise suspicions, and why you can't ask it that way. So start with a list of agents in Central and South America and eliminate names in every country but Belize. Check the grapevine for background on the names you find. Don't ask anyone at headquarters a direct question about Belize."

"That shouldn't be a problem. I've got your drift." Megan understood the importance but still not the purpose of the secret mission Wade had just assigned her. "Where are you going to be when I get the information?"

"I'm back in Houston, staying at a relative's house. I'll contact you. I may be on the road. Just be careful how you source your information and make sure you use a secure line."

"I know how to source information safely. Remember, we trained at the same facility."

"I know. That's what worries me. Those who taught us may well be the ones tapping the lines. Remember in the end the orders all come out of the same facility. "

It bothered Wade that he hadn't heard back from Jack Pisano about his call to the State Department. Wade decided to call Jake.

"Pisano here."

"Hi, Jake, it's Wade. Just wondering if you made that call to the State Department yet."

"I've actually made two calls since I spoke with you. I had long talks with friends at the Feds in Washington, one from the FBI and another from the State Department about the Belize matter. The bottom line is that you're in a jurisdictional quagmire."

"What's that supposed to mean?"

"Belize is a British protectorate – soon to be independent. Other than the partial use of their airbase, there are no U.S. assets in the country, and therefore no direct threat to U.S. assets or personnel. Both my contacts suggested you turn the matter over to the British consulate to handle."

"What about the war games?"

"He didn't see that as a direct threat to U.S. assets. Most assets in the war games are off-shore in international waters. In other words, before the State Department could get involved, there would have to be a direct threat to a U.S. command or embassy post, and you would need to be able to prove a specific threat."

Jake paused to allow the message to sink in. "My State Department friend felt his department would become involved only if the threat was directed toward U.S. personnel or assets. In a friendly country like Belize, the U.S. would look to the U.K. or the Belize government to handle the matter directly."

"No wonder we have such a screwed-up foreign policy."

"He said he'd be happy to make an introduction to the U.K. Embassy in Belize if we had enough evidence. I told him to hold off until I could speak with you again."

Wade could see political wheels spinning with no corresponding progress. He asked, "How do you think the embassy in Belize will respond?"

"My guess is they'll probably do a memorandum. Belize has limited defense forces and relies heavily on the U.K.. Getting the U.K. involved raises the bar, and I don't think you have enough specific evidence at this point. I'm afraid they're going to want to know the what, when, and where about the threat, and especially who's behind it."

Wade thought about Jake's questions and the lack of information he had at this time. He not only couldn't answer the primary questions, he couldn't reveal his source of information or his suspicions about his agency's involvement. He would be laughed out of the briefing room, and if the Agency got wind of his chatter, he'd be fired or permanently terminated.

Jake finally broke the awkward silence. "I'm afraid all we could provide them with at this point is circumstantial evidence pointing to a possible plot."

Wade acknowledged Jake's point. "That's the problem. No one is going to do anything with this, based on the information I have. You're right about unconfirmed sources.

I also can't take the risk of disclosing my sources regarding Agency involvement in the Lockhart murder. At least we tried."

Jake understood Wade's dilemma. He'd been in these situations before. "I don't like it any better than you do, but unfortunately, that's where we are."

Wade had another thought.

"Do you think your FBI friend might offer any assistance if we had more evidence?"

"What did you have in mind?"

"Let's say I was able to get those black cases back here. Could he have them X-rayed and disarmed? If they turned out to be a threat, would he then take action?"

"I would have to ask him specifically about the cases. If the cases did contain a threat, the FBI might go through the same channels I described before. This would all take time, of course,"

"Let's not raise the question about the cases just yet. I need to give it a little more thought."

"Sorry I couldn't be of more help."

"You were a great help. You gave me the answer I needed. It just wasn't the answer I had hoped for. I appreciate it."

"Let me know how it goes."

"I sure will. Thanks."

At that moment, Wade realized he wasn't going to get the help he hoped for, anywhere else either. He could expect the same result from whatever intelligence sources Megan might find. Nobody except a few tourists were interested in a small, politically insignificant country surrounded by jungle and beautiful Caribbean beaches.

The well-armed armadas of the U.K., U.S., Canada, and Australia assembling off the coast of Belize were not being threatened as they played war games. There would be no concern that a few disruptive operatives could cause anything but a minor political embarrassment on shore.

Their scenario seemed ideal from a terrorist point of view. No need for them to confront heavy military assets on the water. A cleaner mission would involve the deaths of onshore civilians and dignitaries right under the nose of the world press. They would be in and out before anyone realized it or could respond. The night was restless as Wade tried to sleep with those thoughts circling in his head.

The next morning, Wade's first wall was to his former training partner Max from the Fort Benning exercise. The overview Wade gave Max over the phone was enough motivation to arrange a meeting later that day in Houston.

As Max walked through the door, Wade rose, and the two exchanged warm greetings commonly shared by soldiers who haven't been in contact for a long time.

"I'm glad you could make it. I didn't want to say too much over the phone."

"I heard enough to know that I'm in if you need me."

"First tell me what you've been up to since Fort Benning."

"After getting my Special Forces training, I had a tour of duty in Vietnam. After R & R leave I returned for a second tour, and I took a bullet in the thigh. I got shipped back to the U.S. and have been in rehab since then. But I'm in good shape now. I signed up for another tour in 'Nam, but the doctors tell me I have to wait another three months before I can return. I work out hard every day and I'm usually at the range three times a day. I can't stand not being in action."

Wade was always impressed by Max's attention to detail, willingness to take orders, and steadfast resolve in dangerous combat situations.

"I understand. I gave you a summary of this mission on the phone, but wanted to give you more details in person. We're up against three, maybe four operatives. I'm trying to get more intel on them now from Yari. I think all the operatives are Intelligence or former military, trained in Russia or Europe."

Max was still a little confused about what the Benning incident had to do with Belize. "So that Mashburn guy was the Lockhart killer, but he was never caught?"

"Right. He spilled his guts to me and I let him go because if I took him out, I'd have killed any chances of getting to the other operatives."

"Do you know who or what their target is?"

"No. Not for sure. That's the problem. The intel is sketchy. It's probably the Prime Minister of Belize or one of the foreign dignitaries. "

"Do you know when they're scheduled to attack?"

"Not certain of that either. It's probably scheduled for one of the ceremonies during the war games. I took two sniper rifles from Mashburn with a 5-power scope, in addition to some small 9 mm arms. Then there are these two black cases that Mashburn dropped at a cemetery in Belmopan. They look like explosives or other devices or weapons that are part of their mission."

"Aside from Mashburn, do you know anything about the other operatives on this mission?"

Wade nodded. "The head guy is a German-trained assassin by the name of Stephan. There are three other operatives coming into the country as well. I don't have a lead on who they are, but Yari is covering all communications between them. We should know more soon. Apparently Stephan is being handled by a former CIA operative who goes by the name of Condor. He's out of Brussels."

"Why is the CIA involved?"

"Not really sure. I can't see any benefit to U.S. interests. It's a real strange mission. Not sure who's running the mission or why. It could be Russia."

"You mean this Condor guy is working for the Russians now?"

"I don't know."

"Unless the U.S. is somehow aware or backing it, I wouldn't bet on this guy Condor living a very long life."

"You've got that right."

Max bit his lip in deep thought before he asked, "Do you have a plan?"

"I have a couple of ideas. We have to first ID the players – I want to know who we're dealing with and who the likely target is. My guess is we'll be reacting to the situation as we get new information."

"Is it going to be just you and me?"

"It looks that way, my friend. We'll need some equipment."

"Not a problem. I can get pretty much whatever we need from the base as long as we can get it into and back out of the country."

"I can take care of that. Let's start making a list."

The men continued their conversation for the next hour. Having both stalked that deadly sniper unarmed months before, they shared a brotherhood. That dark, perilous night at Fort Benning bonded the two men's confidence that they could survive under fire or die knowing each had the other's back.

Chapter 22
Belize City, Belize

The sea bags each man carried were heavy with equipment as Wade and Max entered the pilot's lounge at Ellington. The copilot Wade had befriended on his last flight was checking items off a list.

At Wade's approach, the copilot commented, "Well stranger, couldn't resist another visit to the tropics, huh."

"They keep sending me back. This time I'm taking a diving buddy and some scuba equipment. I'd like you to meet my cohort in crime here - Max. He works with me at the Agency."

Max and the copilot exchanged greetings and handshakes.

The copilot turned to Wade and asked, "You going down to do more interviews?"

"Yeah, D.C. wants some follow-up interviews and a bunch of paperwork filled out."

The copilot identified with Wade's frustration. "Everything is paperwork around here."

The flight sergeant walked in the front door from the tarmac with a clipboard under his arm and turned to the copilot. "Sir, we're almost loaded. It'll be another half hour. I don't have a flight requisition for these two men."

The copilot quickly responded, "These men are CIA, Sergeant. They fly with me on a regular basis. I received the call yesterday. Don't worry about them. Just add them to the list under Intelligence Personnel."

"Yes, sir. I'll let you know when we're ready to depart."

The copilot turned back to Wade and Max. "You see? Everything runs on paperwork. I've got to finish my flight check now. I'll see you onboard in a few minutes. Help yourself to some coffee."

As usual, the two-and-a-half-hour flight was noisy. It was impossible for Wade and Max to hear each other past the ear-cupped head gear. Communicating with hand signals and the occasional shout made pieces of their conversation somewhat intelligible. After thanking the copilot for a good flight, the two boarded a navy bus for a ride to the city center and the car rental agency. Initially they would only rent one car, but Wade thought they would need a second car by the time the other operatives arrived.

Before going to the motel to check in, Wade drove Max by the safe house on Adam Roy Avenue. All was quiet and closed since Mashburn's departure. Only a few parked cars dotted the neighborhood as the afternoon sun bore down on the quiet street.

Wade spent the rest of the day showing Max around Belize City. Max was immediately mesmerized by the natural beauty and ambiance of the historic city, and made more than one comment about how easy it would be for him to move there. They made a stop at the storage rental facility where Wade had stashed Mashburn's weapons, ammunitions, and supplies. Max commented that the weapons grade was high end. He couldn't believe all the documentation, although neither of them could interpret the Spanish papers.

The next stop was to the newsstand to get the local paper. Wade wanted to see if the Adam Roy house had been put back on the market since the robbery and Mashburn's departure. If the house had been relisted, it might mean the mission had been terminated by Stephan or Condor or they had changed the safe house location. They walked into one of Wade's favorite local restaurants while he was reading the rental ads. The isolated table in the corner with a nice view was perfect. Wade looked up from the newspaper.

"I don't see the house listed."

Max was quick to jump in. "That doesn't mean anything. It may be vacant or rented to someone else. We'll have to actually stake it out to be sure. "

"I agree. I want to try something after lunch. I'll need you to cover me."

"Not a problem."

"We'll need to bring our radios."

Max quickly became a connoisseur of conch ceviche and local flounder. They both ate like there was no tomorrow and applauded the chef's skills during the three-block walk back to the car.

After leaving the motel they parked the rental car at one of Wade's side street observation points. The Adam Roy house looked vacant without a car in the driveway and no visible lights on. It was early afternoon. They waited for signs of life but saw nothing. Belize residents really took their siesta time seriously. The early afternoon sun was blazing and no one was stirring on the sidewalk or the side streets.

Each man took time to chamber a round in his 9mm semi-automatic Sig. Wade was in disguise when he reached for the set of keys he had, hoping they had not changed the locks. They coordinated radio frequencies.

As he opened the door, Wade turned to Max who would stand sentry from the car. "I'll have the radio on, so alert me if anyone approaches."

"You're covered."

Max turned the radio dial to the right frequency and checked that Wade's receiver picked up his tone. Wade's disguise was back-up in case anyone he knew, like the maid or real estate agent, happened by. He felt he could talk himself out of the situation if he had to. The fact that Wade already knew the house and grounds made his approach through the garden door into the courtyard seamless.

Thinking they may have changed the locks after the robbery, he had brought tools to pick the lock. He was surprised to find that the door unlocked with his old key. Wade cracked the door, slightly feeling around the edges for wires which might be connected to a Claymore.

With his gun drawn, he eased inside, looking carefully for signs of alarms, cameras, and booby traps, then he quickly surveyed each room. The house was sterile except for an unmade bed in the front bedroom.

He looked in the refrigerator, searching for signs of occupancy. There were two bottles of local beer that hadn't been there when Mashburn left. All the kitchen cabinets were empty and cleaned. He remembered the next day was cleaning day, so they could observe the maid's movements. Wade wondered where Stephan was. After searching each room, he retraced his steps to the rear of the house and exited through the same door he entered before heading to the car.

"What did you see?"

"Nothing noteworthy except for one unmade bed and two bottles of beer. Everything else is clean. I think our man has been here, but I don't think he's using this as his main operation hub. If they kept the same cleaning schedule, the maid should be here tomorrow at 9:00 a.m."

Max knew what Wade was thinking. *We'll be waiting when she arrives.*

That evening the men went to another of Wade's favorite local restaurants. This time they feasted on the conch ceviche, local lobster, and roasted mashed plantains. The next stop was the local library, where Max stood nearby as Wade dialed Yari's secure number from the phone in the outer lobby.

"Hi, Yari, it's Wade. Any news?"

"Yeah, I have some calls to report. I recorded a whole conversation. I think you should hear it - it's between Condor and Stephan. Let me patch in the recording."

Wade tilted the phone away from his ear so Max could listen in. A scratchy sound was followed by a beep.

"This is Stephan. I'm in Belize. I'm at the house, but Mashburn's not here."

"What do you mean he's not there?"

"When I picked up the keys the rental agent said there had been a robbery. Apparently the maid found Mashburn tied to a chair and scared out of his wits."

"What did they take?"

"Everything. The place was cleaned out. All the weapons, papers, maps - everything's gone."

"Are you sure it was a robbery?"

"Yeah, I interviewed the maid. Mashburn gave a police report. She said he was real shaken by the incident and was leaving the country. My guess is the robbers saw the weapons and maps and took everything they could. They'll bring a good price on the black market. I'm guessing they might have gotten scared off by all the military stuff and didn't want to take a chance on killing Mashburn."

Condor replied, "Yeah, I guess that's possible."

Stephan continued his explanation. "I think Mashburn saw that his cover was blown with the police report, and probably thought the only way out was to get the hell out of the country."

"That sounds like Mashburn. He hasn't checked in with me. I'll check to see if he's used the return ticket to Panama.

I don't want that guy floating around. He knows too much. So what's the plan now?"

"I think we go back to the original plan, but that means we'll have to replace the equipment. I assume Mashburn made the drop in Belmopan before he left."

"He told me he did, but who knows. You'll have to check."

"I'll check that out first thing in the morning."

Condor showed his frustration. "It will take me days to replace our supplies."

Stephan wanted confirmation of the mission. "Listen, all I need to know is whether or not I still have a go from the top."

"Yes, but check in with me on a regular basis. And don't get robbed."

"That would never happen to me, my friend. *They* would all be dead."

Yari returned to the line. "What did you think of that?"

"That's great intelligence work. Keep monitoring. We just got back from the Adam Roy house, and Stephan has been there. It doesn't look like he's staying there, but we'll confirm that with a stakeout tomorrow. By the way, I need you to set up a double-secure patch from this line to someone at the Agency for me. But before we do that, someone here wants to say hello."

Wade passed the receiver to Max. "Hi, Yari, it's Max. Good to hear your voice."

"Max! I can't believe you two hooked up again. How are the tropics?"

"So far, so good. But I think things may get pretty intense before it's over."

"You couldn't be with a better guy."

"I can't disagree with that."

Max handed the phone back to Wade for the second call. He got out his pen and pad.

The call to Megan could be his last before he cut off all communication with the outside. He was still anxious and uncomfortable about revealing anything more about the mission, but he had to know what she had found out from her research. While he was waiting for Yari to confirm the patch, Wade suggested that Max go to the periodical section and jot down phone numbers for the American and British Embassies and see what the newspapers were saying about the upcoming war game ceremonies, before the library closed. The patched call went through, and Wade heard Megan's voice.

"Hi, it's me."

Megan was quick to ask, "Are you on a secure line?"

"Yes. Thanks for asking."

"I've got some research results I wanted to go over with you, but first I wanted to make sure we're secure. Before we get into the research, I want you to know that ever since you made that comment about trusting the Agency, I've been more cautious and done a little snooping around on my own."

"What did you find out?"

She gave an audible sigh. "There was an agent in Vietnam by the name of Daniel Spencer who reported to our New York office. He left the Agency and was killed in a hit-and-run accident just after he arrived home in North Carolina. Apparently there was a hush-hush investigation of what was going on in Vietnam before he was recalled. But I could find no mention of that investigation in any Agency documents. From what I can see, several senior people were involved including Spencer's handler, and they all took early retirement or suddenly went on to become consultants with the Agency."

"Be careful where you poke. It's going to get very sensitive when it ties back to the Fort Benning incident. What about Belize?"

"We have one agent recently appointed to the American Embassy, by the name of Art Mellon. From what I can tell he's more of an administrative type, processing documents and doing research projects. There's also an MI-6 agent based in the U.K. Her name is Zara Wicks. Her cover is senior administrative staff to the consul general, and she seems to have some real field experience. She's married to a Belize national who's a surgeon on the hospital staff somewhere in the area. I'm still checking her background through some U.K. contacts."

"Listen, I don't want you to dig any further into this. Let me think about it. I'll decide as we get further along."

"Where are you?"

"Close."

"Close to me or close to Belize?"

"That's all I can say right now."

"I understand."

He paused before speaking his mind. "Please be careful with your research. I don't want anything to happen to you."

"Believe me, I'm careful, but I'm sensing that you might be in danger."

"I'm fine. We'll talk soon."

Wade joined Max in the library, and they both read everything they could find in the local newspapers about the upcoming war game ceremonies. Articles under the peace headlines labeled the purpose of the games as "Building Ties with Friendly Neighbors."

A large looming question continued to bother Wade. He shared his thoughts with Max. "The thing I still can't get my head around is Condor, and whose authority he's working under. If it's the U.S., what's the motive for disrupting Belize relations? If it's another country, he's a double agent. It doesn't seem like a good use of U.S. assets."

Max nodded. "That's been sticking in my craw from the beginning. Who's the enemy here?"

"It would seem that the Russians have the most to gain from disrupting the games."

"That would mean that Condor is a double agent."

"Or that's what he wants everyone to think."

Chapter 23

After watching the maid clean the empty safe house, Wade and Max were certain that Stephan was operating out of at least one other location. Stephan as an operative was obviously much better trained than Mashburn, and still a mystery. Yari couldn't find any intel on the man, not even a picture or last name to go on – just "Stephan."

Wade wanted Max to see Belmopan and get a sense of the layout. As Wade drove he explained the city to Max as his partner pored over several maps. Their first stop was the cemetery to check on the cases. As they rolled past the entry gate, the cemetery looked a little different to Wade. Bushes and weeds had been trimmed and the gravesites cleaned up – perhaps in preparation for visitors.

A burial ceremony was in progress not far from their mausoleum target. They drove to a quiet place on the opposite side of the cemetery and waited with binoculars until the interment ended. The cemetery clean-up made everything easier to see.

Max trained the binoculars on the thicket of bushes next to the mausoleum and wondered aloud to Wade, "Could the maintenance crew have discovered the cases? What do we do if they've been removed by the operatives?"

Wade paused, unsure how to answer Max's question. "Let's take it one step at a time."

"In other words, you don't know?"

"Of course I don't know, and I don't want to spin my wheels thinking about it until I know. It won't be long."

Max kept his binoculars trained on the attendees and made mental notes and descriptions of the guests and their vehicles. His glasses moved back and forth between the departing funeral guests and the service road that ran behind the mausoleum.

Both men knew Stephan had to perform the same assessment if he intended to pick up the cases. It wasn't long before attendees made their way to three waiting limousines parked in a row followed by another dozen private cars. After the funeral procession left the cemetery, all was quiet again. The two men looked at each other.

Max asked for clarification. "How long do you think we should wait?"

"I would give it at least another half hour. I want to recheck the observation positions we previously identified before we go in."

"What are your thoughts regarding whether the cases are or are not there?"

Wade showed a little frustration with Max's question, because he hadn't thought that problem out. "I told you I don't know. If the cases are still in place, it only means Stephan has determined they're safer here than in his possession. That could be because the contents inside are very dangerous or too sensitive to handle. They probably don't want to risk getting caught with them. If the cases are gone, Stephan probably has them, which means we need to track him down, which we'd have to do anyway."

Max agreed with that logic. "That's the way I see it also."

Wade shook his head from side to side in frustration. "You asked me that question so I could tell you that you were right?"

"No. Don't ever tell me I'm right if you don't think it's true. It's just that we think alike."

"It must be the same training."

"Or the same devious minds."

Wade couldn't argue with that.

After scanning potential observation positions, Wade drove slowly onto the service road as Max scanned the surroundings in all directions. Each had their 9mm semi-automatic pistols with silencers loaded, with Parabellum rounds lying on the front seat.

Craning his neck, Wade scanned the dense bushes as he stopped the car. He couldn't be sure. The thick shrubbery created a black cave pressed tightly against the mausoleum's side wall.

With his weapon in hand, Wade left the car and approached the shrubs as Max stood watch. The two cases were still in place. He motioned to Max to join him.

"Gently lift up that case and check out the handle and locking mechanism."

Max complied, but he also jiggled the case a bit, making Wade more than a little nervous. He immediately cautioned Max about the danger.

"Don't do that. It might go off!"

"Didn't you say these cases made it to Belize on an airline flight all the way from Panama?"

"Yes, but for all I know, Mashburn activated them before he put them here."

"They're heavy. My guess is some kind of equipment or explosive device."

Wade's nerves were on edge. Max seemed more relaxed, like he had a better understanding of what he was handling. His hand slowly moved around all sides and the bottom of the case. He studied the locking mechanism up close, as though he could see past the rows of spaced cylinders into the case itself.

Finally, to Wade's relief, Max set the case on the ground. Wade looked at Max and said, "We need to put them back where we found them."

To Wade's surprise, Max responded, "If it's all the same to you, I'd prefer that you put them back."

"Not a problem."

Before returning to Belize City, they spent some time going over the Belmopan map and driving past important administrative buildings. Max spotted something between two of the buildings.

"Look over there. It looks like construction workers assembling stands for the ceremony."

Wade quickly picked up on Max's observation. "The person in the yellow hard hat looks like a construction superintendent."

"Let's stop. We might get some good information on the ceremonies."

Suddenly Wade thought about an approach. "We need a cover – and it can't be that we're tourists, or we won't get any information. Let's think. Who might be out here doing an inspection from America?"

An idea came to Max while the superintendent moved closer to their car. "Why don't you roll up those maps we have to look like building plans? We can act like we're construction inspectors for the U.S. You take the lead. You probably know more about construction than I do. I'll be looking at the buildings for sniper angles."

The two men walked over to the superintendent with plans under their arms like old construction hands.

"Good day, sir, I'm Bill Morris from Collins Construction. The Embassy asked me to come by and take a look at your progress. How far are these stands going to extend?"

Pointing with both hands, the superintendent showed Wade where the stands ended on both sides. "They'll go another fifty-five feet in that direction."

"Have you calculated your weight loads yet?"

"Yes, sir. The metal scaffolding and stands will hold over 140 pounds per square inch. A lot more than the required minimum."

"We always want to be sure. What did you use for the attendance figures?"

"Just under 1,200 people. I don't have the exact number."

"I see you're going five high. Did you use five high to compute your weight loads?"

"Yes, sir. I'll recheck the numbers when I get back to the office. I may be low on the attendance."

"Where will you locate the stage? And how many dignitaries did you calculate for that load?"

Pointing, the superintendent explained, "The stage is going right over there. Including the Prime Minister and his Cabinet members - there will be about forty people on that raised section."

"That looks about right. How are you handling the electrical?"

As Wade continued his conversation with the superintendent, Max checked for trajectory angles from the high surrounding buildings and landscape toward the stage. He identified at least five positions within 300 yards that would make ideal sniper hides.

Max wanted to check out each space for possible ingress and escape routes. He envisioned the viewing area packed with visitors and the enormous confusion a shooting sniper would create.

After the discussion, the superintendent gave Wade his card, and then watched as Wade and Max moved over to the side stairs for a discussion. It looked like they were checking plans against what the superintendent had just told him.

Wade rolled out his papers and pointed. "Pretend we're talking about the plans. I can't believe how much information I just got from the superintendent. I have the whole layout, number of attendees in the stands and on the stage, even where the lighting cables are going to be run. What were you able to discover?"

"I have a pretty good idea of possible firing positions I would take if I were going to sniper this target. We'll have to check out each position, but there are several good options. Now I just need to figure out which ones have the best extraction routes."

"Why don't you mark them on the map and number the buildings from left to right? We'll check each one and the extraction points after the superintendent is gone."

"Give me a minute to code the positions. I need to get the binoculars and a camera."

"Go for it. Remember to look like a construction guy, not a tourist taking pictures."

Max was not a big talker. On the way back from Belmopan, though, he did tell Wade that he'd graduated from the Army explosive school and that explosives had been his back-up specialty in Vietnam. Their conversation continued about shooting positions and escape scenarios from the layout they had seen that day. For them, the concrete, steel, and glass layout was like a living, breathing organism, which they dissected as snipers, much like a surgeon getting ready to operate.

After grabbing a quick meal, the two men headed back to the safe house for their stakeout. This time there was a car in the driveway and a light on in the living room.

"Where has this rabbit been hiding? I just want to see the guy's face."

"We may be here for a while. Looks like he just pulled

up."

"I'm pretty sure this is no longer his main operating house. We're going to have to follow him to find his other hole."

Much to the men's surprise, Stephan was soon on the move, rushing to jump into his car. The men followed his blue sedan to the car rental agency, where the attendant and Stephan conversed for a bit before coming out to the yard to look at vehicles in the lot.

After walking past a number of vehicles, Stephan pointed to a roomy utility-type vehicle. While speaking with the rental agent, he conveniently stood under the light in the parking lot where Wade and Max got a clear look at his face.

He had typical Germanic features and a well-defined lean body type. Definitely fit. This operative was in good shape, with close-cropped dark curly hair and dark eyebrows that seemed too close together for the size of his head.

The car he pointed to was pulled to the front office door, where the agent handed Stephan the keys and Wade turned to Max.

"You follow Stephan in this car, while I stay behind to rent a second car. I'll take one of the radios." Wade reached into the backseat to get a radio transmitter and his weapon. He tucked both under his loose-fitting overshirt. "I'm going to go back and check the house again. Stay with him. I think he may be headed to his second hole."

"I've got him."

Max pulled out of the car lot, following Stephan at a safe distance. Wade entered the front door looking for the gentleman who had helped Stephan. Stephan's car rental paperwork was still on the clipboard sitting on the desk

The sales attendant returned to the small office approaching from Wade's left side. "Good evening, sir, what can I do for you?"

"I'm looking to rent a second car for my associate."

"Listen, would you excuse me for a second? I need to attend to something real quick, but I'll be back momentarily."

"That's fine. I'm in no rush."

The attendant disappeared through a gray swinging door behind the counter, leaving Wade to peruse Stephan's paperwork. He spun the clipboard around to make it easier to read. Stephan's signature was scribbled at the bottom of the page. The last name he'd signed was "Woretz."

He'd just replaced the clipboard to its original position when the swinging door opened and the agent smiled at Wade. "It's been a busy evening. How may I help you? "

"I'd like to rent a mid-size sedan for a week. What are your rates?"

They settled on the rate and a vehicle. After making a right turn out of the car agency, Wade pulled over to the side of a quiet street to hook up his radio transmitter. The two men had already established code names and protocol for the mission, knowing their radio frequency was not totally secure

"Base to Sky, how do you read?"

"Sky here, reading you loud and clear."

"Are you still with the rabbit?"

"You bet. We're seven clicks out of town heading east on Northern Highway toward Belmopan. I'm five cars back."

"Stay on target. I'll check out the rabbit hole and make a few calls home. I'll relieve your watch in the early morning, around 5:00 a.m."

"Copy. Awaiting your next call."

"Over."

Wade cautiously drove by the house before going in. He performed his normal check around the doorjambs for wires. The house remained untouched except for one slip of paper that had fallen to the kitchen floor below the counter, a receipt for hardware parts. The same scribbled handwriting on the bottom of the page confirmed it was Stephan's signature. Wade thought about leaving the paper on the floor, but ultimately decided to keep it for potential handwriting analysis. He found nothing new in the house, and only a single unmade bed. There was nothing more he could do at this safe house so he headed for the library.

The library was closed but the dimly lit lobby remained open. Sitting on the small built-in seat beside the payphone, Wade took a moment to write down a detailed physical description of Stephan before making his first call: approximately six feet tall, slender, with a neatly-trimmed beard; a small scar under his left eye; a small tattoo on his right forearm. He seemed to be in excellent shape, and handled himself like a cat ready to pounce at a moment's notice. By the way Stephan carried himself, Wade got the sense he was well trained as a covert operative.

The call to Yari brought surprisingly little new information. "There were no calls recorded."

"How about credit card transactions?"

"I can't trace them with only a first name."

"That's one of the reasons I'm calling. Our target is using the name Stephan Woretz. His handwriting is terrible, so I may have the last name misspelled. I have a credit card receipt with his signature. I can send that to you for handwriting analysis. He just rented another vehicle from the Island Rental Car Agency. He also used his credit card to buy something from a local hardware store. I'd like any background you can dig up on this guy."

"I'll get to work on it right away. I have a source who can track credit card transactions from that country."

"We may soon have another safe house location for you to trace as well."

Yari tried filling in more gaps. "That's good news, because he's not making calls from the Adam Roy house. I haven't found any calls coming in from Condor's side either. I'm thinking he may be using another line."

"It's possible, but I get the sense this guy runs his own jobs. He may not be communicating with Condor at all. Let's see if we can get another location fix. I'll call as soon as I know something. By the way, I need you to set up one of those secure double encryption patches from this phone so I can call the Agency."

"You got it. Give me five minutes after you hang up."

Wade was hoping Megan's research might have paid off when he dialed her number.

"This is Megan."

"Hi. It's me."

"Let me go to one of the spare offices to use a secure line."

Wade didn't mention that he already had a secure, encrypted patch on their line.

Megan continued from the new secure location. "I think I've discovered which of our Agency's guys was involved with Daniel Spencer in Vietnam. Unfortunately, it goes right to the top. The files are locked down tight as a drum, including related older files at the Pentagon. I have my friend who works there checking. I got one document that shows two people at the Agency signed off on the drug investigation results. I have those names when you need them."

"Did you learn anything about the Belize situation?"

"Yes. Both publically and privately, we support Belize as an independent democratic government. We run everything through the British Embassy, and let them take the lead on most matters. Our interests stem from the fact that their country is near our shores, not Britain's. We monitor everything closely, including their elections and many of their government communications. We have people who also monitor trading partners in the country for commercial ventures to make sure no one with conflicting interests gets too big. We're not going to let them become a pawn of some other country who might not be one of our friends. We especially watch for growing interests from Panama, Cuba, Columbia, El Salvador, and Nicaragua. We're also monitoring Russian influence in the area."

"What did you find out about the politics of the current war games?"

"They seem to be all show with a few political agendas. It's a 'Mine's bigger than yours' parade, from what I can tell. More fanfare than substance. I haven't been able to discover any specific threat."

Wade rubbed his weary eyes and sighed aloud. "My question is who would benefit from a disruption of the war games?"

"Is that what we're talking about here?"

"It's purely a hypothetical question. I'm not sure. I just wanted your thoughts on who might have that kind of motive."

There was a pause before Megan responded. "I'd like to think about that for a while. Other than the countries you mentioned, I can't think of any."

Wade's next question summoned Megan to the dark side. "Can you think about anyone from the U.S. who might have a reason to disrupt the games?"

Megan sounded annoyed when she replied, "I don't suppose you want to tell what you're basing that question on, or what you're up to now."

Wade sensed that Megan felt he was off base and had little to add to support his suspicions regarding a possible U.S. plot. He redirected his thinking to the more obvious Russian, Cuban, and South American countries.

"I don't really know how to answer that question. Just considering all the possible candidates and speculating on who would benefit from disrupting things here."

Megan paused, as if referring to her latest research notes. "That's really heavy stuff. I just don't see evidence that points in that direction."

Wade agreed. "Just me speculating out loud."

Megan said nothing for a long moment. "You don't normally speculate like that. But you're not going to tell me more, are you?"

"Not at the moment."

"You keep your secrets well."

"I learned from the best."

She could see the call was ending. "We'll have to discuss that at another time. I miss you."

"Miss you, too."

Chapter 24
A mango farm, Belize

Before dawn the next morning, Wade followed Max's directions to a location two miles east of Belmopan. Max spent the night staking out Stephan's movements and had swollen red eyes to prove it. Wade got into Max's car and studied the layout. He liked what he saw.

"This is a great observation point. When did he finally come home to roost?"

"About eleven o'clock. He was very wary, closely checking at every turn. He also had binoculars out that second window from the left."

"Does he sense anything, do you think, or is he just cautious?"

"I think mainly cautious, but he may also have a sixth sense. He's not totally comfortable yet."

The two-story house was located at the back of a five-acre parcel. Anyone approaching the house could be seen all along a stretch of gravel driveway leading to the front door. The back of the house was set fifty feet in front of what looked like dense jungle.

Max's observation post couldn't have been better. His car stood at an angle to the driveway off the main road that wasn't visible from the house, and was nestled tightly between two rows of shrubbery, which obscured most of the vehicle. The position provided a direct line of sight to the house through a dense hedge that lined the road behind a row of tall banana plants.

There was little activity to report from Max's night watch except that Stephan had gone to bed early and engaged in a hard work-out early that morning.

Wade commented on Stephan's selection of the second

site: "This is a good location for them. They're closer to Belmopan, and he has a clear line of sight in every direction."

Max nodded. "There's even a possible jungle extraction point at the rear. I want to check that out by approaching from the jungle side at the back of the house. I think there may be trails leading into the jungle."

Wade replied, "And this location is far enough away from the ceremonies not to draw attention. In the confusion after an attack, they could easily extract to this location before splitting up. If they had to use it, the jungle would provide both cover and a secondary extraction route."

Max could see why Stephan had chosen this location for a safe house. "I see your point. They might also use the Belize City house as part of their initial extraction plan. My guess is the police would immediately close all routes in and out of Belmopan, and the area will be crawling with police and military after the incident. The key will be the timing."

Wade was curious. "Was there any movement last night?"

"No. Everything was quiet. He came straight here from the rental agency and hasn't left. He's only used two rooms of the house the entire night."

Wade was already thinking about calls Stephan might be making to the other operatives. "We have to let Yari know about this location. Does this place have a street address?"

"I think there may be a road sign back where it turns off the main road, but I don't see any street numbers."

"I tell you what. You look exhausted. I'll take over your watch. You go get some shut-eye. On your way back, look for any address, street signs, or mailbox numbers that would give Yari a general location so he can monitor calls. If you can't find street numbers, borrow the neighbor's mail from one of those boxes so we can at least get an address code. After you get some rest, call Yari from the library with the location information."

Max's all night stake-out had given him time to think. As he departed he tossed out an idea that surprised Wade. "Listen, I've been thinking about something else I want to discuss."

Wade smiled. "Stakeouts do strange things to people's minds. Let's hear what you've got."

"You know the black cases at the cemetery? I think I have a pretty good idea what's in them. I'd like to try to get into those cases to deactivate the mechanism."

Wade wasn't keen on the idea. "You're not only tired – you've gone mad."

Max was persistent but careful. "Before we do anything I need to confirm my ideas with one of my explosives instructors at the base. He's been a real friend, and I trust him. I'll also need some tools."

Reluctantly, Wade agreed to let him at least investigate the idea. "When you talk to Yari, ask him to set up a secure patch for a call to your friend at the base." He made a face and shook his head before adding, "This is crazy—I can't believe I'm even considering this plan. But we need to discuss your intentions before you do anything rash, okay? I wasn't going to mention it, but I was just thinking about renting a boat, weighting the cases down, and dropping them overboard."

Max frowned. "I don't think that's a good idea. If the cases are missing, the other side will be alerted instantly. In addition we can't be sure what water pressure will do to the detonation device. They may not have to travel far underwater before they explode. That could mean right under our boat."

"I didn't say my idea was a good one – forget I said anything, okay?

Less than an hour after Max's exit Stephan left the house in a hurry. Wade followed, heading south on Hummingbird Highway out of Belmopan. Stephan was quick to pass the slow-moving line of cars on the highway. Wade kept a safe distance, and Stephan clearly wasn't spending much time checking his rear view mirrors. Whatever his destination, he was eager and wasting no time to get there.

Wade hadn't been this way before, so the terrain and local signposts were completely unfamiliar. He radioed his position to Max, but there was no response. As Wade watched, Stephan increased his speed on Hummingbird Highway heading toward Dangriga until he realized he missed his exit. He hurriedly took the next exit, turned around and got back on Hummingbird, heading west. At a safe distance behind him, Wade followed his target as he took the Southern Highway South toward the Silk Grass Forest Reserve. Stephan's nerves seemed on edge. From what little Wade could see, he appeared to be constantly looking at his watch and the maps on the seat beside him. Wade concluded he was definitely trying to make a deadline.

Stephan took the Hopkins Road exit and made a sharp left at a stop sign. The unmarked, two-lane farm road was lined with fences and pastures on both sides. A rooster tail of red dirt kicked up by Stephan's car was visible for miles, so Wade didn't feel the need to follow too closely; the rooster tail would clearly lead the way.

Four miles later, Stephan made a right turn onto another unmarked dirt farm road. The rooster tail dust changed from red to a light tan color that coated the rear of Stephan's car, blocking both his side and rear view vision. Wade easily followed the rooster tail from several hundred yards behind.

Green pastures turned to orchards of yellow fruit trees that now lined both sides of the road. The distant tree line at the base of the mountain marked the far end of the orchards. Stephan seemed lost in the crisscross patterns of unmarked dirt roads and fence posts. He stretched, looking up and down both sides of the road and consulted what must have been directions on the front seat.

Wade didn't want to follow too closely, even though it was impossible to see out of Stephan's dust-covered car. His car would be easy to spot on the empty farm roads, so Wade decided to take a different route that would intersect Stephan's.

His intersect route initially took him away from Stephan's car. After reaching his new observation point, Wade looked back to track Stephan's dust trail, but there was none. Stephan's car must have turned and followed another dirt road to the end of the orchards just before the entrance to the foothills. Wade backtracked until he spotted Stephan's dirt-covered car among a stand of trees, then moved closer to get a better look.

Wade's tires thumped in rapid succession as he crossed the rows of metal pipes that made up a cattle guard. Moving slowly along an old mud trail, he made his way past crisscrossing fence posts until he approached a safe distance from Stephan's car. Up ahead was a stand of tall trees planted to serve as a wind break for the orchards. The trees marked the end of both the orchard and the muddy road he was on.

He slowly drove a little farther, moving his front wheels across a rickety old wooden bridge, hoping it would hold the weight of the car. A small break in the heavy tree line drew

Wade's attention. He pulled his car into the narrow space between two large overhanging branches and moved out on foot to the edge of the trees.

The view through his binoculars revealed the layout beyond the tree line. He saw Stephan's car, covered in dust, parked near a small yellow farmhouse. On the other side of the tree line was a large expanse of open field that curved upward at the base of the foothills. A light-colored strip of compacted dirt ran through the center of the field.

Wade heard a noise to his left and quickly turned with his pistol extended. Two white- faced Brahman-Charolais bulls looked back at him from the other side of the fence. He momentarily gasped in thanks that the thousand-pound bulls were enclosed by a sturdy fence. His new-found friends seemed content, chewing large mouthfuls of lush grass and staring in bemusement at the intruder.

Wade remembered the sign on the post hanging by one nail when he made his last turn: "McLawrey's Mango Farm." On a road hardly traveled, Wade thought he would not likely find other visitors. Turning his attention back to the tree line, Wade wanted a better position from which to observe his target. He decided that any threat would probably come from the yellow house or from behind his own position. He headed toward the windbreak fifty yards closer to the house that offered a better observation and shooting position.

No sooner had he gotten into position when he heard the faint sound of a revving engine from a long distance away. He focused on the roads leading towards the horizon, scanning for fast-moving vehicles, but there were no dust tails or vehicles in sight. The sound grew louder and then faded away.

The distant field was 400 yards away. He looked for

roads covered with brush, hidden from view leading into and out of the field. Nothing he saw suggested a threat. *Surely this field can be approached from more than one direction.*

Quickly scanning the front of the farmhouse he saw Stephan appear in the doorway and walk along a path to the edge of the open field. He cautiously looked around, checking in all directions. Cupping his hands over his brow, Stephan looked up. The sun was just clearing the mountain tops; the temperature was rising and the glare was blinding. Wade trained his binoculars in the same direction. It was difficult to see anything but the white light of the sun that blurred his vision. Even the mountain tops were obscured by the glare.

Back at the car Wade checked his radio transmitter and put in a call to Max. The static in the transmission confirmed that he was definitely out of range. He checked his weapons, making sure both his sniper rifle and pistol were loaded and ready.

He continued surveying the field in front of him and the orchard behind. Wade's biggest concern was someone approaching from the orchard side, cutting off his exit and forcing him out into the open field. He settled in for a long, hot stakeout, leaving the car's front door open like a horizontal sail to catch the slightest passing breeze. He smiled when he remembered he had thrown in bottles of fresh water just before he met Max.

Putting his head back on the seat and closing his eyes was the only rest he going to get until Stephan made the next move. Just as his eyes closed, he once again heard the high-pitched engine sound in the far distance. He grabbed his binoculars and scanned the horizon.

The sound was coming from the glare off the mountain ridge. A glimpse of a silver reflection broke up the glare as a mosquito-sized object descended from the mountain ridge. A Cessna 414 dual-engine aircraft was using Stephan's car to line up its descent over the open field. Clear of the mountain ridge, the plane quickly dropped over the field. The engine sound modulated to a low roar as wheels touched the graded dirt runway and taxied back to Stephan's car.

As the plane came to a stop, Wade quickly scribbled down its tail numbers. The pilot disembarked, and he and Stephan shook hands. After a brief chat, the men approached the rear compartment of the aircraft. It took both men to unload the long and heavy green canvas military bag.

With each man supporting one end of the elongated canvas bag, they marched in unison over to Stephan's vehicle and placed it inside. Their parting words were brief. The pilot walked back to the plane, stopping to check several exterior parts of the aircraft before climbing into the cockpit.

By the time Stephan got back to his car, the Cessna props were spinning fast enough for the plane to taxi its way to the center of the field. The plane turned into the wind as the pilot gunned the engines. The lift was sudden, and the plane dipped each wing slightly before banking right towards the mountains.

Stephan's vehicle retraced its path to the highway. Wade was in no rush, knowing that Stephan was headed back to the safe house in Belmopan, having replaced the weaponry for the Belize mission.

Back in Belize City, Wade joined Max for a dinner of fine local seafood.

"So how did it go with Yari?"

Max unwrapped his silverware and set it on the table. "Fine. I gave him the address and street coordinates, and he said he would have something by the end of the day. He asked us to call him tonight for an update."

"Did you speak with your explosives instructor about the cases?"

"Yes, I think we're both on the same page as to what the cases might contain. He gave me a few ideas on how to approach the mechanism from the outside."

"Wow. I'm still freaked out by all this. Did he say anything about that weird locking mechanism in the handle?"

"It's probably Russian. He's seen it before."

Wade took a sip of water. "What about dismantling or disarming these things?"

"It's pretty complicated, but I'm comfortable with dismantling them."

"In other words, you're saying the details are over my head."

"I just need you to okay the move forward, so I can get the tools I need to complete the job. It's your call."

"I need to think about it tonight, okay?"

"Sure. We just have to find a location to work on the cases where no one is around."

Wade's eyes widened in question. "You mean a location where no one will see us? Or one where innocents won't be harmed if the case explodes?"

"Both."

"Let's call Yari after dinner to see if he's learned anything new. I also have to make a call to my agency. If you don't mind, perhaps you can do some library research while I'm on the phone?"

"Not a problem."

The dinner was awesome, as each man tried a different local fish dish preceded by two rounds of conch ceviche. They made it to the library an hour before it closed. Wade made the call to Yari while Max went inside to continue his research.

"It's me - Wade. Were those location coordinates helpful?"

"They were great. I got four calls just today. I now not only have Stephan's location pinned down, but I have the two other operatives' phone locations as well. I wasn't able to get any confirmation on the name Stephan Woretz, though. It's an alias. The credit card and passport in that name are also bogus."

"I thought that might be the case. What did you learn from the calls?"

"It sounds like Stephan is calling all the shots, just as you suspected. I didn't see any communication with Condor. It's like Condor has now dropped out of this operation."

"Did you get anything more on Stephan?"

"Yes, I had one of our accent specialists listen to the calls. He determined that German is Stephan's primary language from birth. At some point during his youth, Stephan also learned to speak Russian – we know because he spoke to one of the other operatives in Russian. Our language specialist thinks the Russian is very natural. He thinks he probably learned Russian while he was young, but only after he learned German. His English is okay, but probably learned much later in life."

"What about the other operatives?"

"It looks like you'll have the company of two additional people. They discussed a third operative, but Stephan rejected his involvement."

"Do we know anything about them?"

"From the conversation, it seems both of them know and have worked with Stephan in the past. One operative is Bulgarian, and the other was calling from a phone in Chile –

but he spoke with an Eastern European accent. Our language specialist says he's from one of the Soviet bloc countries, but he's not Russian. They all speak English. In fact, 80 percent of the conversations are in English. There were just some references to personal items that we had to translate."

"I want to know what those personal items are. They may be important. But let's not get into that right now. Do you know when they're scheduled to arrive in Belize?"

Yari cleared his throat. "The Bulgarian arrives the day after tomorrow. The guy from Chile is tied up on another job. He's scheduled to come in a day or two after the Bulgarian. They're supposed to confirm all flight information with Stephan tomorrow."

"Good work."

"Are you ready for them?"

Wade sighed aloud. "We've got lots to do, but we'll be ready. I'll call you tomorrow for the flight info."

"Say hi to Max for me."

"Will do. By the way, our target took delivery of weapons today from a small private airplane. Here are the tail numbers. See what you can find out about the owners of the plane."

"Will do."

"Oh, and I need a patch for my call to the Agency."

"Call back on this phone in ten minutes. I'll set it up."

"We'll talk soon."

For ten minutes, Wade scribbled a few notes on his pad before picking up the phone.

He smiled when she picked up. "Hi, it's me."

"Hi, you. I thought you might be calling today."

"I would've called earlier but I was tied up with some Brahma bulls."

"Are those the one with the big humps on their backs?"

"Yes. The ones they ride in rodeos."

"I hope you didn't get near them."

"Not too close. Did you discover anything on your end?"

"I'm not on a secure phone right now on my end."

"Just keep it general. We'll be okay."

Again Wade didn't mention that he had already secured the line.

"There's one U.S. senator who has introduced a bill supporting a stronger U.S. presence in the Gulf of Mexico. He's pushing hard to gain support in the Senate."

"Who's that?"

"Senator Charles Lanier."

"You might check on his background. Did he ever serve in Vietnam, or in any intelligence services? That should all be public record."

"I'll do that. The only other thing I found is that the Russian-Cuban affiliation is cooling off. Cuba expected more from the relationship, including more financial aid from Russia. All they got were a lot of promises. Apparently when the Russians didn't get the missile bases they wanted, they didn't want to play house any more. I also question the involvement of other Central and South American countries. Several are playing footsies with Cuba, but I didn't discover any unusual activity."

"Anything more on Spencer's death?"

"Nothing yet, but I'm working a new angle. I'll let you know when we have a more secure connection."

"I have a busy day tomorrow, and I'm dead tired right now, but we'll talk again soon."

Chapter 25
Isolated jungle location

Max and Wade were in Max's car five miles outside of Belmopan when they turned off the highway. Max made a couple of strange turns onto dirt roads, which caught Wade by surprise.

Then Max stopped the car and turned to Wade. "I thought this might be a good spot."

They both got out and looked around. Max waved to Wade. "This way."

A short path led to a clearing in the middle of the jungle lined by thick overhanging branches and a dark jungle behind, something indigenous Indians might call a rest area. Standing in the middle of the clearing, Wade turned up the palms of his hands, looking confused.

"What's this? When in the hell did you find this place?"

"After we changed watch yesterday, I followed the jungle line along the road. I just had a hunch."

A morning sunrise had just started spreading its rays over the mountainside, but it was still dark underneath the jungle canopy. Wade realized he had given Max the okay to examine the cases more closely, but still wasn't sure what Max had in mind.

"Why here?"

"We have at least 100 yards' clearance on all sides, surrounded by at least another 300 yards of jungle for buffer."

"What exactly are we buffering?"

"In the event the cases detonate."

"What happens then?"

"From the size of the cases, and what my instructor and I expect to be in them, we estimate the explosive damage will cover the entire area and most of the buffer zone."

Wade shuddered involuntarily. "I mean, what about us?"

"If either of these cases goes off, we won't be around to worry about it. But at least nobody else will be harmed."

Max's sobering comment initially passed over Wade's head. A minute later he was lost in silence, when reality set in, waves of trauma that went through him like the explosion itself. Wade stared up at the shards of morning light breaking through the canopy, and then gazed down at the foot-high mist that hovered just above the ground. He felt as if he were looking at his own burial site.

Wade reminded himself that Max had made his statement in a state of perfect calm. It was like he was more concerned about others who would be harmed than the two of them. Wade wondered why he wasn't in that same frame of mind. Before Wade could voice the objections that were running through his mind, his partner spoke.

"Let's check our perimeter."

"Good idea."

"You take that side."

With Max leading, the two men spread out to different parts of the clearing. Each slowly entered the thick jungle vegetation, their 9 mm sidearms at the ready.

They instinctively traveled in a wide, oblong pattern, using hand signals to agree that they would meet at the apex of where the two football-shaped half-circles met. Fifty feet into the jungle, Wade heard a small sound to his right. He quickly turned his head, drawing his semi-automatic from its holster.

Startled by Wade's presence below, a keel-billed toucan dropped a large fruit from his bill. Wade's next step brought the toucan's vocal protest, and a loud child-like scream broke the cathedral stillness, directly over his head.

He jumped back, pointing his weapon toward the sound of the falling fruit as the bird took flight. The experience rattled Wade's nerves, which were already on edge. A few steps later Wade's foot stepped on and broke a twig on the jungle floor. A howler monkey answered with the scream of a child under siege. Wade assumed a crouched position with his weapon extended. He turned toward the sound as the agitated monkey belted out another scream. The noise reverberated within the dense foliage sounding like it was coming from every direction.

Finally, the two men met at the center of their circle. Max was calm, and Wade was inordinately relieved to see a friendly face.

Max was going to need Wade in a relaxed state and decided not to wait for more nerves to develop.

"Let's unpack the car."

Wade wasn't sure what Max meant; Max hadn't bothered to mention that he'd picked up the cases, which were already tucked in the trunk of his car. Max opened the trunk as Wade stared in disbelief.

"When did you get these? I thought we were out here just surveying the site."

"Think of it as a picnic."

The two men each picked up a black case and proceeded to the clearing, then Max returned to the car for the gym bag of tools and a small generator. He pointed to a large fallen tree at the side of the clearing. Kicking away leaves and small brush, he quickly uncovered solid ground. Then he pushed the leaves back to expand a semi-circle around the fallen tree trunk.

Peering down at the trunk, Max eyed the surface. He took out his jungle machete and scraped off some bark to reveal a clean, even surface.

Wade volunteered, "I can get that cleaned off for you. It'll keep me busy."

"We need about this much space."

Max used the spread of his arms to demonstrate the size clearing he wanted. As Wade worked on the tree trunk, Max retrieved the remaining boxes from the car.

The layout of tools for Max had to be precise. He laid a multi-colored blanket of blue and red stylized flowers over the hard dirt, giving the area somewhat of a picnic feel. Max set out each tool on the blanket in precise order, with measured distances between them. With the tools in place, the picnic blanket now looked more like an operating table. Wade helped, speechless and unsettled about what kind of surgery would soon take place.

A thousand questions tumbled over each other in Wade's mind, but he hesitated to ask, unsure that he wanted answers. The precision of the layout was clearly important to Max, and Wade decided not to break his concentration except for one question: "Will you need me during this process?"

"I certainly will. This is a two-man job all the way through to the end. You'll be right beside me all the way."

"I know little or nothing about disarming explosives. The courses I took just taught me how to set them off. "

"I'll take care of the disarming. I just need a steady hand."

Wade held his hands out before him. The visible trembling bore little resemblance to 'a steady hand'.

"You'll get a hand, but I'm not sure about the 'steady' part."

"Take some slow, deep breaths, and let them out slowly."

At Max's suggestion, Wade dropped to the ground, crossed his legs in a yoga position and started slow breathing. His eyes were closed, trying to find the "zone." When Max pulled the cord to start the small generator, Wade almost levitated. His body tightened. *I never liked explosives, even firecrackers as a kid. All of a sudden this jungle clearing will be on fire with human and monkey parts dangling from the branches. The patient is a highly explosive device in a black box, and the surgeon isn't sure about how to conduct the operation. One wrong move and we're all dead.*

Wade shook his head, focusing on the task at hand, and asked, "What happens next?"

"I want to smooth out the top of this tree trunk you scraped to make sure it's as flat as possible."

Wade got up and turned to watch Max. Using his jungle knife, Max went about smoothing the top of the trunk. After cautiously setting one of the cases on the smooth surface, Max checked to make sure it was resting in a stable position before commenting, "I think we're good."

With one hand, Max plugged the cord of the electric drill into the generator and locked in a half-inch drill bit. He was about to drill.

Wade's eyes widened in horror. "What the hell are you doing? Are you going to drill a hole in the damn case? I'm not sure that's a smart thing to do."

"Well, now that you've broken my concentration, I'm wondering if this drill bit might be a little too large."

Wade's nerves were frayed from the uncertainty. "Are you sure we're supposed to drill into it?"

"Yes, I just think I should start with a smaller hole. I can always go larger," Max quickly followed. "Listen, Wade, at this point I have to ask you to stop questioning everything I do. It's going to take all of my concentration to get through this. I can't have you second-guessing me."

"Sorry, partner. I won't ask any more questions. I don't mind saying that I've got some serious jitters, but I'll try to be as quiet as I can. At this moment your concentration while drilling into an explosive box is more important to me than anything else in my life."

"Thank you."

Max asked Wade to move to the other side of the tree trunk to hold the case steady. Wade complied, jumping high enough to clear a small building. A smaller diameter bit was locked in the drill, and Max began slowly cutting through the hard plastic case one slow and cautious revolution at a time. He had to be careful not to pierce much farther than the outer wall. Wade watched, silently counting each revolution of the drill bit.

The bit quietly broke through the interior space to a measured distance. Max withdrew the drill bit in reverse with even pressure and slow rotations. When the drill bit cleared the surface, Wade exhaled as he watched, pale and silent.

Max nodded. "It looks like we have a clean hole."

"That's great." Wade followed with another deep breath before asking, "What's next?"

"We drill another one three inches alongside the first."

"You've got to be kidding!" Wade bit his lip, wondering if Max was going to perforate the entire case. The morning temperature was still cool by tropical standards, but Wade's face was covered in sweat. He checked Max's face for similar signs, but Max was cool and dry as he readied the drill for the next hole.

The second hole was drilled with equal precision to the first, and Max seemed pleased that both holes had penetrated the right depth and angle. Wade's sense of dread remained, anxious for the drilling to end. The thought of watching anyone disarm a bomb in close quarters required a sense of trust that he'd never mastered.

In fact, Wade's concentration in the past few moments was so intense that an entire baseball team could have been standing behind him and he wouldn't have noticed. As if emerging from a dream, he suddenly glanced around suspiciously, jumping to his feet to walk the clearing's perimeter.

Max asked, "What are you doing?"

"I'm checking our perimeter."

"I need you beside me right now."

"I know we have a close relationship but… never mind, I was going to make a joke."

"I don't think we should be joking right now. I need you to hold the penlight over this hole, so I can look for wires."

Wade complied with trembling hands.

"I need you to move the light up and down slowly, going to the extreme edge of the hole."

"Like this?"

With the interior lit by the pen light, Max took his time, examining the entire area before he replied. "That's perfect. You can't see it, but there's a small white wire running parallel to this ridge line on top of the case near the hole I just drilled. Whatever we do, we don't want to breach that wire."

Wade's answer was deadpan. "You realize that if you had drilled a half inch above where you did, you would have gone right through it."

"I know. That's part of the uncertainly and luck in bomb demolition."

"What's next?"

"I need to drill my holes larger, now that I know where the wire crosses."

With the larger holes drilled, Max once again probed the case while Wade held the flashlight. Max chose a slender stick from the ground and shaved off the bark. Using thin tweezers and the stick, he pulled the white wire away from its connection near the front of the case, while Wade nervously held the light.

After changing back to a smaller drill bit, Max turned the case around till he was facing the rear hinges and asked Wade to hold it steady while he drilled out the metal pins holding the hinge in place. Wade complied as Max repeated his routine, slowly breathing through his mouth.

"Can you get to the other side of the tree and hold this steady?"

Wade jumped over the tree trunk like a frog, still tense about what was going to happen next. He grabbed the front of the case to steady it.

"That's great. The pins for the hinges are underneath the plastic, just like my instructor said they would be. I just have to be careful here."

"Please do."

After both pins were removed, Max used a flat wooden chisel to pry up the rear of the case. Now that it was opened half an inch, he peered into the case with the penlight. Slowly applying pressure against the edges, Max got the case opened a full two inches. He asked Wade to hold the entire unit in place as he checked inside, gently moving wires away from the edges.

"I think we're going to be okay for this phase."

"That's great." Wade breathed a sigh of relief, although he had no idea what that meant.

Max took a deep breath and gave an audible sigh. "That handle and locking mechanism turned out not to be wired. I can unscrew the hinges from the inside, and we should be able to lift off the top."

"Good. So that wraps it up, right?"

"No, not even close. Assuming we get the top off, I still have to disarm the detonation device. That's when things will get dicey."

"Oh, my God!"

After carefully unscrewing the hinges from inside using a screw bit with a long extension, the top lifted off. Wade was overwhelmed by confusion seeing the inside of the explosive. The inside looked like the ghostly inner workings of an alien space ship. Max's expression was quite different – more like he was staring at an incredible archeological find for the first time, admiring the clockwork mechanism in a crypt.

"What the hell is it?"

"What you're looking at is a very well-designed anti-personnel explosive device. The two glass canisters on either side contain highly-concentrated white phosphorous crystals, which, when ignited, work as incendiary particles that burn through almost anything at very high temperatures. They don't stop burning until their energy is completely consumed. The ignited particles will burn through a quarter-inch metal plate clear to the other side, and nothing extinguishes them.

"The gray clay-like material in the middle is a C-4 explosive, used to disperse and ignite the crystals. What's ingenious about it is that it can either be pre-set with a timer or detonated with a remote device."

"I take it that's all bad stuff?"

"Very bad. Think of those small white pieces as

crystallized napalm. The C-4 charge is equivalent to one or two sticks of dynamite. The device is not designed to take down buildings or bridges. That's why it's called an anti-personnel device.

"The C-4 is a large enough charge to disperse and ignite these crystals over a range of several hundred yards. Once shot out of their container with a blast, the crystals will burn on their own. If the smallest crystal touches human skin, they'll be seriously burned or killed. This device is designed to cause maximum damage to personnel over a wide area."

"The military uses similar material in bombs and artillery shells as anti-personnel weapons. I've seen them work in Vietnam. It's devastating."

Wade tried to summarize Max's detailed description. "In other words, if this thing goes off in the stage area at the ceremony, all of the officials and most of the attendees will be killed?"

"That's correct. If both of them go off, for sure there will be an untold number of human casualties within at least a 200-yard circumference of each case."

"Was this thing put together by some madman?"

"No. This has military written all over it. If I had to guess, I would say it's Russian - or at least made to look Russian. "

"What do we do now?"

"Disarm the device."

"Okay. Do you need me to do anything now? I have to go pee after all this."

"Why don't we both take a breather?"

"I'd like you to straddle the tree trunk with one leg on each side."

"What? That means the explosives will be right in my crotch!"

"Near it, anyway."

After thinking about Max's request, Wade straddled the large tree trunk, leaning over, with the C-4 explosives and white phosphorous crystals between his legs.

Max gave Wade further instructions. "I need you to hold the yellow wire with the tweezers in one hand and grip the red wire with the pliers with the other hand. Keep them steady and the two wires separated from each other at all times."

Wade complied with shaky hands, while Max peered into the two holes with the flashlight. He followed each wire to its source, trying to decide which one to cut first, keeping a mental image of some diagram in his head.

The stress of keeping the wires apart in such close quarters caused Wade's hands to tremble and sweat to drip onto the case from his brow. He started to ask a question, but Max cut him off before he could get the first word out.

"I need complete silence now."

"Sorry."

"I'm pretty sure we cut the yellow wire first."

"Pretty sure? Look, man, my crotch is six inches away from this case."

"Just kidding. It's the yellow one."

Before Wade could blink, Max cut the yellow wire. "See? Nothing happened. It's okay to release the wire now."

Wade rocked back away from the case and over the tree trunk. He lay on the ground looking up at the jungle canopy, pale as a bedsheet and drenched in sweat.

Max smiled. "There, you can rest now."

After a few minutes of recovery, Wade regained enough control over his nerves to ask the question uppermost in his mind. "I'm afraid to ask, but what's the next step?"

"After I remove the C-4 explosives and the crystals,

than we get to do it all over again on the second case."

Wade just stared as Max carefully removed the wire from the detonation device and removed the C-4. He took out each glass cylinder and gently transferred the phosphorus crystals to another container. He replaced the glass canisters with plain rock salt crystals he'd purchased from the store. Then they repeated the procedure with the second case.

The C-4 was replaced with inactive training clay Max had brought from his base. After replacing and soldering wires like they were connected to the active mechanism, Max replaced the pins in the hinges with new ones he cut from a small aluminum rod in the gym bag.

As a final step, the small holes in the case were filled with a black gooey paste that came out of a tube. The gooey substance hardened quickly, and after some light sanding, the patches were no longer visible.

Max gave Wade the task of smearing dirt over the newly-filled areas so they looked like they'd spent the last several days outdoors in the cemetery. They drove back to Wade's car, and he took on the task of replacing the deactivated cases at the cemetery. Wade had a strange feeling of kinship when he approached the mausoleum. Perhaps he felt he had almost joined its inhabitants. After replacing the cases in their original location, he looked up for a moment of prayer, thanking the Almighty that he'd survived the disarmament.

Max then took up surveillance at the safe house in Belmopan, and Wade returned to the library in Belize City to call Yari and Megan. He realized this might be his last call before their intervention would take place, and to be on the safe side, he decided not to share that fact on either one of his two calls. Wade called Yari first.

"It's me. Just checking in on your progress."

"I've confirmed flights for your arriving guests. Both operatives are arriving in Belize from Panama. One's coming in from Europe, and the other from South America. Both are using assumed names and fake passports. The one from Europe arrives tomorrow, and the other arrives the following day."

Yari gave Wade the flight information for the arrival of the two operatives.

"I tracked down the plane number you gave me. The plane is owned by a couple of guys out of Ecuador. They run a delivery service throughout Central and South America for passengers or cargo, no questions asked. Their flights are said to hug mountainsides and treetops, and they file no flight plans. They seem to have ties with the drug cartels and some arms dealers. Do you want me to turn them over to the authorities?"

"No, not yet. There may be more activity, and I don't want anyone alerted."

Yari sighed aloud. "Sounds like this disruption op or whatever it is, is really going down fast. I think it may be a day or two after the other operatives arrive."

"We're getting very close. The ceremonies are scheduled over the next four days. I just don't know which day they've picked to do the dirty deed."

Yari sounded worried when he said, "If things get hot, do you and Max have an extraction plan?"

"Yeah. We're working out those details now."

"I wish I were down there with you guys, but I know I'd probably just be in the way, screwing things up."

"No, you don't want to be down here right now. Remind me some day to tell you the bomb-in-the-jungle story."

"I'm not sure I want to know."

266

"Do you have any communication from the other two operatives?"

"No. All of my calls are coming from Stephan's phone in Belize. I did learn that the guy coming from South America isn't from there, he's just on assignment."

"Okay listen, I'll need a secure encrypted line to make an agency call."

"You got it. Give me five minutes to set it up."

"We might be out of communication for a while, in case you don't hear back from us, but we'll be okay."

"You two are one hell of a team."

Chapter 26
Belize City, Belize

Wade didn't want to forget anything on his next call. Using a pad, he scribbled some notes before calling Megan.

"Megan Winslow."

"It's me."

"Let me get to a secure line."

Momentarily she picked up the other line.

He dispensed with preliminaries. "Just calling in to see what you've come up with."

"I have several things that look interesting. Senator Charles Lanier, who's pushing the Inter-Americas Defense Bill, has decided to make a speech at the ceremonies in Belize. His press secretary just made that announcement today."

The conversation went into pause while Wade considered, *Could Lanier be the target? How could that be, though, if he just decided to come down here today? Would he put himself in that kind of danger just to make a point? Could he benefit somehow from the attack? Maybe he gets his bill passed or maybe he gets himself killed?*

He finally filled the awkward silence. "Anything else?"

"Lots. You were right about Spencer's hit-and-run accident. I spoke with the detective on the case in North Carolina. He felt it could have been a set up. Probably a professional hit. It had all the trappings."

"Be careful who you talk to about that accident."

"I am, but I think this detective in North Carolina is straight. It's somebody you might want to talk to when you get back."

"Were you able to do more research into whom I should notify about this incident?"

"I got three names. After checking with my contact on their backgrounds, the one I like best is a woman by the name of Zara Wicks. She's attached to the British Embassy in an administrative capacity, but she's really MI-6."

"Why do you like her?"

"She goes by her maiden name, but is actually married to a physician in Belize. This is more than a job for her. They seem stable and very much committed to Belize. One of our agents in the U.K. knew her before she transferred to Belize. He said she was very good and could be trusted. She handled a foreign bombing investigation a couple of years ago in the U.K. and nailed the suspects with top-notch investigative work."

"Who's the other person?"

"James Collingsworth is also an MI-6 who works for Wicks. He's young, with not much field experience, but good with administration. It's really up to you."

"Let me think about it. Are they both in the country so they can be reached through the Embassy?"

"Yes. They both have offices in Belmopan."

Wade paused while he made notes.

Megan broke the silence. "I need to ask you a personal question."

"Sure."

"Why are you doing all this? I mean, why are you once again in the middle of something that sounds dangerous? I don't even know what it is, but I know you. Why don't you just turn it over to the authorities and come home?"

"I thought you understood this when we talked before. I didn't come down looking for this problem. The whole thing came to light while I was here on the Lockhart investigation. I'll turn it over to the proper authorities when I feel it's safe to do so. Why do you think I'm asking you for the names of contacts down here? And by the way, I can't wait to come home."

"Well, that's good to hear. I know you're trying to do the right thing. It's just that unsanctioned activities are not very healthy for you or your career. You should let the proper foreign authorities handle it. It's not your battle."

"That would be great - if I knew who to trust."

"Just be careful."

"Thanks for your help. I miss you."

"Miss you."

After his call, he went into the library to check the most recent newspaper articles. Local news was full of stories on the peace ceremonies and lists of arriving dignitaries. Max soon joined Wade, and they spent the evening digging through the articles trying to find some link that might pinpoint a ceremony for the target event.

Nothing in the news jumped out at them. No single event seemed more important than any other. It didn't make their job any easier that the target could be any one of five separate ceremonies over the next four days. The two men devised a chart listing the times, ceremony, locations, and expected attendees. It seemed Stephan had his choice and was probably weighing the alternatives.

In Belmopan, international media personnel were already arriving from different parts of the globe. Each broadcasting company was setting up equipment and pulling communications cables under and around the raised stage and podium area.

After dinner, the men made another run to check the cemetery. The cases were still in place exactly where they'd left them.

Today was the expected arrival date of the second operative. Max wanted to do more research on shooting angles and extraction points on-site, while Wade followed Stephan to the airport.

Already in disguise, he positioned himself where he could observe the gate for arriving passengers. Two structural posts supported one side of the baggage claim area, so Wade put one of them to good use as a hide. He waited for the loudspeaker to announce the flight number of arriving planes.

Stephan had already driven past the baggage claim pick-up area twice and was circling again. Wade wasn't sure whether Stephan would park and come in, or wait at the curb. After passing the no-parking baggage zone for a fourth time, Stephan's car disappeared, presumably to park.

A few moments later, Wade spotted Stephan coming toward him. He stopped and turned only six feet away. Looking through the line of arriving passengers, Stephan's cold steely eyes dissected each one as if undressing them. He acted like the passengers were his subjects, each with their lives hanging on his approval.

A new thought crossed Wade's mind. One hand remained on the trigger of his 9 mm silenced weapon, under his tan trench coat, ready to take the man out now and escape before a crowd could gather. For the first time, Wade sensed a power over Stephan that he hadn't felt before. His feeling of control made his opponent seem a little less mysterious.

Restraining himself, Wade knew that if Stephan was removed now they would only send someone else. Then Wade caught himself as Stephan nodded to someone he recognized and started moving toward him. Remaining in the shadows, Wade repositioned himself to get a good look at the new arrival. Stephan and the newcomer exchanged formal, businesslike greetings. Unlike Stephan, the new operative was a barrel-chested, stocky man with curly hair.

It was easy to see the two had previously worked together, but were definitely not close friends. For no particular reason, the name "Boris" popped into Wade's mind, and at that moment became the code name for the new operative.

Boris clearly acknowledged Stephan's superior position with his subservient body language. Walking behind and to the right of Stephan, Boris carried his own luggage and waited for directions from Stephan before crossing the street. Wade headed for the same parking lot and followed their car back to the safe house in Belmopan.

Wade and Max spent most of the remaining day identifying possible sniper positions and extraction points. The most obvious shooting positions were discussed and replayed many times. The rooftops of the administrative buildings in Belmopan were no longer unfamiliar to Max; each had been assigned a number and recorded on the map.

Side doors led to stairwells and stairways to roof doors for access at different times during the day and night. Positions were sighted through their scopes from the rooftops to the ground to understand what effect light and angle would play on targets at different times during the day and evening.

Distances were checked and recorded and evacuation routes confirmed. Several hides, some which worked better than others, depending on the time of day, were recorded along with wind direction and speed to account for the afternoon trade winds.

They performed the same calculations from different buildings in order to accommodate longer shots and different angles of drop. Wade assumed Stephan had already done the same target analysis or was still involved in site assessment. In fact, Max and Wade wondered if they might run into each other during the location search, but that didn't happen.

Back in Belize City, Wade and Max had a working dinner over sea bass. After the meal, Wade turned to Max.

"What did you come up with today?"

Max paused before he responded. "I've narrowed my sites down to the three most likely shooting locations."

Wade was quick to interject, "Before you tell me, let me try to guess. I assume you took into account that the three shooters are paid assassins and not on a suicide mission."

"That's correct."

Wade continued, "I've assumed the same thing, which means extraction points and cover for egress are paramount to their site selection."

Max agreed. "You bet."

Wade continued. "I further assume there will be military presence and police surrounding the ceremony area to block off exits after the incident."

"Right again."

Wade took out his map out and with a pencil marked the streets police would likely barricade. Max was intently watching how closely Wade had come to his own conclusions. When Wade finished his mapping, he looked up at Max and asked, "Did I miss anything?"

"No. I think you've covered it all. So what sites did you pick?"

Wade looked back at the map, paused, and then numbered his target sites from most likely to least likely. Neither was surprised that they both picked all but one of the same sites, and all in the same order. Max smiled as he went over the selections. Wade wasn't quite as happy.

He shook his head. "I have an uneasy feeling that we've been too predictable. I think Stephan is just too good for that. We're missing something."

Max responded like his reputation was on the line. "All you can do is try to get into the mind of the shooter. You know that as well as I do."

"Don't take my comment the wrong way. You've done exactly what I think we should be doing, and you did it very well. What I'm talking about now I can't put into words. It's just a feeling that something isn't quite right."

Max heard the uncertainty in Wade's voice. He wasn't sure what else they could do, though, except give Wade more time to think.

Max shrugged. "Why don't I follow Stephan tomorrow to the airport and you take your intuition out to the sites and see if you come up with anything we've missed?"

"That's fine. What I like about the positions we chose for our hideout is that all of Stephan's sites will be visible to us. If we don't split up, I don't see how we'll be able to cover all of their firing positions."

"I agree. Our angle is toward the shooters, not the stage."

"Don't forget, partner. We have to extract as well, and we might have some of the same challenges they do if they're able to get off just one round."

"I'm already giving that some thought. I have some ideas and want to go back there tonight to check on a few details."

The next day Max again followed Stephan to the airport to pick up the third operative. Wade continued watching the safe house and checking the cemetery to see if the cases had been removed. They agreed to meet at 1:00 p.m.

The second airport pick-up went smoothly, much as it had the day before, with a few minor exceptions. After the two operatives greeted one another, Stephan seemed agitated with the new arrival, whom Max nicknamed Jackson.

As was the case with Boris, Stephan seemed to know Jackson, but they were definitely not on good terms. Stephan began lecturing Jackson from the minute he arrived. His agitated demeanor was apparent in the car and continued all the way back to the safe house.

Something must have happened to cause Stephan's annoyance. He wasn't hostile, but close to it. Jackson meekly took Stephan's verbal lashing in stride seemingly, with apologetic acknowledgement and little reply.

Wade and Max met over lunch to compare notes. Max described Stephan's hostility toward Jackson. Wade thought it was an unusual way to start a mission with a fellow operative.

Wade asked Max, "What do you think Stephan could be annoyed about?"

"I'm not sure, but I think it was enough to cause him to have to change some plans. I have to wonder if Jackson screwed something up."

"Perhaps it was his arrival time?"

"I don't know, but whatever it was, Jackson is not getting any favors from Stephan on this assignment."

Max asked, "What happened at the safe house?"

"Boris and Stephan were extremely busy before Stephan left for the airport. I couldn't see through the frosted glass windows, but both men were going from room to room doing something. At one point Stephan backed the car up to the back door, and he and Boris unloaded something. I couldn't see what it was because I was facing them."

Max frowned. "Do you think we should be in position for this afternoon's ceremony?"

"Yes, I think we should be there and ready to act if we need to, but stay out of sight. I don't think it will happen this afternoon because of who's addressing the audience. But they may show up for a dry run."

"We need to check the cases again to see if they're still in place. So far it seems like they're keeping those cases in place at the cemetery until the very last moment."

Wade replied, "I think that's smart on their part. Let's get over to the library and call Yari."

The normally quiet city hummed with more street and foot traffic as tourists and dignitaries poured into Belize City. Even the library hosted more visitors. Wade quickly dialed the number.

"It's Wade. Just called for an update. We saw a little dissension among our new guys today, so I'm just wondering if they made any calls."

"No calls to the outside. Silent as lambs."

"If they're getting ready to take action, they may be under radio and telephone silence. Did you get the private telephone number for Zara Wicks?"

"I sure did. We have an understanding about private numbers with U.K. friendlies, and she's on that list. But I could get my ass handed to me for having her secured private line."

"Don't worry. If I make the call, it will be anonymously. Who knows where anonymous people get phone numbers? I'll be calling you for the encryption patch."

"Great."

Wade joined Max in the library's reading room. There was one article indicating a change in one of the scheduled ceremonies, detailing the new times of the speeches and a different order for the people presenting. They made a copy of the new schedule.

The two men met over an early breakfast the next day to finalize plans. The day would be spent on surveillance, checking equipment, and verifying schedules for the best extraction plans. That afternoon was the first of three days they thought were the most likely to be targeted for the attack.

"I need to check in with Yari to see if there have been any last-minute calls made from the safe house."

"Good. I'll cover the news stories while you're on your call."

The men returned to the motel where they checked and cleaned their sidearms and two sniper rifles before going to the library to contact Yari. Nothing had changed since their last call. They took two cars to Belmopan and parked one at a predetermined space just outside the city for easy extraction. Then Wade took up his position at the safe house after dropping Max off at the city center.

The minute the administrative building opened for business, Max approached the reception counter in a coat and tie, asking for directions to the planning department.

Signage everywhere said the building would be closing at noon for the International Peace Ceremonies. The attractive counter hostess smiled and directed Max to the fifth floor.

With briefcase in one hand and several sets of rolled building plans under his other arm, Max approached the elevator like a seasoned architect. No one got in the elevator with him, so he pressed the button for the fifth floor and exited. But he made a right turn instead of a left as he had been directed.

The plain reddish-brown door opened to a set of stairs, followed by another door which opened onto the rooftop. In the stairwell Max changed into blue coveralls before he stepped out on the roof. With a radio transmitter and binoculars strapped to a waist belt, he moved behind the large gray commercial HVAC unit.

He quickly removed one of the outer doors on the unit, exposing the control panel, and set down his tool kit. If anyone discovered his presence, he was simply a heating and air conditioner serviceman performing regular maintenance.

Max went to the far side of the roof where he was able to see the rooftops of all the numbered buildings on the map. He crouched under the parapet and peered out through a small space between two red roofing tiles. A small reflection caught his attention. He saw additional movement on the top of Building 3.

"Sky to Base, over."

"Base here."

"I have movement on Building 3 east of my position. Over."

"Can you make out the parties?"

There was a brief pause while Max rolled to his right, landing at a better angle of sight. "Boris and Jackson with binocs. No weapons in sight."

"Any sign of the Stephan?"

"Negative."

"Continue observing and keep me posted. I'm moving into position on Building 5."

"Copy."

Max watched as the two men disappeared from that rooftop only to be seen again three rooftops over. It only took them a few minutes to reappear.

"Sky to Base."

"Base. Over."

"Boris and Jackson are now scoping Building 1, no weapons visible. They definitely have keys to these buildings. Over."

"Keep observing and take notes. I'm vacating my

current position on a hunch. Meet me at the rendezvous point in two hours, unless you need me here."

"I've got this covered."

By now Wade was operating on instinct. He retraced his steps to where his car was parked and drove to the cemetery to check the status of the black cases. He confirmed the cases had finally been removed. Wade drove back to the safe house to check on Stephan's whereabouts and found Stephan's car in the safe house driveway, and a flurry of activity was visible inside. Wade could only see shadows moving back and forth between rooms, so there was no way to tell exactly what they were doing inside. With the cases gone from the cemetery and the operatives in place, everything was pointing to an imminent attack.

Chapter 27

Wade and Max met at the scheduled rendezvous point in the afternoon to update each other on the day's activities and decide on the next steps. Both men were on high alert, knowing time was running out before the showdown. Max reviewed the observations he'd recorded from the rooftop.

"Boris and Jackson were together scoping out Buildings 3 and 5. I think they did preliminary angle and drop calculations. I didn't see Stephan the entire afternoon."

Wade tied into Max's last thought. "That's because he was at the cemetery picking up the black cases. I didn't see him carry them into the safe house, but I think they were there. There was an inordinate amount of activity going on as I watched."

Max paused to give that some thought. "When you think about it, they have to assemble the rifles, dope their scopes, and sync their communication devices. They may also have to set the detonation codes on the cases and coordinate signals. They will also have to test and practice their extraction coordinates."

"What's involved in setting the detonation codes on the black cases?"

"As I mentioned earlier, the cases can be detonated with a timer that's already in the case or be triggered by a remote transmission signal. My guess is they'll use the remote trigger, which means they'll have to test and coordinate frequencies and set a code for the cases using those numbered bars on the locking mechanism."

Wade thought about what he'd almost triggered the first time he saw them. "That's good to know. Before you arrived, I was going to spin those scrolls to test the lock."

Max looked at him wide-eyed. "That would have been

the last spin you would have ever made."

After a pause that got Wade's attention, Max asked, "How do you think they'll stage the attack?"

"If it were me, I would stash weapons on the roof tonight for tomorrow's event."

"Good thought. We'll need to go there tonight to confirm."

The men returned to the motel to continue their planning as the afternoon sun fell below waving palm trees. The motel room floor and bed were covered with maps, schedules, and gear. The two men continued to go over timing, command protocols, extraction procedures, and checking weapons and communications equipment.

The evening check of Buildings 1, 3 and 5 confirmed large duffle bags of equipment neatly hidden on the roof deck parallel to the vent ducts on Building 1 and 3. It was clear the operatives had access to the buildings any time they wanted it, which still puzzled both men.

Early the next day, five hours before the scheduled ceremonies, Max was already in position on the roof. He was to remain in position while Wade followed Stephan, trying to determine where the black cases were going to be placed. Even though they'd been disarmed, the placement of the cases might disclose probable extraction routes and how they might approach target shots.

Three large speakers were in place at the foot of the stage to supplement the public address system. The sound from the microphone would travel throughout the large area crowded with guests, visitors, and press.

The Prime Minister of Belize was scheduled to speak after introductory speeches by senior military officers from three countries and members of the Prime Minister's cabinet.

The message shared by all the speakers was in support of stronger Central and South American counties with greater ties to Western powers. The event was being broadcast worldwide by international press in both English and Spanish.

As Max remained in place on the rooftop, Wade covered the safe house. The operatives were still inside preparing. Wade wondered how Stephan was going to handle the placement of the black cases this close to the commencement of ceremonies. He radioed Max that he was leaving his observation post at the safe house to be closer to the city center and the stage. Wade approached the outer platform of the stage from the rear.

An apron of flags from various participating countries hung next to each other along the stage floor. Wade found a seam between two flags and ducked under the stage floor. Quickly moving under the stage from one upright to the other Wade didn't find the cases, which they code-named "party favors."

Wade radioed Max, whose code name was "Sky."

"Base to Sky. Over."

"Sky. Copy."

"Any activity?"

"Negative."

"I'm a little surprised that the party favors are not in place."

"Me as well. Over."

"Maybe they called the party off."

"It's possible."

"Wait…"

The radio went silent. Wade noticed a worker in worn gray coveralls walking alongside the stage carrying a black case. His face was unfamiliar. Wade quickly named him

Coverall.

As Coverall got closer, Wade ducked behind a large metal box housing cables and wires. He still had a good view of the underside of the stage, but Wade could only see Coverall's shoes and the shadow of the case he was carrying.

Coverall stopped, looked around, and quickly ducked under the stage between two flags a third of the way from the back of the stage. From his crouching position, Wade could see Coverall move past two upright posts and place the first case on the ground, against the third support post from the sidewalk. Then he quietly disappeared through the flags to the sidewalk.

A few minutes later, the same man reappeared with the second case, this time on the opposite side of the stage. He ducked under it, placing the case against the second upright post, and returned to the sidewalk, then casually walked away from the stage. Wade remained in place, knowing Coverall would probably be under scope surveillance by Stephan.

Moving to the opposite side under the stage, Wade radioed Max. "We just had two party favors dropped about twenty feet under the stage on the west and east sides. The drop is wearing worn gray coveralls, code name Coverall. Cover him while I get out from under this stage. I want to follow him."

Max used his binoculars to catch the man leaving the stage area. "I have him. He's heading south from your location."

"Stay on him. I want to make sure I find an exit from under here where I won't be observed."

"Affirmative."

Wade saw a stream of light coming in between the flags which joined the steps to the platform. He moved toward the light, believing he might get additional cover from the stairs themselves if he was in Stephan's scope range.

A radio call to Max confirmed that he was still hidden before he exited from under the stage.

Max guided Wade toward Coverall man. The target was moving briskly away from the stage area. Every fifty feet, Coverall stopped and looked around for anyone following, but didn't pick up Wade's presence. Wade kept in constant contact with Max.

"Base to Sky."

"Sky over.

"Is Coverall wearing any wires, or is he transmitting?"

"Negative."

"Keep him in sight. I've got to stay back to maintain cover."

"Roger. I have him in scope, just making a turn to his right at the next block from you. Over."

"I'll maintain this distance."

Coverall was cautious, keeping to a cat-like route between buildings and close to shrubbery as if he knew this terrain very well. Wade wondered, *How could we have missed this guy with all of our surveillance?*

Coverall quickly stopped at the corner, scanning the area for tails, and then continued across the street to a residential area just outside government property. Wade picked up on his stopping pattern and kept several large trees in between himself and the target.

"Base to Sky."

"Sky over."

"I'm crossing Oakleaf Avenue just outside the compound to your west. Can you see me?"

"Roger. I have you."

"Look across the street and up a block. Do you see

Coverall? He seems to have slowed down quite a bit. I just want to make sure I'm not walking up on him."

Max scanned with his scope before responding to Wade. "Hold on. I see Stephan's vehicle parked about a block away on a cross street to the east."

"Can you tell if anyone is in the vehicle?"

"Negative. No one in sight. It's just parked. Your guy seems to be moving toward Stephan's vehicle."

"I'll stay well behind him since you have a visual."

"Sky to Base. Coverall unlocked the rear door of Stephan's vehicle, and is moving a long object out of the back."

There was a pause as Max watched Coverall's activities from the top of one of the tallest buildings in Belmopan. "The object he just pulled out looks like some kind of ramp. Wait – he's in back of the vehicle. He's unloading a motorbike down the ramp. There seems to be a second bike behind it."

"That answers our egress question."

"Yep. They're using small off-road motorbikes."

"All the better to get around gridlock and police barricades."

"He's starting up one of the bikes now. Looks like he's heading back in your direction. Take cover."

"Copy, Base."

Wade froze in position until Coverall passed, and then followed the bike another block to a dead end street. The rider stopped the bike and pushed it over the tall curb. He started it again and passed a concrete fence that led to a natural jungle setting. Coverall turned off the motor and rested the bike against a tree, out of sight from the sidewalk behind the concrete fence. He ran back and repeated the entire exercise with the second bike. Once the bikes were in place, Coverall returned to Stephan's vehicle and drove out of the area.

"Base to Sky. I'm heading back in your direction."

"You might want to consider disabling those bikes before you come back, just in case.

"Good idea."

Within minutes of breaking off his tail of Coverall, Wade positioned himself on his designated rooftop. There had been no signs of Stephan up to that point. Five buildings separated Wade from Max. Each building had been selected to provide a direct line of sight to the maximum number of possible sniper positions. The morning sun had already cleared the mountain peaks and was burning off the gray mist that hovered over the ground.

Facing their targets with their backs to the sun and ceremonies, the waiting began in earnest for Wade and Max. The temperature was already rising. It was going to be a very hot day, lying prone across the white composition roof.

"Sky to Base. Over."

"Base to Sky. Copy."

"I have Jackson taking up position on Building 3. He's armed."

"Does he have a radio transmitter?"

"Affirmative. He's setting up communications as we speak. The device looks military, with a large antenna. Over."

"Any sign of the others?"

"Negative."

"They sure are taking their time."

"Do you think Coverall saw you?"

"Negative."

"Base. I have movement on Building 1."

"I see him. It's Boris."

It was still three hours before the afternoon ceremonies were scheduled to begin, and too early for the general public and distinguished guests to be moving into the visitor area. Television and press personnel were testing microphones and checking video camera cables.

The speakers for the day's ceremony included the Prime Minister of Belize, the U.K. ambassador, military admirals from two countries, and U.S. Senator Charles Lanier, who would soon be sitting in the area reserved for distinguished guests. On the stage near the podium and distinguished guests would be the British Embassy staff, including Zara Wicks.

The long wait would soon be over. Max confirmed to Wade that his position was ideal for covering the two operatives. Wade's position had been selected for the likely appearance of Stephan, but he was nowhere to be found.

"Base to Sky. What are our two operatives doing?"

"They've assembled their rifles and doping scopes for windage and distance. They're also checking their communication devices. Over."

"Are they talking to each other, or to someone else?"

"It's hard to tell, maybe both. The transmitters are heavy duty. I would say definitely military."

"No sight of Stephan?"

"Negative. I scoped the other side of the building to see if I could spot his car, but it's no longer in the general area."

Wade wondered if Stephan was going to show. The thought crossed Wade's mind that Stephan might try to direct his operatives from a distant ground position. He wanted Max's opinion.

"Do you think I should leave now to try to find him?"

"Negative. If he's coming to this party, he'll show up. Let him come to us."

"Have you seen Coverall among the gathering crowd?"

"Negative. He's out of the area. Probably by instruction."

"What do you mean?"

"They probably had him leave the area in case he was spotted or detained. They won't want a recognizable face near the target area."

"I agree. He may be part of Stephan's extraction plan. Remember there were only two motorbikes, not three."

"I copy. I think their extraction might have them going in different directions."

"There won't be an extraction if we have anything to do with it."

"Copy. I meant their *intended* extraction plan."

Moments passed as the tropical sun heated up the roof surface. Max was the first to see movement and radioed Wade.

"Hold on. I think I just saw movement on Building 4, east side. It's not where we expected him to be, but it's Stephan. I don't have a great shot from my angle."

Wade rolled across the roof for a better spot to scope Building 4. "My location isn't ideal, but it's good enough. He's much lower on that building."

Max covered every inch of the Building 4 roof that he could see in his scope. "He's got a lot of equipment stashed on that roof. How did we miss that?"

Wade's angle was slightly better. He called out details while Stephan unpacked. "He's got the green military sack from the plane."

Max also had his scope on Stephan and saw something else he recognized. "You see that long antenna radio thing he's assembling? That's the activation device for the party favors. They would have had to program each case to a specific frequency to activate them this way. I guess my rewiring didn't scare them off."

Wade was now much more impressed with Stephan's skills. "When the hell did they have time to do that? The cases were at the cemetery until this morning."

"My guess is they picked up the cases sometime after we worked on them, did the adjustments, and returned them to the cemetery."

Wade's eyes remained focused on the target only to hear Max continue.

"Stephan's going through a frequency check now. Looks like he believes they're live."

"That's all that matters."

"I have him in my scope. He's setting the two detonation frequencies now."

It wasn't long before crowds started filing in. More cars searched for nonexistent available parking spaces. There was the feeling of an official gathering in the air as speakers played the national anthems of participating countries.

Another hour passed. All the shooters were in place on rooftops. Dignitaries with their entourages began to assemble on stage with exchanges of smiles and handshakes. A live U.K. military band all decked out in dress whites and shining instruments began to play once the recorded anthems ended.

Press correspondents were quick to stick microphones in the faces of dignitaries, still linked by cable to some cameraman's shoulder. No one was ready to take seats yet. Wade scanned the growing group of dignitaries with binoculars.

One woman stood out among the sea of dark-suited men and uniformed military. She wore a cream-colored suit with a matching jacket over a burgundy silk blouse. The lapel of her jacket held an elegant but small bright-red rosebud. This well-dressed woman had to be Zara Wicks. She circulated among the crowd, smiling and shaking hands, with practiced British social skills, giving no hint of her real MI-6 identity. At that moment Wade decided she was the person he would call when the time was right.

Other women on the podium seemed to be administrative types, busily checking off lists and handing out programs. They wore long black cocktail dresses which must have been uncomfortable under the hot tropical sun. Not only were the dignitaries feeling the heat, but both the temperature and tension on the rooftops were also rising at an alarming rate.

Chapter 28

The unanticipated noise from the band made radio communications difficult. Wade was trying to anticipate Stephan's next move. He wanted Max's best guess.

"Do you think Stephan will fire or detonate first?"

"I don't know. We have to be ready either way. We also have to consider what we'll do if he leaves his position early."

"If for any reason he breaks early, you take Boris and Jackson. You should have multiple shots from your position. I'll take Stephan."

"Affirmative."

"Do you have your distances and windage calculated?"

"Down to the quarter centimeter."

"I thought so. Speaking of Stephan, it looks like he just finished doping his scope."

"We need to be ready. They'll probably fire on his command."

There was a brief pause before Wade gave Max his instructions. "Assume your firing position and be ready for my command. We are hot. Hold for green command to fire when ready."

Max immediately replied, "Ready to fire on command. Over."

Preliminary speeches of introduction were starting at the podium. The first to speak was the Belize Minister of the Interior. According to the published schedule, he was to introduce the military guests, and the British admiral would introduce the Prime Minister.

Stephan was splitting his focus between checking his rifle scope and observing the frequency dial on the detonation device. It looked to Wade like Stephan hadn't made up his mind which action he would take first.

"Stephan is on his transmitter. Shooters are in ready position."

Stephan called out orders. Each of his men held their positions as ordered. He picked up the detonation device, pointing the antenna directly at the podium.

A British admiral dressed in a white uniform with medals glowing in the sun rose from his seat to approach the podium. As he adjusted the microphone to his height, Stephan pressed the detonation button but nothing happened. He pressed it again, and nothing.

Stretching out his arm, Stephan extended the antenna getting the maximum distance toward the cases, and pressed it for a third time. Retrieving the device for a closer look, he readjusted the frequency settings and pressed again. Still nothing happened. Stephan shook the device, pressed buttons, and turned dials before slamming it down on the roof in frustration. He picked up the radio transmitter to yell instructions to Boris and Jackson.

Stephan's operatives were already in their firing positions when they began their personal countdowns. Max had his earpiece in place and heard Wade's voice.

"You have a green to fire when ready."

Boris had just moved his finger from the trigger guard to the trigger when Max's round hit his neck, severing his carotid artery, so that he fell lifeless in a pool of blood. Jackson glanced at Boris, looking for a final confirmation. Before Jackson's head returned to his scope, Max's second round struck its mark in his chest. The impact knocked him back into a contorted version of his original shooting position.

Wade glanced back to see Max's successful shots. In the split second it took Wade to return to his scope, Stephan was no longer in his position. Stephan was still on the roof, but his quick reflexes sent him rolling behind a large metal vent. Knowing his shooting position had been compromised, Stephan shielded himself behind the metal ducting while he contemplated his alternatives.

Wade scanned the rooftop, frustrated that he had hesitated. He saw the shadow of Stephan perform another quick roll. The target hugged the metal ducting and roof surface. Realizing his mission had failed, Stephan's only option now was escape and extraction.

Wade kept scanning, trying to anticipate Stephan's next move. He saw only fingers from a raised hand grab the rigid door handle and pull. The door opened wide enough to block the small space between the HVAC unit and the duct. Stephan slithered past the door and down the stairs head first like a snake. Wade didn't have a shot. The only movement was the swinging door left to the mercy of afternoon ocean breezes.

Wade pressed the button on his transmitter. "Base to Sky. The rabbit is on the run. I have him going down stairs. Initiate Extraction Plan 2."

Max's response was quick. "Copy. Plan 2 in progress."

Wade turned to confirm Max's two kills and briefly turned back to the stage, where the ceremonies were going on undisturbed. He pounded his fist on the roof's surface, angry at himself for his split second hesitation. Wade wasted no time in disassembling his rifle and scope for his music case before descending the roof stairs in chase of Stephan.

Instinct told him Stephan had multiple options planned. The question now was which option would seem more feasible now that his mission had failed. The motor bikes were the closest extraction vehicles to Stephan now, but Wade didn't think he would try to use them. In fact, Wade had always believed the bikes were for Boris and Jackson under certain extraction scenarios, but never for Stephan. With his detonation immobilized and his two operatives eliminated, Stephan knew the entire mission was compromised by some group that was just on his heels. He would need to get as far away from Belmopan as quickly as he could. Soon the ceremonies would be breaking up, and traffic congestion around the city would hamper his departure.

Wade continued going through Stephan's options. He might not try to return to either safe house, believing their location had been discovered. He would also assume the international airport would be covered and too risky. Wade reasoned that Stephan's car, wherever it was located, was his best option. The closest safe border of escape would be either Mexico or Guatemala.

Wade had to get to his own car if he was going to catch up with Stephan. He didn't want to draw attention by running, so he briskly walked with his music case in hand like a frustrated musician leaving the orchestra because he'd broken his instrument. Wade finally reached his car and went to the safe house to check to see if Stephan was there. As he expected, Stephan was nowhere to be found. He drove back, retracing the steps Coverall had made, trying to locate Stephan's car. Unfortunately, he was out of options for most probable evacuation routes.

He needed to get out of the mounting double-parked congestion around the ceremonies. The traffic was getting worse, and Wade was running out of options.

Lacking the crowd confusion Stephan had expected, he had to change tactics. Wade tried to put himself in the mind of this rabbit who had gone from being in control to being on the run. Knowing Stephan was no longer on foot, Wade thought about routes Stephan might take to flee the city.

Wade knew Coverall had parked Stephan's car far enough from the ceremonies that his route wouldn't become congested after the attack. He assumed that Stephan would be on foot until he got to his car, so the car couldn't be parked so far away that it was not easily reached.

Wade looked at his maps and plotted locations that met those criteria. He drove up and down the streets that made logical sense to him, but found no sign of Stephan or his car. Pounding the steering wheel out of frustration for missing his shot, Wade sat idle at a stop sign, having run out of ideas. His sights were now set on Stephan and nothing else.

Extraction Plan 2 meant Wade and Max would extract separately, following a specific protocol. The various extraction plans had been rehearsed so many times that Wade and Max could perform them in their sleep. Five different extraction plans called for each man to do designated tasks before leaving town. Each had a prescribed route out of the country.

For Wade, leaving the country now was out of the question. His mission was to find and eliminate his target, and he was on his own to accomplish that task. Wade took comfort knowing Max would be safely back in Houston in a few hours, assuming everything went as planned. Right now he was worried about losing his prey, and after driving past several possible locations, Wade had nowhere else to turn.

Then he remembered a service station at the intersection of two main highways going east and west away from Belmopan. The service station might be a good location to observe that entire intersection. There was only an outside chance Stephan would pass that point, but Wade had no back-up plan.

He backed into a parking spot reserved for cars waiting

for repairs and shut off the engine. Scanning the intersection below him with his binoculars confirmed that it was a good plan. Clearly visible were all cars approaching entrances for the two highways, regardless of which direction they were headed. *Maybe this spot was not such a bad idea after all.*

If Stephan wanted the fastest driving route out of town, he would most likely pass this point. What Wade didn't know was whether Stephan has already passed. He settled in for a long wait.

Looking down at the radio receiver on the seat, he called Max. "How did the extraction go?"

"Not a problem. I'm at the storage unit right now. Where are you?"

"Trying to find the Rabbit. I'm waiting at a service station I think he might pass. It's all I could think of. I checked the bike location before I extracted. Both bikes were still in place. "

Max had confirming suspicions. "I didn't think he would try to use the bikes."

"Why do you think Stephan hesitated?"

"I don't know. I was concentrating on the operatives. I couldn't tell when they failed to respond to his command or when his detonation device failed."

Wade replied, "I think he decided at the last minute to go with the detonation first. When his men didn't fire, he didn't wait around to find out why. Unfortunately, I hesitated, which was my mistake. I think the Rabbit had an alternative extraction plan from the other operatives all along. He wasn't leaving town with those guys. Remember, the original plan was to leave Mashburn's body when they extracted."

"I think you're right. And I'm thinking I should stay and help you finish this job."

Wade was firmly against Max's request.

"That's a negative, buddy. You follow Extraction Plan 2 and get out now. I'll be fine here."

"Your call, boss."

Wade's eyes opened wide. He was drawn to a vehicle he thought he would never see at that intersection.

"Hold on, I think I see Stephan's car. I've got to run. You proceed with Extraction Plan 2. That's an order."

Max replied, wishing he were still with Wade.

"Happy hunting. See you back in Houston."

Stephan drove past Wade's position like he was on a leisurely Sunday drive. Instead of taking the south entrance onto Hummingbird Highway, he took the Western Highway west, a different route from the one he used to pick up the weapons.

This time Stephan didn't seem to be in a rush. Wade followed staying five cars behind on a highway which seemed to have few exits. He was surprised that Stephan seemed to be in a docile mood, rarely checking his rear or side view mirrors. As Wade drove, he wondered how he could feel so confident. Perhaps Stephan hadn't confirmed that his operatives were dead. Perhaps he believed the only thing that went wrong with the mission was that his detonation device had failed. Stephan didn't seem concerned that anyone might be following him, probably assuming he had successfully extracted.

Wade wasn't so calm. That was too simple an explanation of Stephan's attitude. Perhaps Wade was falling into an extraction trap just the way Stephan had planned. He gripped the steering wheel as tension coursed like lightning through his body. His mistakes were his responsibility and he could only blame himself. He was as hard on himself as any instructor would have been as he went through each phase of the mission.

How could I have missed the bikes and let Coverall disappear?

I should never have hesitated taking my shot. It was my mistake, wanting to see Stephan's face when he pushed the detonation device and nothing happened.

His training had taught him better. Chastising himself for waiting to see someone's reaction, he remembered hearing his training instructor's voice yelling: *A split-second delay means the difference between life and death, or the success or failure of your mission!*

As he drove, Wade focused on correcting his mindset. *No more delays for dramatic moments* became a mantra he repeated out loud for the next several miles.

He refocused his attention on Stephan's car when he saw it move two lanes to the right. His car hugged the right lane after passing the Teakettle exit. *Perhaps Stephan is not on this highway to reach the Guatemala border, as I first thought.*

Wade allowed two other cars to pass before getting in the right lane. He wanted to make sure Stephan was going to take the exit and not veer at the last second. Holding his middle-lane position, Wade did one last check of his mirrors to see that he wasn't being followed. The traffic thinned as Stephan's car and then Wade's passed the Spanish Lookout exit. Stephan's car remained in the right lane.

Stephan was not looking in his rear or side view mirrors for tails – he was checking exits. After passing the Spanish Lookout exit, another exit was fast approaching. Wade couldn't see the sign because of a large truck to his right. Stephan waited until the very last moment before sharply veering right across road reflectors to make the Chiquibul Road exit. Wade had to navigate an even tighter turn in order to make the same exit.

The first turn to the south put Stephan next to a beautiful river running parallel on his left. A sign showed the well-traveled but unpaved road headed toward the Tapir Mountain Reserve. Landscapes on both sides of the road were dotted with small banana farms bordering the river that ran west to the base of the foothills at the edge of the Reserve.

Stephan's car was over a mile ahead but easy to follow. It turned left off Chiquibul onto an unmarked dirt road. Wade made the same turn and followed Stephan for another mile to another dirt road. Then he made a right turn on another unpaved road.

Traffic had thinned, and Wade followed cautiously, leaving more space between the two cars. Another right on a farm road, and Stephan's car soon disappeared into thick tree cover on both sides of the narrow road. Stopping at the intersection of two roads, Wade could see that Stephan's car had taken a left onto another farm road. He was reluctant to follow because he would be totally exposed. Instead Wade passed Stephan's road and took the first two-lane dirt road marked Shady Farm Road. The two cars were now running parallel, with Wade following several car lengths behind.

The magnificent, lush scenery on both sides of the river was alluring and would have been distracting if he hadn't been so focused on the goal. Wade stopped his car when he saw Stephan's car stop. Stephan wasn't looking at scenery or for tails. He was stopped in the middle of the road craning his neck right and left, probably for location benchmarks. Keeping a safe distance between them, Wade pulled down the dirt road behind a line of trees separating the two vehicles.

His target seemed to find his bearings and turned right

down a narrow farm road between barbed wire fencing on both sides. Wade waited in a cluster of trees for Stephan to reach his next stopping point.

Wade decided not to follow that same narrow farm road; instead he turned right and ran perpendicular to the road Stephan had taken several hundred yards outside his path. Another farm road brought Wade to a further cluster of trees that provided good cover. He stopped and turned off his engine. The two cars were parallel at approximately the same distance from the edge of an open field at the foot of the mountain with the river to their left.

Pulling his car under overhanging branches, Wade got out and scanned the horizon with his binoculars. The setting seemed similar to his last pick-up site, but it was a different location. This time Stephan's car was parked near a white farmhouse on his far side, with the large barren field between them.

Wade realized he would have to move his car to close the distance between them. He still had to remain hidden, so he carefully scouted the surrounding tree line for alternate routes and cover.

Chapter 29

A muddy road caught Wade's eye. Although he couldn't see where it ended, the road would bring Wade closer to Stephan's car and the farmhouse. Bordering each side of the road Wade passed under the large, dark leaves of banana plants. The road kept winding through the mature banana farm, giving him lots of cover. An opening soon appeared in the dense foliage, and Wade got out of the car to explore. He was still unsure of his exact position. Surprisingly Wade had not been the only visitor to this remote site. Below him were old dried tractor ruts deeply furrowed through once-moist mud. The tracks led to his left, and Wade got back into the car and followed them, his own wheels just outside of the tractor impressions. The road led back to the same tall eucalyptus tree line that bordered the edge of the banana farm.

Wade trekked on foot over ground covered in dried banana leaves and stubble. Finding an opening from which to observe, he saw the farmhouse and a wide flat field before him. Returning to the car, Wade decided it was an ideal place to park, so he drove a little further, until he was close to the open field but still protected by deep cover.

The new position brought his car to within fifty yards of his new sniper hide. After checking several possible shooting angles, Wade returned to his car to assemble his Steyr SSG 69 silenced Austrian sniper rifle fitted with a German 6.5x scope. It was the rifle he'd taken from Mashburn and had on the rooftop in Belmopan. With weapons in hand, he left the comfort of the car and returned to the deeper cover of dense banana plants, where he prepared his permanent shooting position.

Training his binoculars on the landscape east of the farmhouse, Wade saw a small piece of shiny silver metal protruding from a dense cover of branches. The reflection was about five feet off the ground. Wade studied the area more closely and discovered the protruding metal was a portion of a well-disguised airplane wing and fuselage covered in camouflage netting and pushed well back under leaves and branches of the far tree line.

His new position offered a good view of the farmhouse, the plane, and the expanse of the open field. He took his time adjusting his scope and making estimations of range and windage to different target points.

With the sun at his back, he felt he controlled the theater in the front and on both sides of his position. Using his rifle scope, he scanned the area from in front of the plane's propeller to the mountains beyond. The area directly in front of the plane was compacted gravel, making for a hard surface ideal for the plane's weight.

Fifty feet away from where the plane rested, the ground spread out into a smooth ribbon of compacted dirt and decomposed granite that served as a runway. The forty-foot wide airstrip made an ideal runway for small planes, allowing sufficient room for the plane to head in either direction to accommodate whatever wind direction happened to be present.

Two dirt access roads came in from the west and north of the farmhouse. Stephan's car was parked on the road to the right of the farmhouse. It could also be used for evacuation or bringing in addition fire power.

A small white pennant hung from a flagpole strapped to the farmhouse chimney, showing wind direction and speed. Based on the movement of the flag, Wade estimated a light 8-mph wind coming out of the east and used that calculation to adjust his scope.

Heavy shadows from the thick vegetation bordering the field distorted the distances, so Wade knew that making precise distance calculations would be difficult. He estimated the width of the farmhouse and used that estimate to calculate the distances to other points. While he waited, he walked off distances between banana plantings and used those calculations to estimate the distances to points closest to him. He repeated the process until he got several points confirming the distance to the runway and different points between the farmhouse buildings.

Based on those calculations, he estimated the distance to the farmhouse was approximately 450 yards away from his firing position. He could easily be off by twenty to forty yards in his calculations, though, and didn't have much confidence in his estimate.

As Wade was checking his calculations, the front door of the farmhouse suddenly opened and Stephan appeared in the doorway, his automatic pistol holstered at his side. Another man stepped out beside him. The two spoke for a while before walking down a narrow stone path to the edge of cleared field. Wade focused his scope on the man next to Stephan. The face was new to Wade. It wasn't the previous pilot who had delivered Stephan's weapons.

The second man pointed toward the plane, and he and Stephan continued their discussion as they walked

303

into the field. Wade was too far away to hear what they were saying. Stephan seemed relaxed, several times making gestures toward the covered plane. Wade assumed they were discussing the plane's readiness for their departure time. The two men walked back to the plane and started removing the branches and camouflage netting. From the body language of the two men, Wade assumed the other man was the pilot. After the netting and bushes were removed, Stephan started walking back to the farmhouse. The pilot got in the plane, started the engine, and moved the plane to the main part of the runway between Wade's position and the farmhouse. The pilot shut down the engine, got out, checked several parts on the exterior of the plane, and returned to the farmhouse. A smile spread over Wade's face when he saw the plane's new position. It was now less than half the distance to the farmhouse and close enough where he might pick up parts of conversations between the men as long at the plane's engine was silent.

He quickly recalculated his distances and angles to the plane. His only concern was that the plane now blocked his vision of the farmhouse. He considered alternate angles and decided to move his firing position thirty yards to the right, which changed his angle, but still offered a view of the farmhouse and the plane.

Suddenly the front door opened again, and the two men started walking to the plane. As they got closer Wade could hear their conversation. This time Stephan appeared a bit agitated.

The pilot spoke in English with a heavy Spanish accent. "I need to start my inspection of all sides of the plane and wings."

Pointing in the direction of the plane, Stephan snapped, "Well, what are you waiting for?"

Wade's new position gave him better shooting angles from all sides. The only areas that were not visible were one side of the farmhouse and the area behind the house which contained two metal outbuildings that looked like workshops or equipment storage.

The pilot, who was unarmed, slowly inspected the tip of the wing. Stephan turned away from the pilot in apparent frustration and returned to the farmhouse, while Wade counted Stephan's steps as another means to confirm his distance calculations. The second measure verified that he had been off by thirty yards in his previous calculation.

The pilot seemed a little obsessive about his inspection routine, as he spent an inordinate amount of time on details. Wade was able to get a good look at the pilot. He was well groomed, with a short haircut and trimmed beard, which complemented his white guayabera shirt which glistened in the sun. He wore expensive aviator-style sunglasses and seemed to know his way around the aircraft.

The twin engine Beechcraft Baron 58 tail section stood in the sunlight, and Wade jotted down the tail numbers on a crumpled piece of paper which he returned to his pocket. He was far enough back in thick banana plantings to cover his shooting position from three sides.

He happened to look above him. The tall spindly light blue eucalyptus tree leaves danced in the slightest breeze. Wade remembered reading that the eucalyptus trees had been brought in from Australia and planted as wind breaks when commercial banana farming began, in the early part of the century. Wade's immediate thought was that the movement of the blue leaves might give him a better indication of wind speed than the distant chimney flag on the farmhouse.

Wade looked around for a quick escape route from his dark hide. He stamped down the plant material covering the ground, making a path so he wouldn't trip or encounter an obstacle he wasn't prepared for. His extraction paths went off in three directions behind him.

To his right were the decaying remains of an old barbed-wire fence. It was leaning out, almost ready to fall from old age and the encroaching pressure of plant roots. At one time the fence must have served to separate the eucalyptus trees from the banana plants, but the roots of both species had long ago destroyed that barrier. The falling fence was an impediment that had to be avoided if Wade was forced to evacuate in that direction. Of course, it would also slow anyone down who was coming at him from the opposite direction.

Sitting among the dense cover of banana plants, Wade remembered reading that it was the Cavendish variety of bananas that had made the fruit a commercial success in Central America. Poor quality natural soils in Belize made development of large commercial banana plantations less attractive to large-scale importers, so the farms in this country were smaller and farmed by independent growers.

Wade resumed his sniper position, wondering who else might be in the farmhouse or the surrounding buildings. He felt pretty comfortable with his current estimate of the distance to the farmhouse, now at 325 yards. He would probably not be shooting directly toward the house, but that became his reference point for the distance to all his other target points.

Instinct told Wade that the plane in front of him had not been called at the last minute for this assignment. He believed it had been part of Stephan's extraction plan all along and might have been waiting there for several days.

Wade also didn't think Stephan's extraction plans ever included extracting his operatives with him. This plane was Stephan's private getaway chariot.

Stephan and the pilot headed toward the plane, talking as they walked. By then, Stephan was clearly showing some frustration. They picked up their pace at Stephan's insistence, but neither showed a sense of urgency. As they got closer to the plane, the two men separated. The pilot walked ahead of Stephan and began checking the wing and landing gear. He held a clipboard and was systemically going through a list as if he had done it many times before.

Stephan ducked under the engine cowl and came around the wing. Walking in Wade's general direction, he turned to look out at the dense foliage surrounding the outer perimeter. Through his scope Wade could see Stephan's steely blue eyes. They were as cold as Wade remembered from the airport. Stephan's back was to the plane as his eyes scanned the surrounding landscape. He was unsettled, operating by instinct rather than anything he heard. He paced nervously in a semicircle, coming closer to the banana plantings at a difficult shooting angle for Wade.

Wade's eyes were pressed against the rubber ring on his scope. He was focused on Stephan's blue eyes, trying to discern the complex workings of another operative's brain. Stephan's eyes were filled with caution and distrust, laser-like, as if they could melt metal.

The worried look on Stephan's face told Wade there might be something telepathic going on that had brought him to the perimeter. Perhaps it was that sixth sense they both shared. Wade had known the feeling since childhood, growing up in the swamp.

Stephan scanned the long rows of banana leaves moving with the slight nudge from a light breeze. His expression didn't change as he looked into the dark expanse of plantings. Wade wondered what his sixth sense was picking up. Suddenly, as quickly as he'd arrived, he turned back to the plane and walked with purpose toward the copilot's door. When Stephan's angle changed from a side shot to frontal position, Wade had his chance to fire, but he didn't take it. *Why am I hesitating again? Why am I trying to figure out how the man's mind works?*

Approaching the side of the plane, Stephan bent over and yelled to the pilot loud enough for Wade to hear, "I'm ready. Let's go."

Wade couldn't hear the reply if there was one.

Stephan had turned to reach for the cockpit door handle, when Wade noticed something he hadn't seen before – there was a bulge in Stephan's shirt - a protective armored vest. Wade had to immediately change his shooting options. A frontal shot for center mass had been Wade's primary objective, but clearly that wouldn't work. He quickly compared a head shot to a hip shot. A hip shot would give him a slightly larger target below the vest, especially if his leg was extended.

In a jerky motion Stephan backed away from the

plane, showing frustration. He shouted again at the pilot, who was checking ailerons at the rear of the plane. "Damn it! I need to get the hell out of here."

This time the pilot yelled back to Stephan and moved a little more quickly down his checklist. Stephan reached for the cockpit handle, lifting his leg up to the wing step. Wade had to make another quick decision. He wasn't going to hesitate any longer.

As Stephan shifted his weight to his leg on the wing, Wade exhaled slowly while he applied even pressure on the trigger as he had done thousands of times before. The silenced thump of the round leaving the barrel reached Stephan in a fraction of a second.

Stephan spun off the wing in a pirouette landing on his back, screaming in pain. Wade couldn't see where the round had hit. It was either in his upper thigh, hip, or crotch. Wherever it was, Stephan was hit and immobilized, but still alive. Wade readied for his next shot.

The pilot hadn't heard the silenced shot, but heard Stephan's cries of pain. The pilot seemed disoriented, hesitating before looking under the plane. He saw Stephan rolling and holding his bloody lower torso. The pilot crouched and ran to Stephan's aid as fast as he could. Stephan's extended open, bloody hand halted the pilot. Stephan yelled at the pilot, "Start the damn plane!"

Chapter 30

Wade waited for his next shot as Stephan's body rolled and spun below the plane. The pilot was torn, trying to decide whether to follow Stephan's instructions or assist him. Disobeying Stephan's orders, the pilot came to his aid. The two men spoke, with Stephan's bloody hands grabbing the pilot's clean dress shirt to emphasize his point. Wade was unable to hear their conversation, but watched as Stephan screamed instructions. Pushing the pilot away, Stephan rolled behind the landing gear, which blocked Wade's next shot.

The pilot backed out from under the plane toward the opposite side and stepped on the wing as he reached for the handle of the pilot's door. He was clearly unnerved, his hands visibly shaking with fear. Before entering the cockpit, Stephan yelled out new instructions to the pilot: "Start the engine! Call the house for help!"

Standing on the wing, the pilot turned back toward the farmhouse, cupped his hands, and yelled instructions in Spanish. Wade couldn't make out what he said. The pilot wasn't Wade's concern, so he focused on Stephan, who had managed to pull himself up to a sitting position using the landing gear for support.

Blocked by the tire and landing gear, Wade was still without a shot. The pilot disappeared into the cockpit, slamming the door behind him. With one hand on his wound Stephan's other hand shook as he pointed in Wade's general direction.

The plane's propeller made a single revolution, with white smoke billowing from the ports before the engine went silent again. Wade thought the pilot might have had second thoughts, realizing that despite Stephan's orders, the plane would roll over Stephan if he moved forward.

A movement caught Wade's eye in the scope. Two men in camouflage fatigues were running at full speed from the farmhouse toward the plane. Each had an automatic weapon hanging from his shoulder. Wade turned his attention to making scope adjustments for the oncoming threat. He decided it would be better to let them come closer before he took the shot.

He turned his attention to the underside of the plane. The pilot had abandoned his seat in the plane, and had come underneath it to help Stephan, despite his orders to the contrary. Stephan was frustrated with him, but didn't refuse his help. Grabbing onto each other, the pilot was able to drag Stephan to the opposite side of the plane near the pilot's door.

The threat from the farmhouse was quickly edging closer. The two men continued running at full speed toward Wade. They were 150 yards away and were bringing their weapons to shooting positions. Wade moved his scope sight back from Stephan to the oncoming shooters. He scanned behind them to see if there were others following, but saw no one. He quickly scanned the other roads leading to the farmhouse with the same result.

As the two men got closer, Wade recognized their weapons. One man was carrying a Heckler & Koch MP-5 submachine gun, and the other was carrying a Russian AK-47. Both men wore military boots and camouflage fatigues with vests loaded with magazines of ammunition.

The pilot managed to get Stephan onto the wing and somehow pushed him through the door. Following him

311

into the cockpit, the pilot pushed and lifted Stephan's body over the controls into the copilot's seat.

The two armed men took up firing positions, and rounds were now landing all around Wade. Stephan managed to gather enough strength to yell instructions out of the pilot's door. Wade could see him pointing the men in his general direction. Rapid fire continued to split banana plants before landing deep behind Wade's position.

Within a few seconds, the Beechcraft propellers started spinning. The plane lurched forward a few feet, confusing the two shooters and causing them to split their positions on either side of the plane.

Stephan continued yelling directions. But over the sound of the plane's engine, no one could hear. It didn't stop Stephan from animatedly pointing in the general direction of the banana plantings.

Not seeing return fire or resistance, the two shooters were still uncertain about their target. They fired multiple bursts from their automatic weapons in a wide arch, sending broken foliage to the ground around Wade's position.

Wade moved five feet to his right for a better angle at the plane. The approaching men had now assumed prone positions. With his rifle stock resting on the trunk of a recently cut banana plant, Wade scoped the plane one more time as it made a right turn approaching the runway. Wade saw the outline of Stephan's head. At that point he imagined the rest of Stephan's body profile on the inside of the plane's aluminum skin.

He had one last shot, but it would have to be a miracle shot. Adjusting his scope, he imagined where the center mass of Stephan's body would appear in the copilot's seat. This time he ignored the fact that he might still be wearing body armor. The odds of hitting any other body part from this distance and angle were too remote. Perhaps he would get lucky.

The plane started picking up speed. For the moment, he ignored the two men shooting at him and exhaled slowly, increasing his pressure on the trigger. His silenced shot fired, giving no indication of where it landed. Wade wasn't even certain his shot hit the plane. Between the plane's increasing speed, vibration, and distance, along with a slight turn to the left just before moving down the runway, he couldn't be sure. With his vision of the copilot's door now obscured, there was no way to confirm his shot. He had other problems just in front of him.

The two oncoming men moved forward fifteen feet and resumed a prone position. With the plane gone, both men were exposed on open ground. The two men rushing him had been cautious, uncertain of their target and how many men were hidden in front of them. They took turns fanning rounds in his general direction while the other man offered cover, looking for signs of movement. As their bursts were fired, Wade could hear rounds ripping through the plants and leaves around and above his head.

His adversaries were trying to cover an area which they perceived to be fifty yards on either side of Wade. Both men had enough automatic fire power to take out a platoon of men beyond the long banana fence line. They just didn't have a precise fix yet. Wade identified each of the two men by number.

Shooter One stopped firing long enough to carefully scope the surrounding area, looking for signs of movement of any kind. He no longer seemed interested in firing blind. Shooter Two had just emptied his magazine and was in the process of reloading when Shooter One yelled a command in Spanish that Wade took to mean "Cover me."

Wade could see their revised plan was to cover each other, firing into the dense foliage in more systematic segments. Sooner or later, the plan would reach Wade's position. Between alternating firing sequences, they would move closer until they reached the dense cover. Once they were in the cover, they would have the same advantage as Wade, and he couldn't let that happen.

When Shooter One reloaded, he gave the ready command for Shooter Two to run to the next position. When the second shooter hit his second step, Wade fired into his center body mass, causing him to flip backward like a circus clown. He landed flat on his backside, lifeless, face up to the sky with his weapon resting quietly at his side.

Shooter One didn't hear the shot, but recoiled in shock at seeing his partner's back flip and the lifeless body a few feet in front of him. He didn't have a clue where the shot had come from, but emptied an entire magazine whose rounds landed on either side of Wade, missing him by ten yards.

After firing, Shooter One came to his senses and lay as flat on the ground as he possibly could, pressing his cheek hard against the dry compacted soil, hoping it would somehow cover him. His AK-47 was tucked beside him as his only comfort. His eyes followed the small trail of smoke coming from the end of his recently fired barrel.

Shooter One now figured there were multiple

shooters in the dark expanse of banana foliage, but didn't know how many. He heard the plane as it approached lift-off speed, but didn't dare turn his head to look. More tolerable because of his position, the hard dry dirt seemed somehow softer. He was now alone in an open field with no cover.

The shooter's mind was working hard, knowing that he had just loaded a full magazine into his weapon. Now that the plane was aloft, he wondered if a full clip of AK-47 rounds would cover his escape. Something about the hard ground suddenly appealed to him.

He scanned the edge of banana plants lining the open field. Every plant looked like a shooting position. He wasn't about to lift his head; his only hope now was that his low position might offer some protection.

From Shooter One's reactions, Wade realized that he was not used to fighting in the open. He was probably trained for jungle warfare, where dense cover meant everything. The shooter now lay as good as naked on the ground separated by 100 yards of open space between him and dense cover without a leaf to hide under.

Shooter One became either restless or confident enough to fire two short bursts while lying perfectly flat. The rounds landed in the dark vegetation on either side of Wade. In desperation, he must have been hoping for a miracle shot. The random shot pattern confirmed that he still didn't have a fix on Wade's position.

His flat in-line position in front of Wade made for a small, difficult target. There was little Wade could scope except a portion of his head sticking only few inches above the ground. Wade took a quick look above him for one last check of the eucalyptus leaf movement. He made a minor adjustment to his scope for the afternoon breeze that had just picked up.

Seeing the man breathe, Wade mimicked his breathing rhythm. His target turned his head to one side, trying to lower his profile even further. Wade knew that the difference between a hit and miss would be less than one inch at the near 100-yard distance.

There was contrast between the gray ground dirt and the shooter's dark green watch cap. Wade aimed one inch above the contrast line and fired. The target's body didn't twitch, no movement of any kind, and Wade thought he might have missed. Not wanting to expose himself, he remained in position, searching for signs of life through his scope.

A trickle of blood emerged from the watch cap, crawling down like a red centipede and confirming that Shooter One was no longer a threat.

Wade turned just in time to see Stephan's plane gain altitude and bank right toward the mountains. The memory of Stephan's face looking back at the rear of the plane would remain in Wade's memory forever. There had been so much movement, plane vibration, and distraction in the last moments before he shot that Wade lacked confidence. He couldn't see where his round had landed, and he turned on himself in frustration. *The second miss on the same target in one day.*

Wade felt that if Stephan got medical attention soon, he might survive his wound. Perhaps they would even meet on another assignment, in a different time and place.

He turned his attention back to the farmhouse, not certain if more fire power would emerge. He adjusted his scope and scanned the two roads bordering the open field.

Concern ran through his mind. *Perhaps more armed men will soon be arriving from trucks blanketing the field. Instead of the roads, perhaps they're already encircling my flank from the farm side.*

Remaining hidden in his current position was his best tactical alternative even if it meant he would soon be under additional fire. An eerie quiet settled over the farmhouse and his position. He rested his back against a large banana plant, surrounded by its large, overhanging leaves, content to wait for sunset.

Wade reflected on the scene before him. It would be picturesque were it not for the dead bodies lying in the field. The beautiful white farmhouse surrounded by lush foliage and the open green field reminded him of a dream he'd once had about retiring on a country farm with the swamp at his back.

He waited until satisfied that there were no further threats. Walking back to his car, he heard the faint sound of an engine sputter a long distance away. The source of the sound wasn't clear. Perhaps it was a dreaded vehicle backfire that was coming his way. He rushed to the edge of the clearing and began scanning with his scope.

A metal reflection in the sky caught his eye. The flashing metal reflection was miniscule. Grabbing his binoculars, Wade adjusted the focus to the dot and he saw a plane heading in the same general direction as Stephan's plane had been. It was trailing a small stream of white smoke under the right wing, and seemed to be losing altitude.

Within a few moments he heard the sound of the sputtering engine gradually becoming more distinct. The plane banked left, using the stronger of its two engines to

317

perhaps guide it to a landing spot. However, the plane was still over thick, mountainous jungle.

Wade squinted to see the details. In a few seconds the stream of white smoke turned black and expanded in size, now engulfing the entire right wing. He switched to the strong resolution in his rifle scope. He assessed the plane's chances for survival. *There's no way this plane is going to make it over that mountain top.*

The plane lost more altitude and then banked left again just before disappearing below the tree line. A moment later a single column of white smoke emerged above the treetops. The column expanded into a white plume against the purple afternoon sky.

Wade quickly turned his attention back to his mission. The extraction plan called for him to complete several tasks in Belize City before leaving for the airport. He tried contacting Max on the radio, but only got return static. *Max should already be at the airport by now, waiting for his return flight to Houston.* There was no point in hanging around. More uninvited guests might arrive. With no further need to stick around, he gathered his weapons and headed back to Belize City, taking the same route he had come.

He pulled up to the storage locker near the marina to unload his equipment. After wiping down his equipment for fingerprints he transferred everything to the storage locker and headed to the library several blocks away. The call to Yari was a necessary part of his extraction plan.

"Hi, it's me."

"How's did everything go?"

"It's a long story. I'll tell you about it later. Look, I'm trying to get out of here, but I need to make the other call we spoke about."

"Sure. What do you need from me?"

"I need to call the MI-6 woman, Zara Wicks, at the secure number you have for the British Embassy."

"I remember."

"Not only do I need a secure encrypted patch, but can you do something else for me?"

"What? Like make the call for you?"

"No. Can you put my voice through some kind of filter, so it's disguised?"

"I think so. We're playing around with some interesting software that not only disguises the voice but gives you a different language accent."

"I don't care about any of that. I know the call will be recorded. I just want to make sure there's no identifiable voice recognition pattern."

"Would you like a British or a French accent?"

"I don't give a damn. Make it British. I just need you to hurry."

"Give me eight minutes to set everything up. I'll call you back at this number. When you speak to her, just talk naturally. Don't try to do your own accent. It'll mess up the program."

"Okay, okay – just get the damn thing set up!"

Wade didn't have a clue what he would sound like and didn't really care. During the eight-minute wait, he scribbled down some notes. There were lots of details to remember. *Only the important ones matter.* When he looked down at his notes he noticed they were messy, almost unreadable. Looking again, he saw his hand tremble. *It must be from the shooting incident.* He had been as cool as a cucumber during the incident; this must be the aftershock. He took deep breaths waiting for the phone to ring.

The patch seemed like it was taking an eternity to complete. When the phone finally rang, he jumped and immediately picked up the receiver. Instead of Yari's voice, he heard the sound of Wicks' secure line ringing.

"Wicks here."

"Ms. Wicks, I'm calling you anonymously as another intelligence operative who does not want to be identified."

"You've called a British Embassy line that isn't used for outside calls. Where did you get this number?"

"Never mind where I got the number. You're part of the Embassy, but you're also an MI-6 agent. It will serve you well to listen to what I have to say. It deals with an assassination attempt on the Prime Minister and senior officials at today's ceremony. That threat was neutralized by my team. All you have to do is listen to what I am going to tell you, and then you can decide if you want to do anything more about it. I will take less than five minutes of your time. I know this conversation is being recorded, but you may want to have a pen and pad in front of you as well."

A pause followed. Wicks' first thought was that it was a crank call, leading up to some demand or political statement. She'd gotten many of those before, but none had previously started out this way. Everything the caller first said could be easily checked out. If nothing else, the caller had used a creative approach to get her attention.

"I'm listening."

Wade described what had happened and the location of the bodies on nearby rooftops, the location and description of the black cases under the stage, the location of the safe houses, and the storage locker number where she could find the C-4 explosives, phosphorous crystals, and other weapons. He identified the location of the farm where the firefight had taken place and the tail number on the plane Stephan had used to escape, along with the location of the probable crash site. After completing his explanations, there was an unexpected silence.

"Your story is almost too bizarre for you to have made it up. Assuming you're telling the truth, who do you contend was behind this attempt?"

"I don't know. That'll be your job to find out. There are plenty of clues, however. I will tell you that significant resources were behind this attempt, and the individuals who participated have the means to try it again."

"How did you get the intel that this was going to take place?"

"My team didn't have any advanced intel. The threat was discovered quite by accident while we were on another mission in Belize. There was no time to warn anyone – we just reacted to everything as it unfolded."

"How do you feel the threat was planned?"

"Everything associated with your ceremony activities is highly publicized, including who is attending which ceremonies. It even gives the times and when each speech is scheduled to occur. I suggest you do something about that exposure."

"Assuming your story checks out, who do we have to thank for your assistance?"

"No thanks necessary, ma'am. I'm just glad everyone is safe."

"Is there any chance we could meet to further discuss

this?"

"No, ma'am, that's not possible. By the way, that red rosebud on your jacket goes well with your cream-colored suit, but you look a little tired."

The click of Wade's receiver ended the call. Wicks' head suddenly turned right toward the large window on the other side of the room. As she replaced the receiver, she glanced down at her jacket. The small red rosebud was still fresh from the afternoon ceremonies. Wicks slowly got up from her desk, walked around the credenza, and approached the large picture window but remained out of sight.

Does the caller have me in his line of sight? The tall surrounding glass office buildings reflected back an intense glare from the bright afternoon sun. It was impossible for Wicks to see anything. If he was looking at her, he had the sun at his back.

In one sweep, Wicks closed the heavy, lined curtains, cutting off the light into her office. She quickly returned to her desk and dialed her secretary.

"Have the Chief of Security come to my office immediately."

Chapter 31
Greenstone, Alabama

Wade was busy finishing a school paper after his return from Belize three days earlier. He hadn't spoken to Megan since that last call from the library in Belize City just before the attack in Belmopan. He was quietly working on the paper when the phone rang. The harsh ring was then tempered by Megan's soft voice, and immediately shifted his concentration to a sweeter place.

"I hope you're busy finishing your class report."

"As a matter of fact, I'm working on it now."

"How was your fishing trip?"

"Good. I'm glad to be back."

"I bet you are. Can you tell me any more about it?"

"I really can't right now. Just that there were plenty of fish to fry."

"Are you still coming to Washington for the reception?"

"I wouldn't miss seeing you for anything."

"That's sweet."

He changed the subject. "Is the training schedule for D.C. the same as we last discussed?"

"It sure is. Nothing's changed. You'll meet a lot of interesting people at the reception."

"I'm looking forward to completing my training and seeing you."

"I can't wait."

He paused then went on, "I don't guess you've heard anything more about Spencer's activities in Vietnam before his death in North Carolina?"

"Still checking into some files at the Pentagon.

Seems like Spencer's files related to the drug investigation are buried deep under lock and key. You can't even access the area where the files are kept without a special pass."

"I figured that might be the case."

The reception in Washington was the culmination of Agency training attended by agents from around the world. One of the purposes of the gathering was for agents to meet the new crop of recent graduates. It was also an opportunity for recent grads to make connections for permanent postings, and the closest thing the Agency had to an unofficial graduation ceremony. Megan was in charge of organizing hotel activities and coordinating flights for incoming agents. With the reception still two months away, things hadn't gotten very hectic yet.

She was at her desk making preliminary arrangements when her phone rang. It was a call from her good friend Beverly, who worked at the Pentagon.

"Are you and Wade still in touch?"

"Of course. Why do you ask?"

"Interesting. Our office got a communiqué requesting Wade's personnel file. It didn't come through normal channels and wasn't on the request form we normally use."

"That's strange. What was the routing?"

"It doesn't show any routing."

"That's strange. No source or origin?"

"Nope. Just delivered to me through inter-office mail. On my directory, you still show as Wade's supervisor."

"He's finished most of his agency training and is

now completing college make-up papers, so technically he's still under me until he graduates."

"That's a good way to keep track of your man. I'll have to remember that."

"Who do you think is asking for his information?"

"That's the problem – I can't tell from this request. I'll tell you what, since you're still listed as his contact officer, why don't I just send the request over to you? I'll do it by secure messenger this afternoon."

"That would be fine."

"I'll reply to the mail center that all future requests for information on Wade get directed to you. You can take it from there."

"Thank you, Beverly. I owe you lunch."

"Thanks, but who's got time for lunch?"

Frustration had already reached a boiling point for Megan by the time the secure messenger arrived from the Pentagon. From Beverly's description, the request breached all agency protocol requirements. Her hands trembled as she opened the envelope.

Reading the document only caused Megan to stew further. It represented more than someone who refused to follow protocol; this document was an affront to standard procedures, not to mention a personal attack on Agency professionalism.

Megan's mind raced as she read the document, trying to be objective while controlling her feelings for Wade. Under "Purpose" the request stated, "For Covert Assignment." *So ... a mysterious unknown source wants Wade's personnel file for an undisclosed covert assignment. That's not going to happen.* She made notes in preparation for her rejection memorandum.

Undisclosed Assignment – Inadequate Purpose. Lacks documentation of originating source for request, Lacks signature of supervising agent and departmental approval, No training agency pre-approval or signoff, Agent is a trainee and not subject to assignment requests. Her list went on.

She swallowed hard as she studied the poorly-prepared request, trying to read between interagency political lines. It met very few protocol standards, and had been typed on an older form no long being used.

The document requested Wade's entire personnel file as a start. Megan read between the lines. If acted upon, the request would pluck Wade right out of her agency's control and put him under some undisclosed agent or agency. That was not acceptable, and Megan was determined to stop the request in its tracks.

If Megan had learned anything at the Agency, it was the rules of agency protocol. Wade was not officially eligible for assignment until he graduated in October. Aside from protocol issues, Megan had plans for them as a couple, even though she hadn't shared those feelings with anyone but her closest friends.

She and Wade had hinted about getting assigned posts at the same office so they could be near each other to further their relationship. At that moment, both were still reluctant to discuss their relationship because of their positions. She was technically still his handler and under her charge, even though their feelings went much deeper.

Her evening call with Wade was going to start in a few minutes. Megan struggled to decide whether to say anything about the request. *Why should this intrusion ruin our evening visit? After all, he just got back a few days ago from that exhausting trip to Belize.*

She also sensed that his trip had been dangerous. Before the call, Megan had determined that she wasn't going to mention "the request." The call started out upbeat enough, with each telling the other about the day's activities. In the middle of the conversation, Megan felt guilty about keeping him in the dark.

"You seem to have a secret admirer."

"You're kidding! Who is it?"

"I have no idea, and that's part of the problem. Don't worry, your file isn't going anywhere if I have anything to say about it. I'll research this further tomorrow. There's no way they're getting your file."

"Do I have any say in the matter?"

"No. At least not until I get this cleared up. For all I know, this could be an attempted swipe from one of the other agencies. Remember we're under the new 'sharing agents' policy. Worst case, it could be from someone trying to get confidential information about who's going through our training programs. You just cool your jets until I get to the bottom of it."

"All my parts are cool on this end."

Wade's thoughts immediately went to the Lockhart investigation and Belize. *Am I getting too close to the source of agency involvement?* He answered his own question. *The Agency couldn't have reacted this quickly.* His stomach churned with tension at the thought. Trying to maintain a calm personal demeanor, Wade said nothing to Megan about his concerns.

He was still shaky about Megan's involvement in the cover up, but he kept it to himself. Those feelings had nothing to do with his personal feelings for her. Those were real, and he believed she felt the same way about him. He believed the Agency was lurking in the background, however, using their personal relationship to get more information about him – but he couldn't prove it. It was his sixth sense operating again. That sense had kept him alive since childhood, and he couldn't ignore it.

He wanted to take the next step with Megan in their personal relationship but wasn't sure how to do that. Like many other long distance relationships, Megan and Wade sent kisses to end their evening call. For some reason, the kisses that came across in this conversation had a subtle edge he didn't understand. Wade had to find out why if it was the last thing he ever did.

END

ABOUT THE AUTHOR

Joseph D'Antoni is a true forensic and economics expert with years of experience testifying in court cases throughout the world. His clients have included the FBI, Department of Justice, intelligence agencies and some of the largest law firms in this country. He holds advanced academic degrees and taught at three major universities. His fictional characters are often inspired from actual cases he has worked on and events he has investigated.

The author grew up in New Orleans and spent much of his youth fishing and hunting in the surrounding swamps which became his childhood playground and where much of his stories take place.

D'Antoni's next book, *Rogue Asset* is almost ready to go to press and he is well along with another suspense novel to follow. In addition to suspense novels the author has published a fine art photography book, *Louisiana Reflections,* which has received wide acclaim as an introspective photographic study of New Orleans and Cajun Country before Hurricane Rita and Katrina devastated the area. The author is also working on a yet untitled book of poems which he expects to publish by early next year.

He currently resides in Southern California where he writes and works on art when he is not investigating or consulting on forensic assignments.

www.dantonibooks.com

Also by JOSEPH D'ANTONI

LOUISIANA REFLECTIONS

Award winning hardbound fine-art book with pristine fine-art photographic images of New Orleans and Cajun Country taken before Hurricane Katrina.

SILENT SANCTION

The first novel in the Wade Hanna covert intelligence series takes the reader on a journey through Hanna's formative years in New Orleans and the swamp. His life emerges into a covert agent working for U.S. intelligence agencies on dangerous missions all over the world.

INVISIBLE MARKINGS
UNDERSEA VOICES

Two short stories provide insight and supplement to the saga of Wade Hanna's ventures in Silent Sanction.

New!   ROGUE ASSET

The third novel in the series finds Wade Hanna on a dangerous undercover black ops mission in Tangiers, Morocco to intercept an MI-6 agent's arms deal. His relationship with fellow operative Megan Winslow just begins to flourish as each becomes threatened by new unseen internal forces within their agency.

New!   SHADOW CELL

The fourth novel in the Wade Hanna series is expected to be released in late 2015. Forces within the agency require Wade to get very personal as he uses techniques strong enough to offset the power of a hidden cell operating against him within the agency.

For autographed copies ~ dantonibooks@gmail.com

20828329R00200

Made in the USA
Middletown, DE
10 June 2015